H. Leighton Dickson

Dragon of Ash & Stars

H. Leighton Dickson

Copyright © 2016 H. Leighton Dickson

All rights reserved.

ISBN: 1530934591

ISBN-13: 978-1530934591

To Jeannie, Donna &
the Rest of the Laughing Foxes.

Cute, sexy and slightly scary.
Like dragons.

CONTENTS

The Aerie	1
The Storm Fall	Pg 11
The Stick People	Pg 23
Warships & Cannonfire	Pg 35
The Corolanus Markets	Pg 51
The Under Weathers	Pg 64
The Night Dragon	Pg 78
The Death Dragons	Pg 91
The Last Dead Man in Bangarden	Pg 106
Life & Death in the Pits	Pg 117
The Dome of Dragons	Pg 131
Jewel of the Crown	Pg 141
The Crescent Mountains	Pg 150
The Drakina	Pg 162
Rue	Pg 172
Net of Dragons	Pg 183
The Citadel	Pg 194
The Skyroom	Pg 208
Aryss	Pg 223
The Shadow Flight	Pg 236
Night of Dragonsong & Fire	Pg 252
Nameless	Pg 269
Lamos	Pg 282
The Four Hills	Pg 296
Faceless	Pg 310
Skyborn	Pg 323
Dragon of Ash & Stars	Pg 334

ACKNOWLEDGMENTS

A writer is an island; cold, inhospitable, alone.
A writing group is an archipelago; rich, diverse, alive.

Many thanks to the Laughing Fox Writers, CSS
Writers, Northwestern Ontario Writers Workshop
and
The Ontario Arts Council.
Because of you, I am diverse and alive.
Still waiting on rich…

COROLANUS MARKETS
VENITUS
THE UNDER WEATHERS
THE ANQUAR CLIFFS
BANGARDEN
THE CRESCENT MOUNTAINS
THE CROWN
THE DEN
THE CITADEL
TERRA REMUS
ETRENI SALTS
THE NAMELESS SEA
REMUS
ATHA LAMOS
LAMOS
THE NAMELESS SEA
THE FOUR HILLS OF NATHENS

THE AERIE

I don't remember much of my time in the shell, but what I do remember is good.

Warm, quiet, calm. The music of my heart, the rhythm of hot blood, the simmering acid in my belly. I believe I dreamed, but of what, I cannot say, for there was nothing in the shell to dream about. But dragons are a fantastical clan. Our minds have no equal; our imaginations no limit.

I also remember the first time my eyes saw light. For the longest time, my world had been filled with my curled self – legs, wings, belly and tail – black as what I would later call a starry night. Beyond me however, I would sometimes see a film that was rippled and grey. This, I later learned was the shell. At some point, it became too small, or I became too big but the shell was warm and quiet and calm so I stayed. One day, there was a shimmer of motion beyond the film and for some reason, I felt an urge to discover. I had never had an urge before. It was to be the first of many. I pressed the shimmer with the pick of my beak and the world peeled apart into startling brightness. I fell onto a warm rock, dwarfed by a massive trilling darkness that I later called my mother.

There were three others I remember on the day of my hatching – sisters all and green. My mother was there, nudging their flailing shapes, snapping up the shells and the ooze that came with them. They tumbled and chirped over each other and I recall thinking they were pathetic and small. I had no silverstone. I knew nothing of self. I was also small, but I'm certain not nearly so pathetic.

The Anquar Cliffs served as nest and aerie, high above the Flashing Water. There were many cliffs and therefore, many nests for many dragons. I remember watching a golden drakina and her brood of seven eggs on a ledge below our own. While they hatched, I do remember another urge - that of eating them in the shell but I refrained. My mother would have disapproved. Her bites were painful enough if I merely nipped a sister in jest. Still, the sight of the eggs hatching filled me with curiosity and revulsion, although it was years before I realized that I had looked the same way at the time.

Seven eggs is a lot for a dragon and that day, as the golden mother cooed and nudged the many cracking shells, I watched one hatchling flail out of the sticks and onto the stone. It moved awkwardly, for at birth our wings are wet and sticky and very, very soft, and it tipped and tumbled toward the edge of the cliff. I watched as it teetered on the brink, letting out a pathetic cry before the mother rose from the nest, eggs and hatchlings falling from her like scales. A flock of sea snakes swept in, however – their grey leathery bodies twisting beneath their tiny wings and one of them snatched the hatchling from the cliff. The drakina swung her great head and roared, liquid flame spraying from her mouth and turning many of the snakes to char. It was the first time I ever saw dragonfire and immediately, the aerie erupted in chaos as dragons and snakes shrieked at each other. The first snake carried the chick higher and higher until another plummeted downward, catching the hatchling in its talons and together, snakes and baby tumbled through the air in a bloody dance. Finally, they released the hatchling and it dropped soundlessly into the water below the cliffs.

I stayed much closer to my mother after that.

Most days were sunny and hot, the skies blue, the waters bluer and I yearned to fly like the others but my wings were not strong enough. They were an unusual hue, like a smoky night, where you can see stars through the clouds, and I quickly learned that, after sunset, I was almost invisible to the others because of my colouring. There were no other dragons of my shade in the aerie, for most dragons are the colour of the elements – gray, gold, blue and green or a blending of these so that we reflect our surroundings and hide from our prey. I'm not certain, then, how I came to be. My mother was a rock grey with a blue sheen in the sunlight and the drake that held court over our particular cliff was a green, so I suspected early on that I was not his. It didn't matter. Dragons are not given to sentimentality or idle dreams of fidelity. Dragons are interested in food, water, nests and mating with other dragons.

Oh yes, and gold, but that's another story.

The waters around the aerie were full of fish, and while

I know the stick people like to tell stories about how dragons eat their herds and raid their villages, for the most part, that is simply untrue. We eat fish and sea snakes, feathernewts and sometimes shaghorns if they are foolish enough to come close. I do prefer a good fat feathernewt, but that could be simply because of an early diet consisting mostly of fish. While nutritious, fish has a certain oily aftertaste that sits in the belly for hours. My mother was a good fisher and each morning, she would return to the nest and open her mouth and we would scramble in to eat. As the only male, I was the strongest and arguably the most hungry, so I would always be first to gorge on predigested silverfins and bloodbass. My sisters would get whatever was left and after several weeks, I became aware of the fact that I had one less sister than I'd had before.

I told myself it was the sea snakes and thought no more of it.

So for many weeks it was all about the nest and about our mother. Feeding, sleeping, stretching, fighting over fully-formed bits that she brought home in her teeth. Some days she would bring home shards of crystalized arcstone, which I eagerly gobbled up before my sisters could, loving then hating the burn it caused in my belly. On the days that it rained, she would shield us under the cover of her wings. On the days of scorching sun, she would shade us in the same way. She regularly cleaned both us and the nest, and I realized dragon chicks were messy creatures with no regard for themselves or their territory. Still, it was a good life and I was as happy as a young drake could be.

In the mornings, I would wave my wings in the wind

and wait for them to grow as strong as the drakes wheeling through the sky overhead. They preened, those drakes, although there is little thought given to beauty in the dragon world. Pride and strength, speed and skill: those were the marks of a fine dragon. For a drake, hunting ability came a close second after the number of drakinas bred and secured in your own aerie. I'm not even certain the number of hatchlings mattered to a drake. Their mock-battles killed many chicks and maimed even more as they crashed from cliff to cliff. Their tails swept eggs and hatchlings alike into the sea during their raucous sparring.

In the nights, I would push my head out from under my mother and gaze at the twin moons and the stars above me. I didn't know then that they had names, I didn't know then that they had patterns and that you could fashion entire universes out of the glittering, twinkling lights that lit up the night sky. The night was the same as I, the same colour, the same sparkling dance. Like clouds and ash at dusk. I felt an aching affinity for the night. Even from such an early age I wanted to be a part of it.

The night sky was my father, I told myself. The night and the stars and the double moons that winked like eyes in their cycles – waxing and waning, winking and sleeping and wide. The eyes of my father, the star dragon Draco Stellorum, saw all and approved.

As I mentioned, the imagination of dragons has no limit. We are creatures of dreams and fire.

My mother was a large drakina and as such, had secured a nest at the top of the highest of Anquar's Cliffs. Most of the drakes stayed out of her way, knowing she could just as likely render them neuter as kill them, and that, for a drake, would be worse than death. Our drake frequently landed near the nest to preen, cleaning his moss-green scales with the tiniest of teeth, combing the seagrass from his spines with the talons on his back legs and showing off his broad wings in the late summer sun. My sisters watched, entranced. Me – I hated him with every night-black scale on my body and vowed to one day be a better, stronger, more-skilled drake than he.

One evening, the large brown on the outermost cliff began to bellow, a cry that was quickly taken up by the others. The drakinas returned to their nests, settling down atop their fledglings with unceremonial roughness. My mother was fishing and while we waited for her return, my sisters tucked themselves deep into the sticks. I, however, did not, and scrambled instead to the highest ledge to see what could possibly have alerted the entire aerie, more than sea snakes and blue-footed goswyrms. I watched how the drakes postured, watched where they were looking when suddenly, an arrow of dragons crossed the inlet that led past the Cliffs.

Five very large dragons – male and female both – flying like an arrow, led by a great silver drake. It was the first time I'd ever seen a Dragon Flight. It was the first time I'd ever seen a stick.

When I say 'stick', I mean the stick people, the only creatures that could catch and tame and ride a dragon. I narrowed my eyes and stretched out my neck, rising up on my hind legs so I could see. At first, I thought they were spines growing out of the shoulders of the dragons but as they passed, I thought they did look rather more like sticks, with their lean torsos and knobby limbs and funny flat faces. Unlike dragons who are strong as stone and fluid as the sea. We are all the elements combined.

It was then that my mother returned, catching my head in her mighty jaws and dropping me into the nest on top of my sisters. She settled over us and tucked low, as if willing herself to become part of the stony cliff and thus hide us from the Flight.

I marvelled at the thought of sticks riding dragons, however, and turned it over and over in my mind for many days after.

Because of this, I wanted to fly. You weren't a dragon unless you flew. There were lizards and dillies and monitors all over the cliffs but none of them flew. I suppose the sea snakes, wyrms, feathernewts and overmolls could claim dragon-like status but dragons would vehemently disagree. There are many, many creatures that fly on the earth. None but dragons are dragons. Only dragons breathe flame. Fire is what sets us apart from the others. Dreams and imagination and fire.

But back to my story.

One morning, eight weeks after my hatching, I was fanning my wings on the aerie cliff and a great gust of wind caught them, lifting me off the stone and several wingspans over to the nest. My heart thudded in my chest then at the exhilaration. I lumbered over to the edge once more (and I say lumbered, for dragons are most ungainly creatures on land, with our strong back legs and our forelegs knuckled, clawed and winged), spread wide my wings and let the wind take me once again through the air back to the nest. My sisters squawked at me, as mother was out fishing and they assumed her authority as all young drakinas-in-training do. I ignored them, as all young drakes-in-training do. I let the wind carry me over and over across the top of the cliff. It stirred something deep inside of me, so when the next gust of wind came, I unfurled my black wings and sprang into the sky.

And I flew.

I flew up and up and up, over the nest and over the aerie so that the green drake noticed me and launched into the air. But I was fast and young and strong and I soared above him, so proud of myself and my male wings, until the wind died. Those wings, once strong enough to handle the skies, became fledging wings once more and I plummeted like a baby into the nest of the gold drakina and her brood. Only now, the drakina was fishing with my mother and there were six fledglings almost as large as I. They hissed and snapped until I scrambled out of the nest and onto the stone.

I looked up to see the sea snakes coming.

An entire flock of them, twisting and writhing on their tiny wings and I felt an unfamiliar fire in my heart. I summoned it, calling it from deep within. I choked and gagged and finally coughed up a shard of arcstone. I had never blown fire in all of my short life, would likely never do so as a sea snake descended, talons reaching for my black beaked head. I closed my eyes and willed – arcstone and acid, brought them both forth at the same time and felt the heat congeal in the back of my throat. It felt like my head would split open with the pain so I spat now, forcing it forward with all my fledgling strength (which is to say, not much) and felt the roof of my mouth and the slick of my tongue scorch with the heat.

The sea snake shrieked and wheeled away as another dropped from the sky towards me. I did the same, summoning the acid and the stone and spitting them both at the awkward creature, this time lighting the tip of his tail on fire. He flapped up and up until the flock surrounded him and they all went down in a writhing mass of grey scales and tiny wings.

My breath was hot and my chest filled with smoke. I shook my head, retching until the last of the taste was gone and licking my teeth to clear it of ash. Behind me, the nest of six fledglings watched with fascination, their glassy eyes shimmering with wonder and delight. I had done it, I thought to myself. Not only had I been the first fledging in the aerie to fly, but I was the first to call the fire. I was a drake now, not a chick and I shook my head once again, awaiting the day I had a mane of spines to prove it.

And so I rose onto my hind legs and trumpeted the dragon song – a rich, mournful, triumphant cry of victory that, when I look at it in hindsight was likely a pathetic warble, when suddenly, a great shadow fell across the ledge. My mother, large and earth-grey, settled onto the stone before me, her breath reeking of fish. I lifted my face to hers, trumpeted again in defiance. I was a drake. I had flown and produced fire. I needed no mother to protect me and I would take my place in the aerie with all the other males.

She snapped her jaws down on my head and lifted from the ledge, carrying me like a dead thing to our own nest and my sisters. She dropped me unceremoniously onto the sticks and settled down on top all of us like a massive grey stone. We got no food that night. I suppose I should have felt bad for my sisters but I did no such thing. In fact, I felt very content with myself and as I closed my eyes in sleep, I vowed to my father, Draco Stellorum, that tomorrow I would give in to my newest urge.

   I would set my wings to the sea and fly.

THE STORM FALL

My mother left the aerie before dawn. It was easy to tell because of the gust of cold that rolled down in her wake and I was waiting for it. I stayed in place for a long time, partly to make sure she was well and truly gone, but also partly because I was afraid. My wings were strong and my fire was sure; it was my heart that was unsteady and beating so fast. But soon, I lifted my head to study the rooks in the first light of morning and I thought I had never seen such a glorious thing.

The sun splitting the night from the day, the sky from the waters with astounding colours. Reds and oranges, yellows and purples. High above me, the stars. *My* stars, my father, and I felt a yearning for him like I had never known before. I could see shapes and patterns in him now, envisioned in the height and breadth of my imagination. There was the Dying Wyrm – a hook of stars that looked like the death throes of a sea snake. Then there was the Fat Fish, which looked exactly like its namesake – large and round with stars that gleamed like shimmering scales. And of course, there was the magnificent Draco Stellorum – an exultant dragon with wings that spanned the entire night sky. That was my father – Draco Stellorum, Dragon of the Night Skies. His Eyes were the twin moons; tonight one wide, one winking. He was smiling at me, calling me, encouraging me to defy my mother and fly.

As I have said, the imagination of dragons has no equal.

I looked back at my sisters, curled up on each other like twins. I felt pity for them then, although why I did has confounded me to this day. Perhaps I felt superior, young drake that I was. Perhaps I equated them with the mundane life of female dragons, although I was clearly not thinking of my mother if that were the case. Regardless, it was with something akin to fond sadness, so maybe my earlier pronouncement on sentimentality was somewhat wrong.

I kept low and deliberately quiet as I slipped from the nest, made certain not to drag either tail or wings on the stone until I reached the cliff's edge. I gripped it with my wing claws and peered over the side, down at the golden drakina and her chicks far below me. She was stirring and I knew she'd be up in a matter of moments. I would need to be very quiet to avoid her, as well as the flocks of sea snakes that hunted these parts. With a deep breath, I fell forward and stretched out my wings and prayed that yesterday's success had not been premature. Falling into another dragon's nest is never an excellent thing.

I winged down the cliffside, steering away from the nest but plummeting toward the rocky water. With my heart in my throat, I lifted my head and my wings unfurled, catching the wind just before I hit the waves. It was the most exhilarating feeling and I know my words can never do it justice. The lurch of the belly and the release of thought as you become one with the air and the sky and the clouds. The fierce cold of the wind across your eyes, and the glaze of the second eyelid protecting them from burn. I laughed at the sensations - the soaring and the dipping, the whirling and the wheeling. My tail was a rudder, guiding my direction and it followed my thoughts perfectly as I wove in and out of the Anquar Cliffs. It took no time at all to learn when to flap and when to sail, when to tuck and when to reach, the canvas of my wings thin but strong enough to carry my weight. Soon, I passed the Fang of Wyvern, a rocky pinnacle sticking out of the water like a tooth. No dragon nested on the Fang. I don't know why but I knew that if I ever had drakinas, they would nest here simply because no one else had.

And then, finally, free over the open water. I glanced back to see the Cliffs, making sure I could remember my way home. They looked like the scales of a great water dragon and I felt the earth force chime within me. It was like a tug or a pull and I knew that I would always be able to find my way home because of it. The earth force is a dragon's best friend, next to wind and fire.

The sun was higher now, the water a gleaming gold and I dropped to fly just above its choppy surface. I concentrated on the rhythm of my wings, the focus of my breath, the beating of my heart. I could fly like this forever, I told myself. A creature of air and sky and water. The land was a prison, heavy like a stone.

There was a flashing beneath the waves, and I looked

down, delighted to see a school of lemonwhites racing beneath me. I loved the taste of lemonwhites, so flew lower still, stretched out my talons, aiming to snag one but all I caught was water and spray. I flapped faster, dropping my legs into the water and almost flipped wing over beak with the drag of it. I had to think. My people were fishers so there had to be a better way. I angled my wings to take me up, up, up before arcing in the sky as I had seen the drakes do when they'd dance for the drakinas. My wings folded, my tail whipped and I plummeted, entering the water like a pebble. Instantly, all things slowed.

The thickness of the water was unexpected and when I gasped, water rushed in through my nostrils and mouth, filling my throat and splitting my head. Fish battered all around me and I flapped against their currents. Upside down and underside up, I flailed through the water until finally, my head then my body burst through the waves. I retched again and again until the water was out of my chest and back in the sea where it belonged. Dazed, I looked around and realized with surprise that I was sitting on top of the waves. Wings tucked across my back, tail fanned out behind, legs paddling instinctively beneath me. It was a remarkable sensation, sitting here between the worlds of sky and sea, but I realized that that was a dragon's life. Sky and land and sea and fire. It was probably why we were the masters of all. Except the sticks.

I wondered about that.

It was strangely peaceful sitting on the water, watching the great expanse of blue all around me. There were light wisps of clouds in the sky, small white wavecaps on the water. The Anquar Cliffs were just a thin line of spikes on the horizon, scales along the spine of that great ocean dragon of my imagination. The earth force beat in my breast, strong and true like my heartbeat, and I rose and fell on the waves as though the waters were breathing. I was the only living thing in the world at this moment and for the first time in my young life, I was content.

Tickles on my paddling feet and I looked down to see the school of lemonwhites directly beneath me. I wound my tail around my body so that it splashed just below my beak. A lemonwhite rose to the surface and I could see its many black eyes bob and twist as it watched my tail. I arched my neck and dove, spearing the fish with the spike of my beak. Pride swelled my heart as I held it up for all to see; which is to say, no one for I was alone, but still. Vanity and youth are inseparable companions.

I tried to eat it, but in fact, the fish was impaled on my beak and my jaws could not reach. I tried with my tongue but it was too slippery. I tried with my back foot but I ended up head-down in the water, pathetically thrashing. At this point, I was very grateful that no one was watching. Finally, I caught it with the talon of my wing and was able to slide it from my beak and into my mouth.

Nothing can compare to the taste of a lemonwhite that has not been already digested by your mother.

And so, I spent the better part of the day fishing from my vantage point of bobbing water drake. I was happy that the fish didn't seem to have a corporate memory. I was able to use the same technique to catch fish after fish, tossing some in the air until I was quite skilled at snatching them as they came down. Most I swallowed whole but some I crunched, enjoying the salt taste run across my tongue and down my throat. Soon, I was full, weighted down on the top of the water and rather sleepy. I tucked my head beneath my wing and dozed, the morning sunshine warm on my back.

I dreamed of stars, of Draco Stellorum battling the Dying Wyrm and eating the Fat Fish as a Dragon Flight soared across the entire night sky. It was a very good dream.

I'm not sure how long I slept but I awoke to a rocking of the water. Big waters, high waves. I looked around. The sky had grown heavy with clouds and in the distance, I could see the flashing that is called Hallow Fire. It is usually accompanied by Hell Down – a loud crashing roar that follows the Fire. I shook my head and stretched wide my wings but my belly was so full that my wings wouldn't lift. I flapped and flapped but the drag of the water on my legs, tail and belly was too strong. The waves were lifting me higher and sending me lower so that at times I could see neither sky nor the horizon and for the first time in my life, I began to despair.

A sensation made all the worse at the sight of a set of dark scales slicing through the water toward me.

A wave lifted and crested, tossing me briefly out of the water and as a reflex, my legs began to paddle in the air. Once they touched the surface, I found I could run several steps before the water dragged me down again. The scaly creature was almost upon me. It was almost impossible to see because of the darkness of the waves and the darkness of the skies but I could tell that it was large and predatory and approaching me very quickly. I tried to call the fire but a belly full of fish oil prevented it, dousing even my acid with its slimy ooze.

I waited for the next rise and ran along the crest of the wave, beating my wings and cursing my gluttony. The wind was strong, the water stronger, but I urged my legs to be stronger still. I felt a rough surface under my feet and my heart blanched inside of me. The creature lifted me high and tossed me up into the wind, playing with me the way I had played with the lemonwhites. I would end up the same way if I didn't take to the skies soon. A glance beneath me revealed rows and rows of flashing white. They were, believe me, incredible motivation and within a heartbeat, I was skyborn, rising above the huge waves with every beat of my aching wings.

With mouth gaping wide, the creature rushed the surface, leaping into the air but crashing back down with barely a taste of my tail.

There was no triumph however. The winds buffeted me like an angry mother and I remembered that while I was a drake, I was still a small drake, no bigger than the sea snakes that had hunted me. The wind howled and Hallow Fire cracked and I felt like a leaf caught in between, tossed as each saw fit. I briefly reconsidered settling onto the water again but the thought of the toothed creature filled me with dread and so I stayed airborne for the bulk of the storm, all the while my wings burning from strain.

At one point, I tried to fly over the clouds as I imagined the great drakes could do. I flew high, higher, desperately searching for a break in the winds. I needed to see my father, Draco Stellorum. I knew that once he saw me, he would help, but there was nothing but Hell Down, Hallow Fire and the roaring of the wind. The clouds were astounding, however – bigger than anything I could have imagined and rimmed with gold. For one fleeting moment, I glimpsed yellow and blue and pink but was immediately flung back into the dark that flashed with Hallow Fire and thundered with Hell Down. I searched the angry skies, praying even for a glimpse of a Dragon Flight. I would follow them anywhere but there was nothing, no one, so I tucked my wings, dropping back to the fury above the water.

It seemed like a lifetime and when it was finally over, any trace of the sun was gone. I had lost the better part of the day to the waves and the clouds, and night fell so quickly that I had no strength to fly anymore. I returned to the water, floating with my head tucked under my wing and prayed that if the creature did come back, it would eat me before I even knew I had been eaten. And so I dozed restlessly, fitfully, all night until the sea quieted and the sun lifted the mantel of night once again.

When I awoke, there was no land anywhere.

There was no land, there were no Cliffs, there was not even the tug of the earth force within me. There was nothing but sea and sky and a sad, lonely little dragon floating on the water. I remember calling to my mother, willing to accept what would likely be a humiliating return to the nest, but there was no answer, only my pathetic wail echoing across the sea. I was hungry but I would not eat. I was thirsty but the salt stung my throat. I floated like this for a full day, watching the sun cross the sky and dip into the sea, calling the night to follow like a love-sick drake. Follow it did, until the next morning, when the sun peeked out to begin the cycle all over again.

I awoke to the sounds of sea snakes, their shrill voices carrying across the water. There was also the sound of waves against a shore and the smell of fish strong on the breeze. I opened my eyes, blinked out the salt sting, and my heart did a flip inside of me at the sight. It looked like a forest of branchless trees, half submerged, half protruding from the water. At the tops of these trees, a roof of flat wood, wet and smooth, that created a canopy along the rocky shore and cast shadows across the top of the water. Nets hung from that canopy, along with baskets and ropes of twine and sea grass. It was different than anything I had ever seen before, but then again my whole world had been the aerie, so it was to be expected.

The sea snakes circled high above me and I knew they thought me easy prey, which I suppose I was. The fire was back in my belly however, and when one swooped down with talons extended, I welcomed him with a breath of flame. He shrieked and soared upwards when over the sound of the waves, I heard the trilling of dragons. My heart leapt once more so I spread my wings and in two beats was airborne.

From the sky, I could see that the wooden canopies were docks of a fishing village and as I rose over them, I caught my second glimpse of stick people.

I wasn't entirely sure what to think. Like dragons, they moved on two legs but unlike dragons, they had no wings, no scales, no beaks or tails. As I flapped along the wood, they ran after me, pointing and shouting in their odd, unmusical language. I couldn't understand how they could ride dragons as they did – they had no wings or fangs or claws or spines. In fact, they looked quite harmless as they chased me, grabbing nets from the docks as they went. No, with their pushed-in faces and no teeth or talons to speak of, I wasn't impressed at all.

It would be a sad day before I let one of them ride me.

Besides, I was looking for dragons.

I spied the first sitting on a post, her wings spread wide. She was a gold and a little larger than me, so I swept between the fishing huts, flashing my wings before her. She trilled so I trilled back, urging her to join me in the air when I noticed a hemp rope knotted around her legs. It was puzzling, almost as puzzling as the silver band buckled around her throat. It looked far too tight and I thought she surely must be in distress. The look in her eye said otherwise, so I lit upon the post beside her.

A second trill came from the nearest hut and inside, I could see a young drake also larger than I. He was green and blue and trapped in a cage of wooden spikes. It was far too small for him, forcing him to fold his wings and hunch his spine. He also wore a silver band and I puzzled some more until the young drakina began nibbling the sea grass from my juvenile mane. It was distracting and entirely more pleasant than when my mother or sisters had tried.

A crowd of stick people gathered from behind and while I may have been young and foolish, I was not overly foolish. I sprang from the post and up to the roof of the nearest hut. One of the stick people reached for a sack tied to his waist. He was shorter than the others and thinner, with a mane of curling spikes on the top of his head. He looked young, although I had no point of reference at the time. He held a fish up to the early morning sunlight and I remembered that while I had gorged itself on lemonwhites two days past, it *was* two days past. I snapped my beak in anticipation, delighted when he flung it into the air over the roof. I launched and caught it easily, downing it with a single gulp .

The golden drakina cooed at me and I snapped my beak a second time.

He flung a second fish, this time over the docks and I swept down like the Hallow Fire, snatching it before it hit the wood. The drakina was watching with interest so I tossed it into the air and flew in a circle before catching it in my beak and returning to the roof. I was proud of myself for my very newly acquired skill. I was a fisherdrake now. The Fang of Wyvern would soon be mine.

The fellow produced another fish, this one larger than all the others and I snapped my beak again. He waggled the fish in his hand and I leaned forward, clutching the roof with the talons of my wings. He waggled and waggled and the gold trilled and fanned her beautiful wings and the fish slipped out of the hand and onto the dock. The stick people fell silent at that.

I looked around. The sea snakes were circling. They wanted the fish but it was mine. The stick had given it to me, not the snakes, not the other stick people. They stood in a circle around the fish, holding a web of hemp amongst them. I didn't wonder why. Clearly, they were afraid of my fire and thought a hemp wall a sufficient method of protection. It isn't in the nature of dragons to be suspicious, although perhaps it is more in our nature to be vain.

I soared into the circle of stick people, snapping the

large fish in my jaws and with one mighty stroke, swept upwards into the skies. It was then that I felt the hemp fall across my back, weighing my wings like the water in the storm. I dropped the fish and twisted, expecting the web to fall away but I was hauled down to the wood with a thud. I called the fire but the hemp was wet and it only sizzled with oily smoke. The people wrapped the hemp around and around and I remembered the little golden drakina and her bound legs and I remembered the blue and green drake and his cage of twigs and I knew that I had been a vain and foolish dragon. I struggled and fought but the hemp grew tighter and tighter until I could barely move. I cursed my wild stubborn pride and vainly bit at the hands grabbing and poking at my neck. When a silver band was snapped in place around my own throat, I bowed my head and relented.

THE STICK PEOPLE

They are called Stick People because they build their world of sticks.

I learned that the docks were a large fishing market called the Udan Shores on the bridges, barges and waterways of a city called Venitus. Venitus was a water-city, with the sea clawing the edges of the land for miles. Fishing boat, dory and skiff were the ways these sticks got about, and for the most part, they pushed their boats through canals with long poles. Large barges were pulled by dragons, and it was the first time I'd ever seen my people as anything but creatures of sea and sky. It was an affront to my pride and I immediately despised the world of sticks.

It was also the first time I ever thought of my people as a people. I suppose self-identification finds root in many soils.

I was in a cage, much like the blue and green drake. It was small, so small that I was forced to remain curled and it wasn't long before my spine began to ache. I was a sea dragon, used to tall cliffs and taller skies, so these days spent in a cage were a horror to me. There was no food, though the smell of fish was everywhere, and I found my belly rumbling with the thought of lemonwhites and silverfins and bloodbass. At this point I knew I would eat a sea snake and be grateful for it. That is how low I had sunk.

I never saw the stars in those first days, never saw the moons nor the hot sun nor the water. Only the inside of the hut and the cages of dragons. I thought much of my father, Draco Stellorum. I missed him but I realized with surprise that I missed my mother more.

Several times a day, a hard-faced man came with a basket of fish and a long switch. He removed the blue-green dragon from his cage and I could not help but watch the exercises they went through. The hard-faced man handled the drake roughly, checked the silver band and the hemp at the drake's feet. The band restricted our fire somehow, keeping the arcstone from creating the spark that turned our acid to flame. Against our fiery breath, the stick people are helpless.

I watched with narrowed eyes as he slipped a harness over the drake's blue head. Next, he pulled the wings through as though they were made of sticks, like everything else in this world of sticks. He didn't appreciate the glory and the delicacy of dragon wings, for he had nothing glorious or delicate of his own. Unless you counted the golden drakina. She would sit on his shoulder or perch on his wrist, nibble tiny grubs from his hand. He would pet her and coo at her and she would trill back. She was glorious and wicked and wonderful and I found it difficult not to watch her when I had the chance.

Regarding the exercises, I vowed to do the opposite of what was expected of me, so I did. When the hard-faced man put his hand to the blue's beak, the blue lowered his head. When he put his hand to mine, I bit him. I was rewarded with a whack of the switch across my neck. When the hard-faced man offered a spoon of mashed fish, the blue ate, licking it off the spoon with a rough tongue. (I realized then another reason for the silver band – fisher dragons were not meant to swallow any of the fish they caught, merely hold it in our throats until our sticks demanded.) I did not accept the mash offered, however and rather hissed and lunged and was rewarded with the switch to my beak. Where the blue leapt to the hard-faced man's wrist, I flew at his face, straining with all my talons to paint that hard, leathery skin with ribbons of red. I cannot begin to tell you what he did with the switch after that.

I hated the hard-faced man. I hated this village and my life in the cage of sticks, and I vowed to die here, defiant and free at least in spirit, dreaming of my life at the Anquar Cliffs. One day, the blue drake was gone, and I thought I saw him sitting once on the post next to the golden drakina. I didn't care. It would be a year before they would be of breeding age and I would be dead before then.

Many days later, when my belly had long-since quieted and my head was too weary to lift, another of the stick people entered the hut. It was the same one as that first day – the young one that had tossed the fish into the air and lured me into this trap. I supposed I should have hated him more than the hard-faced man, but I didn't. I knew it was my own pride that rendered me here. No one was more to blame than I.

He wore a belted tunic and sandals, with a satchel draped across his shoulder. From it, he naturally pulled a set of sticks. He put those strange sticks to his lips and blew. What came out was music, beautiful sad music like dragons weeping and I found it soothing to my ears. It was good music to die to, I reckoned, and closed my eyes to welcome my end.

Then, he began to talk in a voice that sounded like the roll of waves on the shore. I didn't even open one eye. He could slit my throat and take my hide as a prize, although with its bruises, I doubt it would be a worthy thing.

"Stormfall."

He repeated that single word, over and over and I grew to understand the shape of it, if not the meaning.

"Stormfall," he said. "Stormfall. That's what I would call you."

I ignored him, wishing in fact that he would slit my throat. At least the silver band would be gone.

"Serkus calls you Snake, but you fell out of the storm, so Stormfall."

And then I felt something on my tail, a light something at first and I could smell a sharp tang above the odor of fish. I opened one eye to see him rubbing salve onto the wounds on my tail. I could have moved it if I wanted. I could have slid my tail into the cage and tucked it against my body but I didn't care. It felt good and I felt bad. It made sense to do nothing.

"You are a fine dragon," I heard him say. I didn't

understand the words, but I understood the meaning, if only in the crooning tone of his voice. "A very fine young dragon indeed. I'm sorry I let them catch you but I can't let you go now or Serkus will beat me the way he beats you."

He brought his face close to mine, studied me through the wooden bars. I opened both eyes now and blinked at him. He did look young, I thought, although I knew nothing of stick people. Dark curly hair like seaweed, dark eyes, dark skin like mine. If I had my fire, I think I could have burned it all off with one breath but I didn't care to. At least, that's what I told myself.

The boy bolted upright as the hard-faced man entered the hut, the blue perched obediently on his arm. He moved his stony eyes from the boy to me, and back again, before sliding the drake into his cage on the floor beside me.

"You think you are a match for this black snake, soul-boy?" he snapped in a tone that I understood all too well, despite my lack of verse in stick. "You want to try to make him a fisher?"

"I did well enough with Skybeak," the boy answered. "You said I did."

"Because I was teaching you."

"Then let me try. It's no use killing him."

The hard-faced man nudged my cage with his boot.

"A dragon not tamed is a dangerous thing," he said. "Best to kill them before they eat your flocks or your village or your family."

Lies, I thought to myself. All I wanted was fish and sky.

"Let me try," said the boy. "If I don't have him willing

in harness and tether by the wide moons, I will take out his heart with a fishknife."

"By the Open Eyes?" The man shook his head. "That's four days."

"I can do it in three."

When I think back on these things, I realize dragons aren't the only creatures with an abundance of vanity and pride.

"Three days it is." The hard-faced man turned to leave the hut, looked back with a wicked grin. "If he eats any of the fish or damages the nets, it comes out of your pocket, Rue. Or your soul."

"He won't," said the boy.

Rue, I told myself. He was called Rue.

It was, I realized much later, my first introduction to names. It was to be a deep, twisted and profound relationship. But back to my story.

"You have two seasons left, Rue," said the hard-faced man, "To get both your freedom and your soul. Don't risk it all for a wild dragon. A soul is a valuable thing."

He paused.

"Worth at least six months of fish."

And then he laughed.

The boy called Rue lowered his eyes but I saw his fingers curl.

Still laughing, the hard-faced man left the hut.

We were alone, the boy, Skybeak and me. From his little cage, the drake trilled and I watched as Rue reached in to rub the blue head, running his hand down to the chin, to the itchy spot between the spines. Skybeak gave a contented sigh, closed his eyes in pleasure.

Oddly enough, I didn't hate this blue drake. He was a captive just like me. He had made choices to live and not die and even though he spent his nights in the lair made of sticks, he spent his days serving at the side of the beautiful drakina. He seemed content but I wondered if he had ever flown the open skies. I wondered if he had ever caught his own lemonwhites or burned the tail of a sea snake or had seen the Dragon Flight soaring across the open waters. I could never accept this as my home, could never live off the mashed remains of rotten fish instead of hunting for myself.

Rue moved back to my cage, slid a wooden panel down from the top to pin my head and neck to the bottom. I didn't fight it. I didn't care. He fastened it with twine and carefully, opened the latch, reaching his hand in toward my face. I knew I should have bitten him then. My life would have been much different. Instead, I growled (which in dragon sounds much like music) but it did not deter him and before I knew it, his fingers brushed my jaw. I growled again as he traced the long, elegant lines of my beak, from my chin to the bony ridge circling my eye. I blinked slowly as his hand traced down my angular cheek and through the spines to the soft spot of my throat, all the while repeating the same word.

Stormfall.

He applied the sharp-smelling salve as I closed my eyes. I would growl more tomorrow, I told myself. I would burn his face off once I had regained the strength to do so. I had no idea what the next three days would bring, nor how my life would change by the wide moons. For now, I desperately wanted sleep and so I did. But the moons are like the tide – there is no stopping them once they are on their course to rise.

***

Rue carried the cage out of the markets to a remote part of the shore, where sand and stone met weeds and waves. Tiny sink-lizards darted along the beach, hunting insects that flittered above the surf. The wind was strong and cold and I found myself wondering how he was going to attempt to do this when the wind was a dragon's ally. Regardless, I didn't care overmuch. Once I could, I would be free.

He laid the cage down onto the sand and knelt beside it, sliding the wooden panel down across my neck again before opening the latch. I hissed at him, baring my teeth and wishing I had the flame to scorch his skin off. Within two moves, he had affixed a harness to my face, tightening leather straps around my jaws and fastening them behind my head. I had no horns at this point so I was effectively muzzled, prevented from biting, snapping or even spitting a wad of acid. He raised the panel and sat back, tugging on a cord that was attached to the muzzle. I didn't budge. I wouldn't give him the satisfaction. He would have to drag me out onto the sand to begin his lessons. Which is exactly what he did.

I braced myself against the wood but he was so much stronger, and soon I was beak-first in the sand. My wings sprang out from my back, free for the first time in days. Yesterday I was wishing for death. Today, however, was another day and I leapt into the air, bringing my wings down in frantic strokes as they caught the wind and pushed me higher. Soon, I was far above the boy and the beach and I was free until a yank on the muzzle jerked my head earthward.

I cursed my foolishness. Of course there was a method. He had trained dragons before and I was new to this game. I twisted my neck and tucked my wings, racing down towards him with talons extended but he ducked and flicked my legs with a reed as I swept by. Not harsh, but a reminder that they were stick people for a reason. I growled and flew high, reaching the end of the rope once more. I began to fly in circles, dizzying circles above his head, around and around and around, keeping the tension on the rope and searching for a weakness. But as I looked down, I saw him wrap the rope around his waist. He dropped to sit in the sand, pulled a small package out of the satchel across his chest. Immediately, I smelled salted silverfin and I slowed my circles, my belly waking up to the idea of food once again.

He sat quietly, this stick boy, chewing the silverfin and ignoring the dragon flying at the end of the rope. He was clever too, I had to give him that. It didn't take long before I swept in and dropped to the sand in front of him, folded my wings across my back. He didn't look at me, just continued to munch on the silverfin until it was all gone down his odd flat hole of a mouth. I suspected they had teeth, the stick people. Not true teeth like dragons. No fangs or tusks of a mature male, that much was true, and I wondered how they could eat anything as chewy as a silverfin. Lemonwhites, however, were a different story. They would fall apart with the slightest pressure.

"Six months worth of fish," he said softly. "That's all my soul was worth."

I narrowed my eyes, watched him eat the silverfins and thread the leather straps.

"My father sold it to Ruminor when I was born, before he sold me to Serkus. With all this buying and selling, you'd think I was valuable."

My mouth watered watching him.

"A dragon is worth far more than a soul-boy..."

I wondered if they were also meant for me, these new leather straps. It didn't matter. I would soon be rid of this muzzle. No bindings could keep me contained. I was a wild drake. I racked the straps with my talons but the leather was strong and I was weak. Chewing, he looked up at me, reached into the pouch for another fish. Held it by the tail and waggled it like he had that first day in the village, causing the scent to waft in my direction. If I could have, I would have snapped my beak but I could barely open my mouth and I felt the juices well up between my teeth. I feared I would drool because of this cursed muzzle and that, for a dragon, is a terrible degradation.

Rue tossed the fish to the sand at my feet and I grabbed it in my talons, tried desperately to put the flesh to my mouth but the muzzle prevented it. I thrashed furiously and battered it with my beak but to no avail. I launched into the air, wishing I could just leave this prison of torment or die trying. I flew in dizzying circles once again but this time to the music of the wooden pipes. It was sad and lonely and beautiful, like me. I flew for hours and hours until the sun was high in the sky and I could fly no more and finally, I plummeted to the sand, welcoming the warmth on my belly and tail. If I couldn't have the fish, at least I would take this one pleasure before I died.

After a long while, Rue rose to his feet and crossed the space between us. I lifted my head and hissed at him. The muzzle was tight and there was sand on my tongue but I didn't move. I didn't retreat. I merely watched him, knowing that at any moment, I could leap into the air and be out of his reach. If only for a time, though, because I was tethered and he was strong.

He crouched in front of me, held out the leathers.

"Stormfall," he said. "This is a body harness. It will free your head and allow you to eat."

I hissed again, although perhaps less vehemently.

He reached out his hand, stroked my neck, ran his hand along my shoulder, still raw from the hard-faced man's lashes. He gently laced the leathers around my wings and under my chest like the blue drake. I let him, knowing that ultimately, without teeth or fire I couldn't win. For some reason, I forgot my talons. I could have shredded his face and throat but I never thought about it. I tell myself I was exhausted but I suspect there was something more in the forgetting.

He cinched the second harness tight and I growled at him. He stroked my head, the spines that would one day mature into a mane of spikes, untied the muzzle and slid it off my face. I debated biting his nose off but it was then that he held up the fish.

It was a lemonwhite.

I hated him.

He pulled out a short fish knife and slid the blade into the fish's mouth, slicing it into long, ribbon-like strips. He held one out to me and I growled again.

"Eat, Stormfall," he said, his voice rolling like the waves on the shore. "It's small enough for you to swallow, even with the fisher collar. I won't mash it for you. You are a wild dragon and deserve respect."

My belly growled this time and I snapped the slice from his hand, throwing it back into my mouth but it caught the wrong way in my throat. I shook my head and it went aright, sliding down like water. It felt like nothing, and I looked back at him, angry and proud and demanding.

Smiling, he held up another slice.

WARSHIPS & CANNONFIRE

It was amazing how fast I could fly when the sky was clear and the waters calm. I learned how to release thought and focus solely on breathing in time to my beating wings. It was a furious rhythm, allowing no room for distraction and I found I could push myself so that even my second eyelid would burn from the wind. But while it was furious, my spirit soared in those times and I skimmed the surface of the waters in search of a target. In those days, my target was fish.

During the last weeks of the dry season, I became the best fishing drake in all the village. Rue was a good trainer and I learned how to snatch two silverfins at once from the surface with my talons. I learned that the red flash in the water meant bloodbass and I would soar up high, arcing and diving deep to catch as many as seven in my mouth at the same time. I knew how to spit acid at the sea snakes and how to pull the heads off sink-lizards with claw and beak. I knew the school patterns of lemonwhites and the feeding habits of blue mollies and I knew which fish to avoid because of venom in their spines. I found that out the hard way.

I learned how to drink the waters of the ocean. I far preferred the fresh water that Rue gave me from amphora back in the fishing hut, but I realized that I could, in fact, swallow mouthfuls of ocean when necessary and strain out the salt through tiny slits in my beak. The salt often crystalized, looked like stars glittering along my face.

Best was that I learned to taunt the big scaly things called Black Monitors – the same creature that had tried to eat me on the night of the storm. I led them a merry chase, my tail dragging atop the ocean waves until they swam into rocks or reefs or sandbars that I had spied from above. They never died but still, I was proud of my new skills and thrived under Rue's patient hand.

I would have been happier if they died, but then again, I was young and proud and male.

Because of Rue, I learned about life in the village. The Udan Shore was part of Venitus, a larger city of water canals and glass blowing and many, many boats. Everyone in Venitus seemed to hate the hard-faced man, whose name I learned was Master Fisher Brazza Serkus. I refused to acknowledge that he in fact had a name, preferring to think of him as simply the hard-faced man. I was still as proud as ever and wild, even though I wore the silver band.

I learned that Venitus itself was in the nation of Remus and that the stick people of Remus bought and sold everything, including each other. As a child, Rue had been bought by the hard-faced man for peeling the shells off tiny beaked shrimp. He had proved good at his job and worked his way up to his current position of apprentice fisher dragoneer. Once his apprenticeship was complete, he would be free to leave the village and find work elsewhere and then, perhaps a life. He was young but not so young, and I would catch him glancing from time to time at the girls who sold hemp along the docks. They would smile and wave but wouldn't approach. I never thought that it might have been me, perched on his shoulder with my wings wide and teeth bared, although perhaps I suspected, just a little.

I also learned that fishing dragons didn't last long in the village, for within a year they would outgrow any of the skiffs that the stick people used. In fact, the best I could expect from my life here was to breed the golden drakina (whose name I learned was Summerday) and then be sold as a barge dragon along the canals or as a cart dragon to an inland farm. I tried my best not to think of this, believing in my bones that Rue would free me before selling me as a cart dragon, but I didn't know this for fact. While he was kind, Rue was a stick and I was a dragon. Life meant very different things to both of us.

And so one evening, I returned to Rue's skiff. He was alone in the little boat, the shoreline barely a slash across the western horizon. I landed on his knee, releasing the fish in my talons and bringing up the others from my crop. The baskets were full after a good day and as I settled onto my perch at the prow, he pulled several strips of silky lemonwhite and fed me by hand. Because of the band, I could never swallow the fish I caught so Rue always fed me strips. I felt very lucky. Skybeak, Summerday and the others were always fed mash. I couldn't imagine eating mash from a bowl. It was an affront to my wild, proud and vainglorious nature.

And so we sat one evening, Rue playing the pipes and I warbling along in my beautiful dragon voice, both of us enjoying the sun set over the water. Soon, it was twilight and the sky filled with streaky clouds and stars and my father, Draco Stellorum, and we just sat, the boat rising and falling on the quiet breathing of the water. The village was a long way off and we would frequently go back after dark. I think he was lonely, this stick boy, and a dreamer for he would often gaze for hours at the horizon of empty sky. We would venture further than any other fisher team and I wondered if he had ever thought to escape, to flee his master and begin a life somewhere he had never been. Every night we returned home, however, to the hut and the dragons and the docks and Master Fisher Serkus. Fortunately, the beatings were few now that Rue was growing and I was trained.

At one point that night, Rue lowered the pipes.

"There's going to be a war soon," he said quietly. "Serkus said that Lamos is trying to steal our dragons. He said we should not go out too far and to pray that Ruminor will keep us safe when we go."

I had heard the name Ruminor before. A god, I presumed, a spirit who ruled the skies and taken the moons as sister-wives. I was learning much from my time with the sticks.

"I won't pray," said Rue. "It's Ruminor's fault if there's a war. He made the world for his sons but gave dragons to one and not the other. That's a terrible thing to do. We shouldn't have to pay the price if war comes to Remus. Ruminor was a bad father."

He paused, searching his thoughts. He was a quiet boy, not given to many words. This was the only time he talked, when we were alone on the ocean at night. I think the water made him feel safe and the stars made him free.

Sometimes, it was so quiet that I could hear his thoughts.

"Not that I know about fathers," he muttered. "Mine sold me when I was born."

He shrugged.

"Doesn't matter really. I have shelter, I have work. And I have my own dragon. That's better than a father."

He ran a hand along the crest of my skull, the warm nubs where my horns would grow. He raised his dark head to stare at the sky and sighed.

"I don't believe the old stories about Ruminor and his sons, anyway. They're just old myths and rules. Don't tell Serkus. He'd have me whipped, even though he doesn't believe them either."

I couldn't tell the hard-faced man. I wouldn't even think his name. Names were, and still are, profound things.

He'd stopped patting me. I pushed my head into his hand so he resumed.

"I do believe in dragons, though," he smiled. "Dragons are beautiful and proud and strong and clever. Sometimes I wish I had been born a dragon."

I loved these nights on the water. I loved his hand on my neck, the sound of his words. Like waves on the ocean. With his music and his love of the sea, I often wondered if

Rue was part dragon.

"I've been learning about dragons. Well, mostly about Selisanae of the Sun. Every morning, she rises from the ocean to chase Ruminor's wives from the sky. She reminds me of Summerday sometimes."

Summerday. I could easily believe she was daughter to the sun. Just the mention of her name made me sit a little prouder, arch my neck so my spines stood out.

Vanity, thy name is dragon.

"She was one of the First Dragons, Selisanae was. Serkus calls them the *Veternum*. Selisanae, Nerisanae, Stellorus and Anquarus."

The last two struck a familiar chord. My father and my home. Odd how the words were so similar. Maybe Rue was part dragon after all.

"I believe in the *Veternum*," he continued. "But Ruminor?"

He grunted.

"I don't believe in him because I don't have a soul. If he gave it back, then maybe I'd believe but he doesn't, so it's his own fault."

Rue often talked about souls. I didn't know what they were but apparently he didn't have one. His father had sold it to that Ruminor before selling him to Serkus. It was complicated and beyond my dragon reason. I knew about fish, however. I snapped my beak. He passed me a slice of lemonwhite.

"Soul-boys – that's what they call us." He sighed again. "Soul-boys, because we don't have a soul. Doesn't matter. I don't need it anyway. I have you and you have soul enough for me."

I would give Rue a soul if I knew where to find one. All a dragon needed was water, sky, flame and fish.

"I'll be free soon though and Serkus will make Ruminor release my soul. Only two more seasons. I'll have to pay Serkus for you so I might have to work another season, but I'll do it. I'll take you with me, Stormfall. I promise you that. When I'm free, you will be too. I may not end up with my soul but at least I'll have my dragon."

Freedom sounded good. Lemonwhites sounded better.

"Can you imagine where we could go on our own?" he asked, passing me another strip. "To Capua or to the Etreni Salts or maybe even all the way down to Terra Remus. I could buy my own skiff and we could live on the beaches and neither of us would have to work for anyone ever again. I don't need a soul to be happy. I think all I need is a dragon."

All I needed was fish. I snapped my beak again.

He grinned and fed me another.

We sat longer, rising and falling on the water and eating lemonwhites. By right, they belonged to the hard-faced man, as did Rue and I and all the fish we caught. In spite of this, I would have happily eaten them all but at one point I realized there was a sound on the water.

I lifted my head, gazed around in the darkness.

"Stormfall," Rue asked. "What do you hear?"

He reached for a lantern, but paused.

The creak of wood, the splash of oars, the rush of waters, the flap of canvas in the faint breeze.

I spread my wings but he scrabbled forward, wrapping me in his arms and pulling me into his chest. He closed my beak with one hand.

"Hush," he hissed. "A ship…"

I blinked, not understanding. I didn't fight him, though. It was Rue and he was my stick. The rush of waters grew louder, became a roar. I darted my eyes across the expanse, looking for a sign. There was black and there was blackness. I could feel the air moving forward, pushed by an unseen force.

There. I spied it just to the east of us - a flash of rigging in the starlight. It was almost on top of us and I struggled now, flailing against Rue's arms. He released me, hauling back on his oar and turning the prow just as a massive vessel swept across our path. I launched into the starry sky, flapping just above the water and hoping I was invisible because of my night-black scales.

Three vessels with billowing striped canvas sails and ten oars per side, row upon row. The prows were curved inward with large painted eyes that watched me as they surged past. On the decks, men pushed large iron objects and there was an odour that brought back early fledgling memories of arcstone.

One of the shipsmen shouted, pointed at me as I swept too close. It was a language different from Rue's and I flew higher until I was out of sight. From the sky, I could see Rue's tiny boat bobbing in the wake of the three great vessels so I waited until he was far behind before swooping down to my perch on the skiff.

"Lamoan warships!" gasped Rue and he lunged forward, snapping my harness to a pull-ring at the prow. "We have to warn the village! Maybe we can beat them to the shores! Fly, Stormfall! Fly!"

He threw me into the air and I whirled above the skiff,

feeling the harness snap taut against my chest. I heard his oars splash and I threw all my strength against the leathers as together, dragon and boy set the small boat racing across the waters toward the village. But two oars are no match for forty, and one small dragon no match for wind-catching sails. They easily out-paced us, leaving us battling their white-capped wake as we struggled to keep up.

In the distance, I saw a flash like Hallow Fire, followed by a boom like Hell Down and behind me in the skiff, Rue let out a strangled cry. I flapped harder, feeling the strain in my wings and the chafe of the leather against my chest. Another flash, another boom and fire began to glow across the horizon. Posts and beams, docks and huts, we watched the structures of the village catch and blaze. Soon, Rue leaned back on the oars, dragging us until we slowed.

"Stormfall," he whispered, his voice hoarse and cracking. "Stormfall, come back."

I did, grateful for the rest, and I lit on his knee, eyes still fixed to the burning village very far away. He dropped his hand on my head, silent and still. From our vantage, we could see silhouettes of buildings blazing with flame, timbers crackling and splitting, roofs crashing down on the living things within. Most disturbing were the shadowy figures, blazing as they leapt into the water. Plumes of steam rose as the waves sizzled and smoked.

This was stick fire and I was stunned at how deadly it was. Another flash, another boom, another explosion in the village. And so we sat for a long time, rocking on the waves, our faces made hot by the distant flames, our backs cold from night on the water. As the village burned, we could see men from the ships running from hut to hut, could hear laughter and screaming in equal measure. I thought I heard the shriek of a young dragon and I feared for Skybeak and Summerday. There were other fishing dragons in the village, so I convinced myself it was one of them.

Another sound now, coming from the night behind us and I sat up, looked to the sky. Rue said nothing. I'm not certain he even noticed. I chirruped loudly and unfurled my wings. Rue looked up and gasped.

Whommpf, whommpf, whoompf, steady and low and strong, a Dragon Flight swept like an arrow across the stars above us, a great silver drake at the tip. I could see the intricate harness, saddle and leathers that kept the riders in place and my heart threatened to burst at the sight of them. They continued on over us and I knew tonight there would be a battle that I would be both honoured and horrified to witness.

As they arced down over the ships, seven dragons unleashed their fire and the sails erupted in flame. There was chaos on deck as the great iron objects spun, flashing and booming in the night sky. One, a stone-gray drake, went spiralling down and I could see his rider leap from the saddle as they hit the water. The drake bellowed, thrashing as arrows pelted the waves. The rider cried out under the deadly hail before he disappeared beneath the hull of the ship. The last I saw of the dragon was the tip of his tail as he too slipped into the black.

Rue had a grip on my own harness but I strained against him, twisting and snapping, until he finally unhooked the rope. Released, I was instantly airborne and beating my wings madly to catch up with the Flight.

Another flash and boom and I ducked, the heat searing my second lids as a great iron ball tore past me to shatter the wing of a golden drake behind me. He spun as he went down, hitting the waters hard, the spray cooling me as I swept through. His rider did not leap and both were met with a volley of arrows, turning the whitecaps red before they slipped under the seething waves.

Above us, the dragons circled, spraying fire and as I neared, the heat was worse than even the hottest day on the Anquar Cliffs. The sounds from the battle were deafening– the booming of black iron, the roar of the fires and the shouting of the sticks. Another blast of cannonfire, another volley of arrows. Five dragons raining death down on the flaming warships, and me, a little night-black dragon in the middle of it all.

I saw the silver drake land on the top deck of the lead vessel, setting everything alight with his breath as he swung his great head. Two sticks spun a cannon, taking aim at him from the deck below. I barked a warning but the battle roared louder so I tucked my wings and dove like a spear.

The first stick screamed as my talons raked across his face and I wheeled, disappearing with a flick of my tail into the night. *Fragile,* I marvelled. His skin tore like lemonwhites under my claws. The second stick cranked the iron, so I dropped onto his head, striking at his eye and piercing the pulpy flesh with my dagger-sharp juvenile beak. A string of slime and ooze trailed when I pulled it out and I shook my head, sent it sailing across the deck. The man howled and dropped to his knees but I was gone; a wraith of ash and stars and cool night air.

Before I knew it, the great silver drake was in the air beside me. His head was larger than my entire body, his one wing-beat to my ten. I knew he saw me, for his wide pupil constricted, but his rider yanked on the rein and he banked hard, circling to rain fire once again across the foremast of the ship. It pitched forward, crashing onto a set of barrels and black powder spilled across the deck. Suddenly, there was a great flash of light and I tumbled through the air, a boom cracking the night like Hell Down. I caught the hot wind and soared upwards, watching as the hull split in two under the flames. Slowly, both halves pitched forward and followed the drakes down to the depths.

The remaining ships began to pull away from the docks, abandoning any men to the fire, the boiling water and the enemy, but the Dragon Flight was relentless. Their flames scorched the ships over and over until both vessels groaned and shuddered, tipping stern over prow and sliding into the dark water. The Flight then swept the seas, torching any men left bobbing in the waters. It was as bright as midday, but the light was that of the burning docks and the flaming timbers and the golden reflection of it all on the surface of the sea.

I hovered for a long moment, watched the Flight leave the wreckage and wing their way towards the village. In my heart of hearts, I longed to follow but I was too young and far too small. But they had captured my imagination – dragon and stick flying as one, our fire harnessed without a single silver band to be seen. Perhaps the most powerful, most noble dance in the history of the world and I had shared in its steps, small as they may have been.

With a flick of my tail, I wheeled in the air and returned to the skiff, lowering myself silently onto the prow.

Rue sat, eyes empty, watching the glowing city as we rocked on the waters. I snapped my beak at him, hoping for a reward. He did nothing. I hopped over to perch next to him, snapped again. *Nothing.* I had done well tonight. I had assisted in a battle. I deserved a reward, praise, a stroke on the head.

Nothing.

His silence was confounding.

Finally, after several hours of sitting in the boat, bobbing up and down on the surface of the water, he reached for the oars to take us home.

***

There was little left of the docks that morning and our fishing hut had burned to the ground. Bodies lay fallen among charred wood, arms and legs twisted at awkward angles, smoking like coals. These sticks died in contorted positions, and I realized it was the same as with dragons. When we die, our spines constrict and our heads twist over our backs. I couldn't imagine the manner of pain produced by immolation. Some things are too terrible for the imagination of dragons.

I perched on Rue's shoulder as he wandered through the remains. I wasn't certain what he was looking for, but he was my stick. He needed me and I was proud to be needed. When I think back on it, I realize that I was bound to him in ways that had nothing to do with the silver band at my throat.

Other villagers wandered across the docks, some gathering usable items, some looking for loved ones, all wailing in despair. The docks were the only part of the village that I had known, but Venitus was a large center and city people floated by on their dorries and skiffs to glimpse the destruction. They were lucky that the pirates did not get further into the city but then again, they were lucky only because of the Dragon Flight.

"Boy!" came a voice and Rue turned to see a man in silver armour crunching through the debris toward us. I recognized him as the rider of the silver drake and I spread my wings at the sight of him. I'm not sure why. Perhaps to make myself look bigger and therefore more impressive. Perhaps as a threat to keep him away from my stick. I don't know. It had been a long night and I was tired.

"Ruminor smiles on us," said the man in greeting.

"Ruminor smiles," said Rue, bowing swiftly. "How may I serve?"

"Your dragon, may I see him?"

Rue glanced at me then back at the rider.

"Why?"

"Your dragon saved my life last night, and that of my drake, Ironwing."

Rue glanced at me again before gathering the hemp rope and passing me over to the rider. I hissed angrily but perched on the man's gloved wrist. I was big but he was strong.

"What have you named him?"

"Stormfall, Master Rider."

"Interesting name."

"Yes, Master Rider. He blew in on a storm. With his

colouring, it seemed to fit."

The rider checked my teeth, examined my spines, the stumps where horns would crown my skull as I aged. I hissed again but it was a vain protest. This man was skilled in the way of dragons.

"Taken from wild, then?"

"Yes, Master Rider," said Rue. "I caught him for my Fishing Master."

"And you trained him yourself?"

"I did, Master Rider. He's a very good fishing drake."

"Hmm." He passed me back and I hopped to Rue's shoulder, home. "His colouring is advantageous. Gods-damned Lamoans never saw him coming."

"The fish don't see him either," said Rue. "That's why we go at night."

"My name is Cassien Cirrus, First Wing of the Eastern Quarter Dragoneers," said the man. "When he's older, bring him to the Citadel. We could use a night dragon like him."

"A night dragon…" repeated Rue, tasting the words on his tongue.

The stick reached into his armour and produced a coin. He placed it in Rue's hand.

"A pass into the Citadel. Bring it with you when you come."

He turned to leave.

"But what about me?" called Rue. "What will I do without my dragon?"

The man shrugged.

"Perhaps we could use a young dragon like you too."

He flashed his teeth and left us to approach a gathering

of city officials down the docks. In the distance I spied a gleam of silver as the great drake cleaned his scales on the sand.

Rue studied the coin in his hand before slipping it into his pocket and I folded my wings across my back. I was hungry and too tired for imaginings. I longed for my wooden cage where I would fall asleep under the trills of Summerday.

I wondered if I would dream, and if so, I hoped it would be of the Flight.

Suddenly, the world pitched beneath me and I tumbled forward to the dock, a crack like Hell Down ringing through my ears. Rue staggered and went down as well as the switch of Fishing Master Serkus rained blow after blow upon his head and shoulders. I screeched and sprang from the dock, wings beating against his chest, claws extended. I would rake out his eyes like I had on the ship.

But I froze when I saw his face. The face that had always been hard as mountain rock was now gone – fleshy, raw and blackened by flames. With a savage backhand, he whipped the switch across my beak and stars exploded like Lamoan cannons behind my eyes. He swung a net of hemp across me and I dropped back to the charred wood with a thud. Rue cried out and threw himself, fists flailing, onto the man but Serkus struck him to the dock with savage ease. I thrashed against the netting as he kicked me over and over and over. The blows were hotter than the fire on the docks, but soon, even the heat faded and Rue's cries drowned under the pounding of my ears until there was nothing but ash and stars and blackness and silence.

THE COROLANUS MARKETS

I was in another cage now, traveling on the back of a cart pulled by noxen – strong buck-like creatures with low horns and no imagination. They were happy to pull carts. They were happy to eat grass. They were happy to be in harness and happy to be free of it. I easily understood the myth that dragons ate noxen, for if I'd had the chance, I would have killed and eaten them too. I think they would have been happy for their deaths as well.

We rattled along the road through foothills of yellow grass and red rock. I could see mountains in the distance; great white peaks that were impressive yet so very different from either the Anquar Cliffs or the Udan Shore. This dry land was alien to me and I found my scales flaking in the arid wind. I missed the water that had shaped my early life, but it wasn't the only thing I missed.

Next to me in an identical cage was Summerday. She had survived the attack on the village, for which I was grateful, but she had not trilled, she had not cooed, she had not done any of the things that had previously marked her as a glorious young drakina. I realized quite soon then that she was blind. Something had happened on the night of the attack and rather than slit her throat, the hard-faced man (whom I now called the no-faced man) was going to sell her as a breeder, taking whatever he could get for her. I didn't know if it was the right thing. While a dragon lived, there was always a possibility of life out of the ashes. Once dead, a dragon merely fed the earth and the many creatures that lived on her.

Skybeak was not here, which told me much.

The worst thing, however, was the fact that I had not seen Rue since that morning on the docks and I prayed that the no-faced man hadn't killed him. I couldn't imagine how he could have, not with Rue almost grown, but sticks lived by very different rules than dragons. They killed dragons easily, but I wondered if killing each other was allowed by the laws of their land or their god.

Without Rue, I felt torn in two, like a sliver of lemonwhite left to dry on the shore. If he was alive, I knew he'd find me and free me from this terrible cage. We'd live on the ocean and fish forever, he'd promised and I believed him. But if the no-faced man *had* killed Rue, I hoped he was with his soul somewhere where spirit dragons flew to the song of his pipes.

I would have protected him with my life had I been given the chance. I would have given my life for his.

There was no fighting this cage. I had tried and I had failed. The bars were rattan and very strong and the little acid I could produce would only sizzle the smooth oiled surface. And so I lay, curled upon myself and cursing the life of a dragon. I should not have left the aerie, I told myself. I should not have been so vain. But vanity is like youth – it fades in time, to be replaced by ache, stone and ash.

But then again, I would never have met Rue. I would never have flown alongside a Dragon Flight, battled warhsips, learned about sticks. I couldn't regret my choices. They had been mine and had been right at the time. Still, I was so very young. What did a young dragon know about life?

After several days on a terrible lurching road, I saw the signs of another village, this one larger than the Udan Shore but smaller than Venitus itself. Huts high up in the mountains, farms along the hills, fields of noxen and tallybucks, and more carts that joined us on the road. That night, the no-faced man pulled into an inn as the rains started, taking his noxen into the stables but leaving Summerday and I under a tarp on the back of the cart.

The no-faced man had left us each with a small wooden boards blobbed with mash. I was very hungry and tried to eat it, but my tongue rebelled and I pushed the board out through the bars to get the scent away from my nose. It was then that I heard the first sound from Summerday – a snapping of her beak that drew my attention. The no-faced man had missed the mark and her mash board sat just outside the cage, beyond her reach. She could smell it but couldn't see it, and she battered her head repeatedly against the bars of the cage as she tried to reach. I was not a sentimental dragon but the sight of such a glorious drakina reduced to this filled me with an ache of an altogether different sort.

I glanced down at my food. I wasn't going to eat it so I nudged the board with my own beak, edging it towards her cage. I nudged it again and again, until it caught against the base of the bars. She heard it bump and flattened her head, spines lying elegantly against her neck. I had to try harder. I slipped my beak beneath the board, tipping it up and the mash slid down, down the board to blob at the base of her cage. It was gone in a heartbeat and I felt a wave of satisfaction, not so much in the act of helping her but in the act of thwarting the no-faced man.

My anger burned again and I vowed to kill him even if it meant death for me, which it would. Sticks could kill dragons, but dragons were forbidden to kill sticks. If dragons were a proud people, sticks were prouder still. Perhaps we were similar in that regard.

Maybe I would kill him for Rue too. I would kill him for Rue, for Summerday and for me.

The rain continued all night and water seeped under the tarp to run through the cart. I didn't mind. I was a fisher dragon and water was my friend. I stretched my neck under the bars and let it roll onto my tongue. I felt bad for Summerday however – she couldn't catch the water and after many hours of missing the raindrops that fell through her cage, she stopped, lowering her beautiful head onto her claws, defeated. She went thirsty that night and after the meal of rotten fish, it was heartbreaking.

At first light of morning, the no-faced man climbed back into the cart and we rambled off again. I was grateful he didn't bother to feed us but wished he had removed the tarp. While the rainy season meant cooler weather, it was hot under that heavy cover. My wings and legs were aching from the confinement, and I longed just to be able to stretch and flap and fly. I dozed and my dreams were filled with longing and fire and Rue.

By noon, the rain had ceased and noise from the streets had intensified. I knew that we were no longer on rural roads and I was elated when the cart jerked to an unceremonious halt. I raised my head when the tarp was thrown off and blinked as the light poured in from above. My cage was yanked from the cart and I could immediately smell dragons.

It was a market, bustling with sticks and animals and carts and stalls and despair. Brown puddles splashed under foot, wheel and claw. Waterlogged canopies hung from poles and masonry walls were streaked from the night's rain. Still, the sun was strong, making the air heavier than ever. I was glad to be out from under the tarp.

The no-faced man threw my cage up on a wooden platform between three other young drakes. One, a large red, hissed and flung himself against his bars, but I spat a mouthful of acid at him and he recoiled, showing me his back. The others were grey-greens and I don't think they even noticed me. They lay with their heads on their wings, uncaring and dull and I wondered at the apathy of dragons. It was an entirely foreign concept to me. Then again, I had wished to die those first days on the Udan Shore. Perhaps apathy was not so different from grief. Both crippled like chains.

A moment later and Summerday's cage was wedged between us. Surprisingly, the red drake hissed at her too and I wondered if he were as blind as she.

The stick people gathered round a sandy circle, shouting and laughing as one-by-one the half-yearling drakes were auctioned off. The red was sold to a fighting pit and I thought that it was a fitting end for the foul-tempered creature. The grey-greens were sold as a pair to a family of arcstone miners. They would spend most of their lives underground now, detecting and grading the stone for the men who mined it. Apparently, arcstone was as vital for sticks as it was for dragons, although what they did with it, I still don't know.

Next, it was Summerday and I craned my neck as the no-faced man pulled her from her crate. She wobbled awkwardly on his wrist and he gave it a shake so that she unfurled her marvellous golden wings. A murmur of approval rose from the crowd and for the first time, I wondered if sticks had an appreciation for finer things.

"What is her story?" asked a woman from the back row. "Can she pull?"

"She's a fisher," said the no-faced man. "Best I ever had. But she can pull, given the right harness."

"Why are you selling her, then?"

"I ran a fleet on the Udan Shore of Venitus," he said. "Lost everything to pirates in the last raid and needs to pay my debts. See?"

And he gestured to his non-existent face.

Another murmur. Clearly, news of the raid had made it to this foothill town. I could hear the word "Lamos" from the crowd and a rumble like distant thunder of Hell Down. One man spat upon the ground.

"She's blind, see?" said the no-faced man. "Lost her eyesight in the fires so she's no use to me as a fisher. But as I said, given the right harness – a fixed harness, mind – she can still pull."

The woman stepped forward, accompanied by a lady in waiting and two men, obviously guards. She was in cream linen, with gold belt and gold laurels in her golden hair. If I had been a stick, I'm sure I would have been impressed. As a dragon however, I knew she would burn as easily as the next.

"Ruminor smiles on us," she said and the crowd murmured.

"Yah, Ruminor," said the no-faced man.

"Your blind drakina," said the woman. "How can she pull?"

"She's a fine thing," said the no-faced man. "And so are you. I'm assuming you're not using her to pull a plow, harvester or tiller, are you?"

"Certainly not. I'm from Bangarden."

The crowd murmured approvingly. She noticed.

"Ruminor smiles on Bangarden," grinned the no-faced man.

"He does indeed. My husband is a senator and as such, I have a golden pilentus that is always pulled by a golden dragon. I have four, you see, but the golds – well, they don't come along every day."

"Your headstalls have blinders, yeah? Well, she don't need them. If you have a fixed trap and a good driver, she'll do well by you."

"How is she for handling?"

"As I said, best I ever had."

She whispered to one of the men before turning back to the podium.

"Twenty-four denari and nothing more."

"Twenty-four denari?" barked the no-faced man. "She's worth twice that!"

"She's blind," cooed the woman and I suddenly hated her more than the no-faced man. "No blind dragon is worth a single coin so be grateful I'm offering what I am. She'll have a year of service in a fine household and I have a golden drake that is around her age. Perhaps we'll get a few clutches out of her before she kisses the axe."

I would tear out her eyes before I killed her.

"Sold," grumbled the no-faced man. "Treat her right. She's a good girl."

But the woman was gone, whirling off into the crowded market with her lady at her heels. One of the men stepped forward to complete the transaction and I felt an unexpected tightening in my chest at the sight of her – beautiful wicked Summerday, sold to pull a vain stick carriage and likely die before her prime. Life was hard on dragons. So few of us reached maturity and once again, I thought of the Dragon Flight. Large, majestic, mature dragons living with a noble purpose.

And, I thought, no silver band around their throats.

Just like that, she was passed over to the woman's guard, a muzzle strapped around her beak and her wings bound in leather. He bundled her under his arm and pushed into the crowd. I lost sight of her in a heartbeat and for some reason, my world was a little darker without her.

I was the last of the half-yearlings and the no-faced man hauled my crate roughly to the podium. Like Summerday, he yanked me out and made me perch on his wrist. I was heavier and I could tell his muscles were straining under the feat, but still, he snapped his wrist and I stretched my wings for balance. There was silence from the crowd.

"What in Hadys is that colour?" asked one man, a stick with more rolls on his chin than there was on the shore. "Black? Since when is there a black dragon?"

"He's perfect for night fishing," said the no-faced man. "Or night hunting. The prey don't even see him coming."

I remembered the words of the silver rider. A Night Dragon, he had called me.

"A night dragon?" echoed a voice and the crowd parted on a small man with long grey hair and skin almost the same shade. He had a cane and was wearing a hat that looked like an upside-down cone. "Wouldn't that would be dangerous?"

"Dangerous? This one ain't dangerous. He's ominous."

And once again, the no-faced man shook his wrist. I flapped instinctively to keep my balance, cursing him and his theatrics.

"My name's Gavius and I'm from the Under Weathers," said the gray man. "We've been having troubles with a dragon taking our flocks. How would I know this one wouldn't do the same?"

The no-faced man ran a hand along my scales. I snapped but he batted my beak and I relented.

"Look at his scales," he said. "Why do you think he so scarred up?"

No one answered.

"He was on the docks when the cursed pirates attacked," the no-faced man lied. "He tried to save my dragons but the cannons were too much for him. He risked his life for the others, but all he ever ate was fish."

Lies, lies, all lies. Except the part about the fish.

"So I can guarantee you, Master Farmer Gavius, that this dragon will not eat your flock. In fact, he'll protect them. He's the best drake I've ever had."

Acid. Flame. Teeth to the throat. Talons to the belly. All the ways I could kill him.

"I thought you said the gold was your best?" came a snicker from the crowd.

"I lied," he said. "That horanah was rich and I wanted her money."

"Yah! You're full of shat, Serkus!" said another.

"That's what his wife says!"

And the crowd laughed at him. Almost as good as death, I reckoned but he bared his teeth, held me up all the higher.

"The First Wing of the Eastern Quarter Dragoneers staked a claim on him," he shouted above the crowd. "And you can get two hundred denari for a Flight Dragon recruit."

"Why don't you train him then?" came another and the crowd murmured once again.

He stepped forward and I felt his puckered eye fall upon me.

"I don't have the heart, see," he said quietly. "The boy who used to fish with him…"

My heart thudded in my chest.

"They were inseparable, see?"

Rue. He was talking about Rue.

"That boy, he was like a son to me…"

His voice cracked. A woman crooned in sympathy.

"I just, I can't bear to look upon these proud, valiant, Lamoan-fighting black scales…"

I had no breath, no heartbeat, no thought. What was he saying?

"So I needs to find him a home, see? A home where he can be treated fairly, with someone as proud and valiant as my poor, lost fishing boy…"

I didn't know what to think. He was lying. Surely, he was lying about Rue. But I didn't know.

I didn't know.

There was silence for a long moment, before Gavius nodded and raised his cane.

"Twenty."

A knife smile split the raw face and he shook his wrist so that I flapped one last time.

"Give me thirty for my poor lost fishing boy."

"Thirty!" called a large stick from the back.

The bidding was hot and animated but all I could think of was Rue. He couldn't be dead. The no-faced man was lying. And yet, why wasn't he here? He had said we'd be together. He had promised we'd be free.

He had been bought and sold in a market just like this as a youngling. I wondered if he had been afraid like Summerday, or apathetic like the grey-greens, or bewildered like me. Not for the first time, I marked our similarities but also our differences, and wondered what it was that enabled people as frail as sticks to rule creatures as magnificent as dragons.

"Sold!" shouted the no-faced man. With great pleasure that he slipped the muzzle on over my beak, tugging the laces tight behind my head. One day I would kill him, I thought to myself over the tugging and the straps. I would summon all the fire in my dragon chest and finish the job the pirates had started. Whether Rue was alive or dead, I would be happy to watch him burn.

He passed me over to the grey man.

"This collar looks tight," said the grey man. "When does he need a new one?"

"Not for a few months," the no-faced man lied. "It's a fisher-bolt, see? Supposed to fit good and snug. Besides, this fella is slippery and can spit acid with even the littlest room."

"Noted," said the grey man. "He have a name?"

Stormfall, Rue had said. *You fell out of the storm so Stormfall.*

"Snake."

The grey man shrugged, slid the wing-leathers down over me and once again, I was confined. He strapped me in across his back, so I could see where he had been. As he began to make his way out of the dragon market, I could see the yearlings brought in now – greys and blues, greens and browns, all of them as beaten down as the noxen that had pulled my cart.

In the swarming, bobbing mass of people, I did see a flash of gold. I imagined it was Summerday flapping desperately in harness and fixed poles, an elegant golden whip coming down across her back. But it was only a flash and I have a vivid imagination.

I closed my eyes then, and let the stick carry me away from this horrible place to my new home in the Under Weathers. But a part of me was gone, left behind on the Udan Shores, bound up in the fate of a lost boy without a soul.

THE UNDER WEATHERS

It was dark and raining when we reached the district called the Under Weathers and as we traveled, I thought we might possibly be headed back to the sea. My ears popped frequently and if I kept my eyes open to the road behind me, I grew dizzy from the low pressure. The air was a welcome change from the Corolanus Markets however, and the rain made everything lush and green. Moss grew up rocks and down tree branches and rivers rushed alongside the road that gradually became a path then a shaghorn trail and then little more than a narrow footpath.

We saw no one else on that road for the entire day. It was a silent, solitary journey through foothill and forest, but the rain was constant and warm so I was content. Dragons are creatures of water as much as sky, but I did wonder about the stick. His conical hat and hide boots were soggy to the point of shapeless, but he walked without slipping, so I couldn't complain.

This land of the Under Weathers was very hilly, with low mountains and odd rock formations rising from shallow lakes. There was fog everywhere. At one point, I thought he was going to take us directly into a mountainside but there was a fissure and we slipped right through. It was perfectly black in this cavern and I could hear the hissing of goswryms overhead. Soon, we were out the other side just as the last of the sun sank behind the foothills. He paused a moment, wiping the rain from his face.

"Here we are, Snake," he said. "The Oryza Fields of Gavius Grele. Been in my family for generations."

And he turned his back so I could see ahead for a change. There were fields as far as I could see, some flooded, some dry, and some that stretched up the hillsides of scrub and grass. The mountains surrounded this little valley and I thought it rather pretty and pastoral. Strange smells carried on the rain and I wondered what sort of living this man made from the earth when suddenly, I smelled dragons and my heart leapt in my chest.

In the distance, there was a thatch-roofed farmhouse, several outbuildings and what looked like a silo several flights high. Lantern-light flickered at the window and stick people gathered in silhouette at the door. They looked very small.

Gavius turned and continued down the path toward the farmhouse. They ran to meet us in the rain, those little stick people, splashing through the mud and shouting with voices that were very high in pitch. I instantly thought of fledglings with their sharp, high chirps andrealized they were children.

"Ruminor smiles, avus!"

"Ruminor smiles on us all!"

"Did you get one, avus?"

"Avus, can we see it?"

"What colour is it, avus? Did you get a blue one like you said?"

I was surprised at how small they were. And how many. They reached up to touch my feet, my tail, my belly. I couldn't hiss. I couldn't spit. I was a bound dragon. Indignity was my life now.

"Open the aviary, Tacita. He is young and needs rest."

The children raced away from us toward the silo – a tall stone building with curved walls and a metal mesh roof. Suddenly, a warble went up into the night, picked up by another and then another. It was like music to my ears and my breath caught in my throat.

Dragonsong.

The grey stick called Gavius Grele swung me from his back, his old fingers working at the tethers that bound my wings.

"They are serenading you, Snake," he said. "They are giving you a poor dragon's welcome."

As the door rolled aside, one of the little sticks lit a lantern and placed in front of a surface that reminded me of very quiet water. I later learned that this was called silverstone, and sticks used it to reflect light in miraculous ways. Soon, the entire tower was filled with warm gold. My heart leapt at the sight of three dragons of various ages, each in their own cage. Each cage was easily one sixth of the silo, and soared all the way up to the metal mesh roof. They trumpeted and called and I hadn't heard such a thing since the wars between the sea snakes and the dragons on the Anquar Cliffs.

Everything within me wanted to serenade back but I was wearing a muzzle and the best I could do was a pathetic hum.

"Neve," Gavius said. "Our Snake is hungry. Fetch him a small meal of grubs and diced kidney. But very small. His collar is a fisher-bolt and I think it's too tight. I'm not sure how we'll fix that. I should have bought one in the village but I wasn't thinking."

The little stick called Neve raced off to do his bidding.

Gavius carried me into one of the empty cages, set my talons upon the damp chaff bedding. He released the bindings from my wings and they sprang out as if of their own volition. Next, the muzzle, and once off, I threw back my head and sang as I had never sung before. The three dragons launched into flight, up to the metal mesh roof (which I realized was open to the sky and rain and stars) and then swooped back down again in a display of dragon joy.

My feet next, and once free of the hemp, I lit from the straw and soared up, up, up to the mesh roof, filling my chest with cold night air and rainwater. In the pen to my left was a grey yearling drake with the beginnings of horns and we battered our beaks along the mesh walls in greeting. In the pen to my right, an old green drake with stunted wings and dwarfed legs and many scars along his scales. Across from the three of us, a red drakina of about three years. She was too large for her pen but that didn't stop her trilling along with us. I would have happily continued to spiral and soar but a strange, mouth-watering scent reached my nostrils. I dropped to the straw to investigate.

"But he's not blue, avus," said one little stick.

"No, he's better," said Gavius. "He's a night dragon."

"Oh," they all said at once.

They had spooned a pungent mixture of mash and grubs into a wooden trough and slid it through a panel in the pen. I cocked my head at the sight of it. I was a fish eater for the most part, occasionally tasting sea snake, goswyrm, dillies and jakes whenever Rue had a mind to share. Never this strange green-brown medley that smelled like the inside of a dead ghorn.

"What's his name, avus?"

"The man at the auction called him Snake. What do you think about that, Tacita?"

Gavius noticed my hesitation and reached a grey hand in, plucking several tiny oily bits in his fingers. He tossed one in the air towards me, which I caught easily. The children clapped and squealed and I was proud of the fact that Rue had taught me well. I swallowed instantly, unsure of the taste on my tongue, but when he tossed another, I crunched down with my tearing teeth. Dragons are not grass grazers like noxen or leaf nibblers like goswryms. Dragons are flesh eaters and our teeth are made like little daggers or arrowheads or spears. Crunching was a foreign concept, like slurping mash or pulling carts.

"Snake is not a good name for him," said the little stick called Tacita.

"Well then, what would be?"

But crunch I did and I shook my head at the scattering of tastes through my mouth. It went down fine, however, and I snapped my beak at him, catching and swallowing the third piece before plunging my jaws into the trough with relish.

"Blacky," said Tacita.

"Smoky," said another

"Cloudsnake," said Neve.

"Draco Stellorum!" cried a boy and they all laughed at that.

"Draco Stellorum," repeated Gavius. "Dragon of the Stars."

I would have approved but I was busy.

"Nightshade," said Tacita.

"Nightshade," repeated Neve.

"Nightshade," repeated Gavius. "Well then, I think our new dragon has a name."

I didn't care. My belly was full and I eagerly licked all the green-brown juices and grub legs from the trough. And that night, when I climbed into the hemp nest just above the floor and folded my wings across my back, I hoped that wherever he was, Rue was as happy and well-fed as I was at this moment. And when I dreamed, I dreamed of water and fish and Summerday and my wild and future home on the Fang of Wyvern.

***

Pulling a cart does not come as naturally to dragons as fishing, but I did learn many things in those first weeks on the oryza fields.

First, I learned that there are two kinds of harnesses – fixed and free. Fixed traps are used for young dragons and when the terrain is even. They involve three light poles that fix the harness to the cart, one pole on either side (attached to the harness under the wings) and one beneath, (attached to the harness under the chest) to keep the dragon flying just above the ground. The underpole can be adjusted to varying angles and while restrictive, it's actually very helpful. Learning the art of steady flying is difficult for young dragons and we need all the help we can get.

Free traps are simple – dragon harness attached by tethers to the cart. These are good for plows and tilling unstable ground. They require a dragon that knows his angles, for it is very easy to become tangled in the loose set of leathers. Fortunately for me, Gavius started me out with a fixed harness and we got to work immediately in his large acreage of oryza, a type of grain that requires flooding to grow. Planting is done in the spring and is very labour intensive. It doesn't require dragons however, just many little sticks. The plowing of the fields, the mixing of the shat fertilizer and the tilling of the soil, those were jobs for dragons. The threshing of the kernels from the husks – that was also a job for dragons.

Gavius also had a flock of Silky Shearers that he used for wool, milk, cheese and meat. This, along with the oryza, fed his family and ran the business. Dragon shat is acidic, and when mixed with the milk from the shearers, produced a fertilizer that was perfect for the oryza. It was the job of his children and grandchildren to spread in it the water that soaked the fields. Everyone had a job at Gavius' fields. There was not one day of rest.

The old green drake with dwarfed legs went by the name of Stumptail. He had been on Gavius' farm since he was a yearling, and the work was becoming hard on his joints. He could pull a cart like a nox however, walking on all four limbs with an odd, jerking gait. As I have said before, dragons on land are cumbersome things and I would watch him walk, head bobbing as he pulled the plow. Whether it was a limp or a rhythm, I couldn't tell, but his legs seemed sound, his knuckles strong and his body solid. He had no tail and his horns, spines and talons had been filed down so that there was nothing dragon-like about him. It made me question my fate here on the farm, where a dragon became more like a nox in order to fit. Still, he had few vices and was old, so perhaps life had not done so poorly by him after all.

The young grey was called Stonecrop. He was being trained to take over from Stumptail and was a happy young drake, filled to the spines with nervous energy. He was always chasing his tail or scratching his shoulders or chewing his feet, and every night he climbed up the mesh walls of his pen, then down again, up and then down. I couldn't imagine life for him on a farm, pulling plows and tilling fields under harness every day. It didn't seem suited to his nervous personality and I wondered if he had started out that way or if life had conspired to make him so. Not all dragons thrive in the service of sticks, I've learned over the years. More are destroyed than are kept and Samus the plowhand threatened us always. Kissing the axe, he called it. The fate of working dragons.

The red drakina was called Ruby and she was the resident thresher. She had the spines of a mature dragon but with filed horns like the others. She also had a temper that kept the drakes away from her and I realized that was why she was on the far side of the aviary with an empty pen on both sides. It made me wonder about drakinas in general. Other than my mother, sisters and Summerday, I had little experience with them. It seemed like such a bother to attend worrisome, wicked or brooding females when the entire ocean was filled with fish.

The work was hard. I didn't take well to pulling a tiller at first and must admit it is not in the nature of dragons to pull. It is ours to soar and wheel in the skies, to dance on the clouds and swim in the sun. This type of agrarian flying was hard and disciplined, with short, tempered beating of the wings. No stretching, no soaring; just slow, steady flight. But Gavius and his family treated me kindly, so I was happy and well fed and I grew under their care. After a few weeks, the sores from the harness became callouses as my body moulded itself to the farm.

I had never lived through a rainy season, having not yet been a yearling when I'd arrived and the weeks of constant rain wore my spirits down. The skies were dark in the morning and dark well before the end of work. Some days, the sun never shone at all and I despaired of ever seeing blue sky again. Fortunately, the aviary was well drained so while it was always wet, our nests were sheltered and relatively dry. I found there was nothing I loved better than climbing into my nest after a long, bone-weary day in the fields. Closing my eyes to the singing of the dragons was (and still is) a blissful thing.

The little stick named Tacita had taken a liking to me. She was the first to bring my mash in the morning, squatting by my pen to watch as I ate. Sometimes she would show me my reflection in the silverstone and together, we admired my beauty and colour. Other times, she brought a slate, reedpaper and charsticks and would sketch for hour after hour. She always showed me her charrings and invariably, they were of me. My profile, my eye, my talons, my beak. Sleeping, eating, pulling. I especially liked the ones of me soaring across the moons, for I hadn't soared since the Udan Shore.

I wondered if she dreamed of elsewhere, like me, like Rue.

But Tacita wasn't lost and she wasn't a slave. She was free and happy and I often wondered if this could have been Rue's life had he not been sold to Serkus. At night, she would sneak in to the aviary and sit outside my pen, hugging her knees as if they would keep her warm. Sometimes she sang with me, her high thin voice mirroring the memory of his pipes. She had dark hair, just like him, and large dark eyes like the moons of my father, Draco Stellorum. Soon I began to look forward to her night visits and sometimes fell asleep to her singing.

"I'm glad we didn't get a blue dragon," she said one night. "I like you better. You're like the night sky and the night sky is big and dark and very sad. It's okay to be sad. I was sad when my parents died but avus is good to me. At least we could all stay together."

She fell asleep beside my pen that night. If I could have, I would have stretched my wings to cover her. Still, I exchanged my perch for the straw of the floor and slept with my back to hers, warming her as best I could until morning.

Life could have been worse for me, I realized.

The silver band had become too tight however and

now I could only eat very small meals. It had become difficult to breathe as well, but the low fields were heavy with rich, damp air so what I *could* breathe was good. Still, it presented a problem, for the band had no way to be loosened without being removed entirely and it seemed Gavius didn't have a second, larger size for me. I wondered how you could have a farm with dragons and no proper equipment for their care. Then again, they were poor and I was growing.

He left for Corolanus one rainy morning, leaving Samus the plowhand in charge of the farm. I was pulling the tiller through a field that had been left fallow for a year. It was on a high slope and the soil was heavy from the rain, so it was a difficult job even under the best conditions. Behind me, Samus was driving. I didn't like working with Samus. He was lazy and made the dragons do more than our share. However it was not in my nature to complain, so I put my shoulder into the work, flying hard and strong up the hills in the rain. Harder yet was the tilling downside, for that was when you really needed your stick to keep the device from sliding forward and crushing your feet or tail under its heavy iron blade.

I knew now why Stumptail had no tail. Tillers, plows and long, elegant dragonlines simply didn't mix.

We had lost the sun early and it was almost time to quit for the day. My shoulders were aching from the down-strain of the fixed harness and my wings were burning with exertion. Low and steady, flap and flap. Exhausting, especially with the silver band cutting off my breath and I couldn't fill my chest with air, only rapid shallow gasps. But still I worked, low and steady, flap and flap. I couldn't wait to be done for the night.

The soil was hard and slick and on the second last run, Samus stumbled. He dropped onto the ground and stayed, muttering under his breath but behind me, the tiller began to slide forward and I realized he had let go of the gripholds. In fixed harness, the poles began to carry me on down the hillside.

I whipped my tail beneath me and dipped my wings back, trying to brace my feet in the wet hillside but the tiller was heavy and I was already light-headed. Samus shouted as I slipped forward and downward in the mud. The metal blade churned hot on my scales and I beat furiously to right myself but my wings beat vainly against mud and pole and grinding blades. Suddenly the poles snapped and the tiller lurched forward, plunging the broken ends into the ground and taking me with them. Pain shot like arrows through my haunches while mud and the silver band cut off all breath in my chest. I was being crushed into the hard, slick soil and for a moment, like me, the world did not breathe.

There was a shadow as Samus grabbed the long gripholds, hauled down with all his weight but it was not enough. The forward angle was too high, the arc too deadly as they rose slowly, ominously, into the air above me. He would be forced to release them soon, else risk his own death. This slope was so steep that once it fell, we would plunge down the hillside, shattering tiller and dragon alike.

Suddenly I was surrounded by the shrill voices of many little sticks, grabbing at the harness and pushing against the tiller's frame. I saw the flash of a blade as the boy, Niro, leaned in close, his face covered in mud. I felt the jerk as one by one, my harness leathers snapped free and the many little hands grabbed at me from beneath, tugging wings, pulling legs and finally sliding me out from under the crushing weight.

Samus shouted again and the little sticks scrambled out of the way as he released the holds. Immediately, the tiller flipped upside-down, harness leathers whipping, metal blade screeching as it plunged down the hillside, bumping, crashing and finally smashing its way to the bottom.

I stretched my wings, jaws wide, chest burning, desperate for air.

"Nightshade!" cried Tacita.

Too tight, too hot. There was no air. "Samus!" cried Farida, one of the taller sticks. "He's choking!"

"The band is too tight," Tacita wailed. "He can't breathe!"

Burning, stabbing, threatening to burst.

Farida turned to Samus.

"The metal cutters!"

"No!" he shouted. "An unbanded dragon is death!"

"He won't hurt us!" cried Tacita.

"Get the axe," shouted Samus. "It's the only way."

"No," wailed Neve.

Tacita scrambled to her feet and disappeared down the slope.

Despite their little hands, I sank into the mud. No air, no food. The life of a farm dragon was too hard and I welcomed the kiss of the axe if only it would end this agony. My thoughts were spinning and my chest ached as though under water. My head was heavier than the entire world so I laid it down, tasting mud and rainwater and old, dead oryza.

Stars popped behind my eyes, bursting like Lamoan cannons. Fire and crash, boom and burst, Rue falling to the docks under the no-faced man's blows.

I didn't feel the tugging of the band. I didn't feel the metal slide beneath my scales but suddenly, my chest filled like a balloonfish and my head almost split in two. Smoke rolled out of my mouth and I heard cheering from all the little sticks. I'm certain they planted many little kisses all over my face, but it was a fleeting thought, and I surrendered to their embrace, weary but breathing.

And more importantly, unbanded.

THE NIGHT DRAGON

It was the middle of the rainy season when the night dragon came.

I was sleeping in the aviary when I heard the cries of the shearers. They are stupid creatures, like noxen but less happy, and truthfully, any dragon who could eat them would be right to do so. But these were Gavius' shearers and I was loyal to Gavius, and so when I heard the bleating, I raised the alarm. It was too late however, for in the morning seven of the flock had been butchered with only two eaten. That was curious. I couldn't imagine a dragon wasting anything as tender as a shearer.

He didn't come back the next night, nor the next or the next so life went back to the way it was. Gavius always rose before the sun, along with Tacita, Farida and Samus. Together they fed us, cleaned the aviary and got us into harness for the day's work. Gavius had purchased a new collar in Corolanus – a tiller-bolt, it was called and it fit me quite well. In those weeks, my appetite flourished and my growth nearly doubled. Now I was as large as a shearer, each wing as long as Gavius was tall. My scales were growing thicker, my spines longer. My skull was itchy too and I knew I was beginning the first buds of horns.

Almost every day after work, Tacita would show me my reflection in the silverstone and I marvelled at my handsomeness. Self-importance is much more relevant when one has at least an idea of self.

The red drakina had gone into season and while I was still young and barely aware, it made Stonecrop irritable and restless. At all hours of the night, the grey dragon climbed up and down his mesh walls, cooing to her and singing songs of love. Stumptail snarled and spat little wads of acid at him. Unfortunately, my pen was between theirs and his wads would end up sizzling the chaff on the bottom of my floor. Every morning, Samus grumbled about what a messy dragon I was but I didn't speak stick and had no way to correct him. Besides, he was lazy so I was happy he had work to do, regardless of blame.

One night, I awoke to the sound of bone on metal. I looked up from my nest to see Ruby clinging to the mesh at the top of the pen, her long spiked tail slapping from side to side. Through the bars, there was another figure silhouetted by the moons and my heart stopped in its chest. I knew it was the night dragon, butcher of shearers and lover of red drakinas, gnawing at the bars with his dagger teeth. I thought for a long moment, knowing that if I raised the alarm I would have an enemy for life in Ruby but that if I didn't, Gavius would lose more shearers. Gavius was good to me and Ruby was miserable at the best of times so the decision was truthfully not a hard one.

I am wont to say that I debated just a little for the sake of peace in the aviary.

So I bugled the alarm and Ruby's head snapped down in my direction. She hissed, her lashing tail threatening to take out some of the stones in the wall as the night dragon lifted from the roof. Stumptail grumbled and Stonecrop yawned but outside in the rain, I could hear the thundering beat of wings and the terrified bleats of shearers. I knew Gavius had lost more of his flock and it was all because of Ruby.

The next morning she was horrible, snapping and growling even at the sticks and I wondered at the reasons for having a drakina when there were so many useful drakes around for the purchase. Still, I told myself that Ruby was simply a strong, dominant dragon. She probably would have ruled an aerie had she been free and not for the first time, I thought of my mother.

That night, however, Gavius did not put me away as usual. No, after he fed the others, he led me to the shearer pens carrying a large spear, an axe and an oil lantern for light. It was still raining, but being night it was a cold rain and I can't say that I enjoyed it overmuch. (Neither did the shearers, having a dragon so close.) Gavius led me by the harness into one of the rain shelters. There, he leaned the spear against the wall, placed the axe in the chaff and dimmed the lantern. I curled into the chaff and in a manner that reminded me of my days with Rue, we settled down for the night.

The sound of rain on a thin metal roof is a pleasant thing. I longed to gaze at the stars but Gavius had a basket filled with sliced moorsnake, a favourite of mine from the swamps. He sat with his back against my flank, feeding me slices of snake and telling me stories of the early days of the farm in a very quiet voice. Truth to tell, I wasn't paying attention. The moorsnake was superb and I was happy to be away from the hissing, snarling drakina. Besides, there was another smell coming from the basket and it had set my heart racing.

Arcstone.

A working dragon is never given arcstone. It's against the rules of sticks. With our fire, we are powerful and would never submit to a life of service. So when he slid the bolt from the collar and it dropped to the ground with a thud, I knew then that I was not simply enjoying an evening out under the stars. No, tonight I would be taking on the night dragon.

Much later I came to wonder if this hadn't been his plan the moment he laid eyes on me in the market. After Serkus' exaggerated tales, it sounded perfect – a dragon brave enough to fight Lamoan pirates and able to hide in the night. It would have been a good plan, the perfect solution, with one exception. I was just a yearling.

In fact, I wasn't even sure I could fight Stonecrop and win. No, I take that back. I *could* win against Stonecrop. But against Stumptail? Against Ruby? And more importantly, against a mature dragon that killed for play?

"I can guarantee you, Master Farmer Gavius," Serkus had said. *"That this dragon will not eat your flock. In fact, he'll protect them."*

The liar, the user, the beater of helpless dragons and soul-boys. Gavius went to the market to get a blue dragon and came home with the 'Hero of the Pirate Raids.' Only the 'cannons had been too much.' The no-faced man had spun a story that had hooked this man like a gullible grey fish.

I hated the no-faced man more than ever.

Gavius pulled a small piece of the flaky silver rock and held it up to my nostrils.

I had no idea what to do. I wanted the night dragon to find another willing drakina and leave the shearers of the oryza fields for another night. I wanted our farm to go back to the way it was, the routine and the rain, the singing and the sweet sleep after a long day's work.

Gavius nudged me, offering the arcstone once again.

I took it and swallowed, embracing the burn that it caused as it went down my gullet and into my crop. It was a terrible sensation, eased only by the exhalation of a breath of fire. No one really knows how we make the fire, not even very old dragons. It has to do with the arcstone and the acid in our bellies – when they meet, you can either swallow or spit, and once the spit hits the air, it erupts into flame. A dragon can spit acid even without arcstone, but it is nowhere near as impressive.

I ate another piece and then another, felt it stick to my tongue and coat my back teeth. Once swallowed, it is never completely gone. It can live in the crop forever.

The night was cold and I lay my head down across my wings. Gavius was sleeping. I could tell because of the rhythmic noises he made when he breathed. I could have killed him then, I realized. I could've set him on fire and taken off into the night but I didn't. Gavius and his little sticks had been good to me and I was a dragon of integrity. My pride was all that I had in this odd, stick-run world, and I would guard it with my life.

It was late when I heard the first bleat. The rain had stopped and I lifted my head from my wings. The shearers were restless, bumping around like confused goswryms and I knew that I would eat them too if I lived in foothills like this. It was then that I had a fleeting moment of self-doubt. Dragons have no concept of ownership. Territory, yes. Ownership, no. Food was food. You fought for it and if you caught it, you ate. If not, you went hungry. I was never certain how the sticks managed to barter their foodstuffs. It didn't make sense, but then again, I wasn't a stick.

I heard the sound of wings overhead and looked up to see a shape pass across the moons. I also heard the groan and screech of metal and knew that Ruby was once again trying to gnaw her way out of her pen. I chirruped quietly and Gavius opened his eyes. He pushed off my flank, grabbed the axe and staggered to the wall where he had leaned the spear. He looked at me.

"Are we ready, Nightshade?"

Ready, I thought to myself? How could I possibly be ready?

I rose to my feet and shook the chaff from my scales. My belly was burning with the arcstone and I knew the fire would be strong and yellow-hot tonight. It was a good feeling, for I hadn't blown fire in over a year, not since the marauding sea snakes under the docks of the Udan Shore. Once learned, however, it is a skill no dragon forgets.

More groan and screech of metal and together we left the shelter, looking to the aviary to see a shadow on the roof. My heart caught in my throat. He was large, perhaps five years old and easily three times my size. There was no way I could harm him, let alone frighten him. There was nothing I could do.

"Remember the docks," said Gavius in a quiet voice and he laid a hand on my neck. "You fought those Lamoan pirates when you were much younger. You are a brave dragon, Nightshade, and you are the colour of the stars. You are invisible."

He was right. While I was no hero of the pirate raids, I did save the silver dragon and his rider, tear out a throat and some eyes on the ships. All I needed to do was get this night dragon on the ground and Gavius, with his axe and his spear, would do the rest.

I unfurled my wings and leapt into the sky.

High, higher, the wind under me, careful not to beat too quickly and make a sound. There was no rain now and I blanched at the thought. We dragons are sensitive to sounds. Sometimes the rain was a friend, creating a constant drone under which I could fly. Other times there was a muffle as it hit my body, interrupted on its way to the ground. I could see the farm and all the fields gleaming silver under the wet moons and I flew higher still until the aviary with its interloper was right below me. Through the bars, I could see Ruby's teeth and claws, glimpses of her dark red beak. The metal was almost chewed through and I realized that they had been at this for months. Dragon teeth are very strong and I was impressed to the point of second thought.

Ruby was a captive drakina who wanted her freedom. It was natural, it was understandable and it was a death sentence. She had a band. She would die within weeks without its removal, and as much as I disliked her, I couldn't let her die.

I tucked my wings, summoned the fire and dove like an arrow toward the head of the night dragon.

He turned his face and I breathed the fire, blinding him first and raking second, feeling the soft round flesh of his eyes slice under my talons. He bellowed and shook his head, scorching the air at my tail but I dipped down when I should have swept up and the flames missed me by a scale. I felt the heat, however, and knew that one mistake on my part and I would end up like a charred, twisting seasnake. I circled back around from beneath, spraying fire across his eyes a second time. His wings beat down and the force of them caught me, slamming me into the wire mesh of the roof. Stars popped behind my eyes at the sudden pain, when Ruby clawed through the mesh, raking long red ribbons along my back. I sprang off, dazed but spiralling into the night sky, praying that I was as invisible as the sticks said.

The drake, whom I realized was not black but inky blue, launched from the roof as well, spraying fire in my wake and I rolled to avoid being scorched. He was seasoned, could follow me by scent alone so I swept downward to the pens, hoping to lose him in the mix of their strong aroma. Beneath us, the shearers scattered in terror. His wing beats were so strong that they caused the air around me to push out and suck in, battering me by force alone. My head was spinning and I misjudged my altitude, my wingtip catching the roof of the first shelter and stars popped behind my eyes. I spiralled to the ground and the flocks scattered as I hit the ground. Blindly, the drake followed, shattering the shelter into a hundred pieces under his weight. I sprang into the air but was yanked to the ground yet again, wing snagged in a piece of twisted roof metal.

The indigo dragon rose to his feet, towering over me like a mountain.

It was then that the aviary shattered upward as Ruby burst forth from the mesh. She clung to the roof for a brief moment, clutching the twisted metal that had once been her prison. The indigo drake swung his head and bellowed and she bellowed back before launching herself skyward. Shouts from the farmhouse as Samus ran out, lantern in hand.

She arched toward him spiralling in the air, her wings almost dusting the ground. I watched in horror as she snatched him from the doorway, in her talons and flew up, up, up before letting go.

I did not see him hit the ground.

Above me, the indigo dragon turned back and coiled. I could see his acid breath ignite across his tongue and I shrunk low to the ground, fearing the rush of scorching flame. Suddenly his head jerked back as a spear savagely burst from his throat. Fire spewed from his mouth like blood and he tried to lift from the ground but Gavius was there, hauling him back down to the earth. The drake sprayed fire in all directions, flames catching wood, grass and shearers alike. Gavius released the spear and swung the axe now, striking the inky head once, twice, three times. The dragon roared, part of his beak severed when Gavius slammed the axe down once last time deep into the great blue skull. The drake rocked back on his legs, clawing at the spear protruding from his neck like a harpoon and sprang into the sky, spinning and twisting as he went. It was with horror that I watched him crash backwards onto the roof of the farmhouse. It collapsed inwards under his weight and screams rose like the flames from within.

Gavius bolted across the field.

I was still stuck on the wedge of tin that had pierced my wing. My back was torn and bleeding but there was nothing in the world now like the screams. Farida and Niro, Neve and Tacita. Mostly Tacita. The drawings and sketches, the silverstone and the kindness. She had fed me for months, patted me when I was weary, sung with me like a friend. I rolled and thrashed and sprang into the air, dragging my pinned wing as I made for the farmhouse.

A massive weight struck like a fist and once again, I struck the ground. It was Ruby, crushing the breath from my body and trying to break my spindly neck with her jaws. In the moonlight, the silver band gleamed at her throat and I knew that while she was larger, she was vulnerable. I sprayed my fire into her face, increasing the heat from yellow to white until I was dizzy from the effort. Her lids sizzled and puckered under the flame and she released me, shaking her head and backing up into the shattered shearer hut. I rolled to my feet, dragging the tin and blasting fire until her spines were smoking and she sagged back down into the debris with a howl.

A sharp boom cracked the night air as the blazing farmhouse collapsed in on itself. I could see the indigo dragon's legs and tail thrashing above it, watched with a breaking heart Gavius silhouetted in the flames. The house was an inferno, the heat pushing him out at every turn.

There were no screams anymore now, only the roar of his burning home and soon even the indigo dragon grew still. The farmer sank to his knees, merely a shadow in the fierce light. He stayed that way for a very long time.

Beside me, Ruby moaned, clawed at her eyes with her wing talons. Finally, Gavius rose, picked up the axe and crossed the field, ending her life with a merciful few strokes.

I sat there by her lifeless body as the farmer stumbled over to the aviary. I could hear the cries of both Stumptail and Stonecrop and prayed that they hadn't kissed the axe too. They were blameless. In fact, as I looked down at Ruby, her lifeblood making rivers in the darkness, I realized that she was blameless too. She was a dragon, meant for better things than threshing and plowing. She had yearned for a life beyond Gavius' oryza fields and the wet pressure of Under Weathers. The indigo drake had been wild and only doing what wild dragons do – soaring high in the limitless sky, eating what they can catch and mating with other dragons.

It was the sticks who complicated things and what was worse, tonight, I had helped them.

Thunder from the aviary as Stonecrop burst out of the doors, wings wide and he immediately took to the sky. Thankfully, I saw no flash of silver in the moonlight and he spiralled over the farm again and again before becoming no more than another star in the night. Stumptail next, an old dragon who couldn't fly and he lumbered away from the aviary in his odd, lop-sided gait. Despite the rain, flames were travelling swiftly across the winter grass and he leapt into the flooded oryza fields like a water dragon. I watched the moons gleam off his scales until he too disappeared in the darkness.

A *whoomph* from the aviary and I turned to watch as it began to glow. Soon, flames leapt from the doors and sparks rushed from the open mesh roof. Gavius had set it on fire. I didn't know why, I didn't understand so I waited patiently for him to come out, to lay a hand on my head, to drag the dead drakina to the flames and dispose of her body with honour but he never did. He never came out and the aviary stones sizzled and popped under the heat.

A final boom from the farmhouse as the rains began anew. Papers floated down on the night breeze, edges bright, centers black, and I recognized the charred sketch of a dragon soaring across the moons.

I remembered tasty grub mash and silverstone reflections, soft kisses on my cheek and songs at midnight. I laid my chin down across the sketch and did not move for the rest of the night as the wet fields boiled all around me. Ash rose on the night breeze up to the sky where it looked like floating stars.

Ash and stars and my father, Draco Stellorum. I was very sad and I realize now that I was mourning. I didn't know it then. It was a strange sensation, huge and empty and sharp and heavy. I had never mourned before, not truly. I had never mourned the loss of my aerie or my freedom or Summerday or even Rue but now, wave after wave crashed over me until I thought I would drown in sorrow like the ocean.

And so I mourned for all of them now, covered in blood and ashes and wishing life were very different for dragons and the sticks that ruled them.

I barely felt it then, when other sticks came sometime the next morning. They dug through the wreckage and pulled me from the ash. They freed my wing from the wedge of tin, put a band around my throat and threw me into another cart. I never saw Gavius, his children or his fields again, nor any of the dragons that had lived or died there.

Truth be told, I did not miss the dragons.

THE DEATH DRAGONS

There was a plague in the town of Bangarden, and therefore great need for funeral dragons. Because of my colouring, I was a perfect choice and the price for me this time was well over fifty denari, although it made little impression on me then. I understood now the apathy of dragons. What little pride was left in my young body was quickly being turned to ash, my fledgling imagination to stone.

The smell of death was my constant companion in this place on the plains and I learned about the many rules of city life. Working carts like plaustri and carpentri were pulled by noxen, whereas finer carriages like ciseri, bennai and pilenti were pulled by dragons. Those dragons on the right side of the road had their harnesses fixed at steep angles, whereas those on the left side (going in the opposite direction) were fixed level. It made a certain sense, for dragon wings are wide whereas streets are narrow. It was a very common site for drivers to halt mid turn and lower the traps before changing direction but it made the streets even more congested than they already were.

My new owners were a family of funeral practitioners, run by a patriarch, Allum and his three sons. They ran a fleet of death carts and I had to admit, in this plague town, it was a lucrative business. They drove around the city on Death Days, calling for corpses. Sticks motioned to them from their houses, and they would carry out dead slaves, servants and unloved relatives, tossing them on the back of the carts before moving on. People paid for this service and were told that the bodies were taken for communal burial. I can assure you that they were burned in Allum's furnace, where the ashes were sold to other sticks for use in fertilizer, soap and silver polish.

That was the way of business in Bangarden.

Now I had been sold as a funeral dragon and as such, didn't pull the death carts like others did. I was reserved for those who paid for a private burial. Then, Allum would take out his best carriage – an elaborate roofed vehicle made of ebony wood. We went out several times a week to the Banners, neighbourhoods in Bangarden reserved for politicians, businessmen and their families. (I learned much about stick society in Bangarden. Whereas powerful dragons nest up, powerful men nest large.) Once there, we would wait for the rituals of death to end. Then, a party carried out the dead to lay them inside the funeral carriage and we would head off to the burial grounds, followed by a throng of wailing sticks. I was allowed to fly low during these times, for given my size and spectacular colouring, all traffic would stop and allow us to pass. The mourners apparently liked this and I believe Allum was paid well for this service. I had my own pen at night because the other dragons were unhappy and it was feared that they might damage my valuable pelt.

That, I realized, would not be good for business.

Day after day, I waited for the rattle of the harness that would allow me to be out in the wet winter sun. I never had realized how much I loved the sun until Bangarden. Well, truthfully, until the Under Weathers and the advent of the rainy season but at least there, I could be outside in the air and fly, even if pulling a plow or a tiller. Here, I stayed in my pen until an important stick died, necessitating the services of a funeral dragon. My pen was not open to the sky as in the Under Weathers, but roofed and dark, without even a window to see stars or moons. I slept more often than not and grew deaf to the incessant chatter and squeals of the other dragons.

My new name was Hallowdown and I must admit I liked it. A combination of Hallow Fire and Hell Down and I thought it fitting for a drake of my colour and stature. I was a year-and-a-halfling now, and growing larger every day. There were four others all under two, which is the perfect size for pulling a cart. I could only imagine what happened to the death dragons over the age of three. I admit that I don't remember seeing any older in my brief time in the markets, nor in my days on the streets.

I sometimes wondered how one would kill a three year-old dragon. By then, our horns are in, our necks are fully maned with spines and the spikes on our throats are strong and hard. A simple slit of a blade would not do it. I did remember relative ease of dispatching Ruby with a few strokes of an axe and it made me sad when I realized how I knew this. I had helped to kill the indigo dragon and in doing so, I had helped to kill Ruby. My obedience and my integrity had cost the lives of two dragons. Although I tried not to think of it, I must admit that there was little else to do but think.

That line had been crossed so subtly. With all the indignities I had witnessed in my short life, I had found it easy to lose myself in the service of sticks. The moment I'd smelled the firestone, I had made a choice. I could have feigned ignorance. I could have flown away the moment the band had been removed. I'd thought I was better than other dragons, smarter, more respectable and therefore not subjugated by the sticks whose only weapons were mesh and whips and dreaded metal bands.

It was apathy, I realized, as I lay there listening to the other dragons quarrel and fight. As selfish as they were, the sticks understood how to work together to accomplish a task. Dragons don't think much beyond themselves and their own needs.

I believe I grew quite cynical and esoteric in those days as a funeral dragon. Time and death, it appears, does that to a dragon.

I was also growing hard in my spirit. I had been free for less than one sixth of my life and the memories of the sea and the stars and other noble things condensed into small stones, like lumps of coal that simmer and grow cold. I thought often of Rue and Tacita, Summerday and Ruby. Freedom and loss and beauty and pride; my early world crushed to embers under the formidable iron wheel of life.

I also thought often of the no-faced man, of Gavius and his axe coming down on a defeated Ruby, of dragons bought and sold like fish, dragons in pens and under harness. I only needed to call these things back to mind, and those coals would blaze anew. It was a different kind of fire, one that had no need of arcstone and thrived in spite of the silver band at my throat.

Or maybe, it thrived because of it.

"Come now, Hallowdown," came a familiar voice and I opened my eyes to see a young man entering the dark aviary. "Who's the finest funeral dragon in all of Bangarden?"

I rose to my feet and shook the straw and chaff from my scales, reached my wing-talons out before me and stretched long in the spine and tail. The pen wasn't large enough for me to fully extend my wings. In that respect, Gavius's aviary was considerably superior, but I was the only dragon to have a solo pen, so I couldn't complain.

I was happy to see it was Junias the middle son, rather than Kellas or Nonus or even their father, Allum. All were experienced dragoneers but Junias had kind hands, and with the new head-harness I was wearing, that kindness was an important consideration. He entered the pen and I bowed, curling my wings in and lowering my head in respect.

That, I learned, was what working city dragons did.

The death dragons began to shriek when he slipped a hand into his pocket and pulled out a sliver of dried goswyrm. I took it, shredding it slowly as to savour the taste on my tongue. I had learned that respectful behaviour usually went well for me, all things considered. And since I was a dragon with integrity, I always gave respect until a stick or dragon lost it. Then, I have to admit my pride would reign and those little coals would flare and grow white hot. Character flaw or simply life, I cannot say. Or perhaps, more truthfully, I would not.

Junias checked the silver carter-bolt band at my throat, ran his hand along my neck and scratched the maturing horns. They itched terribly and I released a long rumbling sigh. Back feet were awkward for scratching and more than once, I found myself envying their hands.

He laughed, lifted the head-harness with the wedge of metal that I now wore in my mouth.

This, to dragons, is the ultimate indignity. Such glorious, majestic and powerful creatures controlled by a slip of metal between our teeth. It was called a 'bit' and I will admit it made controlling us much easier, for as large and powerful as we are, our heads sit at the end of our very long necks. As such, they are easily turned and where a dragon's head goes, so goes his body. I had been wearing bits for months now since being brought to Allum's aviary, so I opened my mouth and accepted it, bristling at the sharp tang of iron on my tongue and the grate of the curb against the roof of my mouth. With Junias, his kind hands meant less friction and therefore, a much more pleasant drive for me.

I always hated the sound of Kellas or Nonus's sandals on the floor. I would rarely be able to eat on the nights after they drove because my tongue and palate would be bruised for days. If I had hands like the sticks, I would push the metal into *their* mouths. But if I had hands like the sticks, then I would *be* a stick and all things would be reversed.

As you can see, I had much time for thinking.

Junias led me out past the other dragons, their shrieks and hisses bouncing harmlessly off my night-black pelt. I secretly yearned for the days at Gavius' though, when Stonecrop and I would play bite-beak between the mesh, or I would happily watch Stumptail's acid spit-wads streak across the pens. Dragons don't do well in confinement. We were made to fly in open skies. Something the sticks apparently did not understand or appreciate.

Maybe the Dragon Flights understood that. Maybe that's why I thought of them so much.

The black carriage was waiting in the courtyard, its ebony wood polished to gleaming and its fittings painted a liquid gold leaf. I took my place in the traces, standing quietly as he fastened the harness across my back and under my wings. This carriage also had a wooden brace for my feet and I found it very useful to press against while keeping the momentum forward and low. It also had a T-shaft, a groove beneath the carriage for my tail, eliminating the need to bind or dock it as with other death dragons. All in all, it was a well-designed vehicle, I thought, but when the only other things I knew were plows and tillers, skiffs and dorries, I was no expert.

The poles next, affixed to both sides of the harness. There was none underneath. I was an experienced cart-dragon now with no need for the fixed brace. I had often wondered if I could carry the thing upwards to the stars given the inclination, but I'd never had the inclination, so I never tried.

Lastly, the draw-reins. I hated the draw reins. They ran

from the bit through rings on the breastplate and up to the drivers. Draw-reins allowed them to pull our heads down to our chests, making for an attractively arched neck when pulling a carriage. It was uncomfortable to fly with head tucked into my chest and by the end of the day every muscle in my body ached from the unnatural position. I never knew if there was another function for the draw-rein. They never spoke of it, just attached it and drove. Once again, I was thankful for Junias and his kind hands.

He climbed aboard and rolled a black canvas awning over his head. It was the end of the winter season and that meant a lighter rain from morning to night. As a dragon, I welcomed the water as a friend, an ally, a kindred spirit but after so many months, I longed to see the sun once more. I never saw the moons or my father, Draco Stellorum. In the rainy season, there were far too many clouds.

With a flick of the rein we were out into the city.

Bangarden meant 'Fine Garden.' It was a city built for high-born Remoan politicians and their servants. Streets cobbled with worn stone, palms on every corner, cedars in every fine yard. Travertine homes, limestone walls, marble statues. Here, there was politics and there was the plague and as a result, there was also civil unrest. Both took their toll on men and dragons alike.

This rainy morning, I saw another funeral carriage pulled by a drake named Towndrell. Towndrell was a grey with a faint pattern of indigo stripes across his back and legs. His tail had been docked just below the rump and to me he looked like a winged nox. He had a large, kind eye however and was as fine-tempered as any dragon I had ever met. I had liked him the moment we'd met, carriage to carriage at a large family funeral. He was respectful and earnest and longed to serve his driver to the best of his ability. His driver, Philius was an angry man – harsh with the bit and harsher with the whip. I often wondered if the stripes across Towndrell's back were not a coat pattern but rather scars left by a lifetime of angry men. I would believe it had he language to tell me.

I also believe I once saw Summerday. This was a city that prided itself on wealth, position and appearance, and truthfully, nothing could be finer than a golden dragon pulling a golden pilentus. She had the draw-reins pulled tight so her neck arched magnificently, and her spines looked like the rays of Selisanae, Dragon of the Sun. Unlike Towndrell, her tail had been coiled and bound, mirroring the arch of her neck and she flew without blinders under the constant cracking of a golden whip. I called to her but her drivers were hard and if she heard, she had no opportunity to respond. Or perhaps, she cared not to. The no-faced man had hated me, and she had been devoted to her master.

Such was the life of dragons.

Back to my story.

This morning, I saw Towndrell in the town square flailing against the braces. His cart's rear wheel was wedged in a rut in the cobbles. The streets were old and well-worn and even in the finer areas of town, there were large gaps between the stones. In the rains they filled with mud and became treacherous sinkholes for wheels. We tried to avoid them but sometimes our drivers did not pay attention. The road rarely obliged even the most diligent of dragons.

I watched as Towndrell struggled to pull the wheel loose, watched the whip come down across his back again and again, making stripes in his leathery coat. Blood from his knees splashed into the puddles and ran between the cobbled stones like a river. In the carriage seat behind me, Junias muttered a curse. He hated poor treatment of dragons but he was a junior driver and usually kept his opinions to himself. Now, there was a crowd of spectators gathering around the carriage, some shouting at the driver, others shouting at the dragon. This was Bangarden. Everyone had an opinion. Everyone was to blame.

The rain came down, the traffic had ground to a halt when Junias surprised me by leaping from the driver's seat, leaving me stranded on my side of the road. Without a word, he tromped through the rain and pushed through the crowd, reaching Towndrell's carriage and leaning his back into the wheel. The driver cursed him and shook his fist, but within moments, a second man appeared and then a third. Together they worked the wheel free from the sucking mud and the crowd cheered as they finally placed it on steady ground.

He laid a hand on Towndrell's neck.

"Go easy on him, Philius," he called up through the rain. "He can't get his weight into the trace with the draw-rein so tight."

"Oh forgive me, wise Master Junias!" snapped the driver. "But you've forgotten what it is like to work hard. Not all of us have night dragons to impress the senators."

"Treat your dragon well and you'll impress the senators, Philius."

Junias turned but Philius brought the whip down

behind him with a crack. The crowd shrunk back, waiting and wet.

"You've forgotten your rank, Junias Allum," Philius snarled. "You are new money and proud show. The Prefect will remember those who have served him long after night dragons lose their fashion."

The crowd parted as a thin-haired man in a fine cloak stepped out from among them, a servant holding a nox-skin parasol over his head.

"The Prefect is an imbecile," said the man. "He remembers nothing. But the senators; well, the senators are another matter."

The crowd mumbled at his words. A few men laughed.

"*This* senator will remember that your dragon was thin and bloody while *his*," the man grinned, waved a ringed hand at me. "His sleek and fine. That's what *this* senator will remember, even if the Prefect doesn't."

"Forgive my impatience, Senator Aelianus." Philius bowed his head, glowering under his brow. "But Ruminor does not smile on us all."

"In Bangarden," said the senator. "It is enough for a senator to smile on you."

"A senator who will one day be Primar," said Philius.

"Perhaps," said the man. "But today, Ruminor has other things to deal with."

"Like the terrible state of these streets," grumbled a man from the crowd.

"Like Lamos," snapped another.

"Like the plague, idiot," growled another.

The senator raised a gold-ringed hand.

"Times are hard for Remus," he said. "But the Remoan

people are stronger than hard times. We will outlive this plague and rise to crush Lamos under our boot!"

The crowd roared and some shouted. Others began to push and quickly, the senator was ushered from streets now grumbling and growling and roaring in the rain.

In the midst of it all, Junias looked up at Philius.

"Just care for your dragon," he said and pushed his way back through the crowds to climb, soaked and muddy, into the driver's seat. With a tug of the rein, he pulled me back onto the road. I did manage to throw a glance in Towndrell's direction. I'm sure I saw the whip come down one last time across his back.

***

The funeral was long so it was late when I was let into my pen that night. The mash was cold but still I ate. I was a working dragon. Little was left to my choosing anymore and food was the one thing I looked forward to after a long day in the traces.

I crawled into my nest of straw and despite the hissing, hooting of the others, fell into a deep sleep almost immediately. I dreamed of Towndrell – his kind eye and docked tail. The whip painting patterns across the grey streets – painting, cracking, stinging, bleeding. Summerday, beautiful and proud, sinking under a pilentus of molten gold. The mud sucking wheels and wings and death dragons and cities and Rue and the Sleeping Eyes of my father, Draco Stellorum.

There was an unusual scent in the aviary.

I opened one eye.

I was a night dragon, accustomed to seeing in the black and I lay quite still, waiting for the glint of movement in the court. There was the sound of dragons moaning in their sleep, the hiss of rain on the roof, the hum of crickards in the courtyard. And *there,* the crunch of straw as something moved across the floor outside my pen.

"I'll teach him," muttered a voice in the dark. "Bloody prideful boy talking to me like that, showing me up in front of the senator."

And suddenly, a torch sprang to life beyond the bars, the face of Towndrell's driver gleaming in the firelight. I raised my head, blinking at the brightness.

"I'll burn the pretty pelt off you, night dragon," he said. "Then the market will be fair and I can earn back my business without Allum's sons to taunt me."

A grumble from one of the death dragons far to my left. A hiss to my right. I narrowed my eyes, snarled. After Ruby and the indigo drake, I dreaded the thought of fire unleashed in such close quarters. Locked inside these pens of mesh and metal, we would sear as easily as fishing docks. We would burn as thoroughly as wood.

Philius' face flickered as he held the torch up to the bars of my dark pen. He was going to slip it through the bars and drop it onto the dry chaff on my floor. It would catch and burn like wildfire, and in such a small enclosure, I wasn't convinced I'd survive. My heart slowed, my muscles tensed and coiled, ready to spring. I studied it, the angle of the stave, the rise and fall of the flames as they leapt and danced before me. I could almost feel the fire bite the roof my mouth and my throat stung as acid raced up from my belly.

Slowly, as if under water, he slid the torch in through the bars.

He never saw me coming, never imagined in all his years that a dragon might do what I did then, lunging from my nest like a cannonball and crashing into the bars with a clang. He never in his wildest dreams could have imagined my jaws coming down on his wrist, completely enveloping the torch in his hand.

He screamed but I could not hear him. He tugged but I could not feel him. The world had shrunk, instantly condensed to the war between my teeth as acid met oil-soaked flame.

Flames, hot and stinging, bit the roof of my mouth, danced over my tongue, savage and raging and caged. My eyes bulged from the pressure, my throat expanded painfully above the silver band until I thought I would burst. It was a furnace of scorching acid and I released it all in a massive fiery blast into Philius' stunned face.

He staggered backwards, tripping to the sandy floor before scrambling wildly to his feet. He fled into the courtyard like a madman, hair flaming, arms flailing as he went. Tongues of fire leapt to the poles and the oiled leathers lining the walls and the night filled with the shrieking of death dragons. Still, it was the rainy season. Water buckets sat filled outside every door so when Allum and his sons appeared, the fires were out within minutes with a minimum of damage to either poles, walls, roof or dragons.

I'm not certain they ever knew what had happened. They certainly never knew how a spent torch and man's hand ended up on the floor of my pen. I never saw either

Philius or Towndrell again. Later that week, I did see a thin grey dragon being loaded on the back of a death cart. I can't be certain but I believe Towndrell was flying with my father, Draco Stellorum, in the wild expanse of the skies, finally free of lash and leather and the dreaded silver band.

THE LAST DEAD MAN IN BANGARDEN

According to the legends of sticks, the high god and creator of the universe, Ruminor Deiustus, took two wives – Luna and Lara, the sister moons of the world. From them, he fathered two Celestine sons – Remus and Lamos. Remus was the clever one and beautiful and his father had gifted him with Selisanae, the Golden Dragon of the Sun. To his son Lamos, who worked in the underworld forging iron into swords, he gifted nothing but smoke and ash and iron and labour. Soon, the sons battled over Selisanae but Remus was victor, refusing to kill his brother in a regrettable show of mercy. Instead, he exiled Lamos to the harsh and fiery mountains across the Nameless Sea. His descendants have lived there ever since, forging cannons and trying to steal dragons from the prosperous people of Remus. At least, that's how the legend is told in Remus. I imagined it would be much different when told in Lamos, if it was told at all.

I often thought that Selisanae reminded me of Summerday. Given the chance, I'm certain I would have fought for her myself.

There was strife in the city of Bangarden.

The plague had worsened and the politicians had called priests from other cities to offer sacrifices, consecrate temples and call for fasting and prayer. Still, people were dying tenfold every day. Bodies piled up on the streets, impeding traffic and filling the wet air with the stench of rotting flesh. I imagine it was hard for the sticks and for the politicians that tended them, but for Allum and his sons, their business was thriving. Almost every day now I was sent out to the Banners and I enjoyed being able to stretch my wings, even if it was in the traces.

One morning, I heard Junias' sandals on the aviary floor and I looked up. He was unusually quiet as he slipped into my pen, offering me the goswrym without his customary greeting. He rubbed my horns, scratched my chin and slipped on the bridle before leading me out to harness me in very fine leathers. As he fastened the draw-reins, I wondered at his silence. Like Rue, he wasn't a talkative fellow, but there was something about him that filled me with unease. He led me into the walled courtyard where the funeral carriage waited, along with his father, brothers and to my surprise, his mother Avea.

I had rarely seen Avea. She was a small woman and strong but today, she wrung her hands as if to make them warm. She was wearing a palla cloak of dyed wool and gave me a wide berth as her husband fixed the draw-reins into place.

"We will be home late," he said. "There will be a large

celebration to mourn his death. We don't wish to offend by leaving early."

"Don't offend," said Avea. "It is an honour to have been chosen."

"No one is sad he's dead," said Kellus under his breath. He'd polished the last of the ebony wood so that it shone like silverstone.

"Kellus!" snapped his mother. "Don't say it."

"It's true," said her son. "None of us will mourn him. He was a terrible Prefect."

"They're all terrible Prefects," said Nonus as he oiled the wheels.

Kellus laughed.

"We do not speak ill of politicians," said their father. "We're being well paid for this, so keep your tongues in your heads, all of you."

Avea wrung her hands again.

"Cara says there are whispers in the streets."

"Bah," grunted her husband. "This is a politician's town. There are always whispers."

"Not like today," she continued. "The senate has doubled the guard."

"And there's a Dragon Flight in the city centre," said Junias.

A Dragon Flight! My heart thudded in my chest at the words but I was mindful not to react. A Bangarden dragon was known for his composure and restraint.

"What's a Dragon Flight going to do?" said Kellus. "Light the funeral pyre?"

"Kellus!" snapped his mother again. "Ruminor forgive you!"

"Ruminor thinks it's funny."

And he blew her a kiss. All but Avea laughed at that.

"Should I take out a death cart today?" asked Junias.

"No," said Allum. He and Kellus stepped up to the carriage seat while Nonus climbed into the back. "Let the dragons sleep. There is only one dead man in Bangarden today and that's the Prefect. The rest of the city can die tomorrow."

And with that, Allum pulled the draw-reins so that my jaw was pulled down to my chest. My spines stood proudly against the arch of my neck and my back curved unnaturally.

"Oh, he does look fine, Allum," said Avea and to my surprise, she patted my shoulder. "Ruminor has blessed us with such a fine dragon."

For the very first time, I didn't curse the strain of the draw-rein.

The whip cracked in the air above me and with a deep breath, I pressed onto the brace, bringing my wings down in one great stroke. A second and then a third, and soon the carriage rolled forward, out and onto the streets of Bangarden.

***

It was the end of the rainy season and already the days were brighter. Still, I spent most of the day standing outside in the warm mist, watching the streetwyrms land to scratch for seeds and my belly began rumbling for food. In Allum's aviary, we were only fed at night, a practice I didn't fully understand. The first light of morning seemed the best time to me but then again, I'm not a dragoneer. Perhaps they think they get a better day's work from us when our bellies aren't full, but by midday, it was difficult to think of anything other than your next plate of mash. As unappetizing as that sounds, that was my life and I prided myself to say I did it well, being a dragon of integrity and all.

The Prefect was the magistrate of the city and from what I understood, he was not so terribly old. His house was very large, gated and at the center of the city. Black drapes hung from every window, black lanterns from every post. There was a mob gathered outside but all stood a respectable distance away from the carriage, a fact for which I was grateful. If I could have, I'd have blown fire in a great circle, forcing them back even farther but naturally, I was banded and the pleasure of fire was denied once again. There were centurions everywhere – soldiers with swords, spears and large scutan shields standing between the mob and the house. People gave them as much berth as they gave me.

I heard a sound and held my breath as I looked to the sky. A Dragon Flight was wheeling above, flying in high perfect circles over the Prefect's house. I marvelled at their skill as they passed each other, wingtip to wingtip, banking steeply and riding the air with a minimum of beats. They stayed high and I looked around at the crowds, wondering at the meaning of it all.

Dragons don't understand much of stick politics. Our world is about speed and skill, strength and longevity, so the older and larger a dragon is, the more power he or she has. And for dragons, power only means more nests and more breeding and more eggs and more cliffs in which to house more nests. If another dragon challenges us or interferes with our plans, we fight. But the fighting leads to swift resolution – either submission or death and life goes on. We are not a complicated people. So while I didn't understand the mob that had gathered outside the magistrate's house, I could easily feel the tension that simmered like a riptide beneath calm waters. It reminded me of how storms gather all the clouds into one dark place before the first crack of Hallow Fire.

Because of the draw reins, my head was bound tight, so I cast my eye around the mob as sticks pushed towards the walled gate. I growled at them and they shrank back. When the soldiers hiked their weapons to threaten me, I snarled at them too. I admit to a certain satisfaction when they stepped back as well. Standing at my head, Kellus jerked the rein but I did not growl at him.

I could hear the great doors open behind the gate and I breathed deeply the smell of death. This was not the sickly sweet smell of plague, nor the rancid, musky odor of disease. No, this had a powdery sharpness to it and I wondered if he had been poisoned. Nobody had liked the Prefect, according to Allum's family. The mob shifted and murmured, growing blacker like those stormy clouds as the gates opened now on six men carrying a body wrapped in black. A crowd of mourners followed, wailing and posturing and flowing like a black tide. At the sight of the body, the crowd rippled like the waves on a dark ocean and I knew the Hallow Down was set to strike.

The lurch as the body was laid into the back of the carriage and I Nonus closed the rear hatch and spring up into the back. Allum climbed onto the driver's seat and Kellus followed. Immediately, the carriage was surrounded by mourners and mob. I saw one man push another, only to be struck with the hilt of a centurion's short sword. The crowd roared and pressed forward but the centurions held them back.

A clay jar shattered at the wheel of the carriage and the soldiers fell upon the thrower. I snapped at another man who staggered too close but the head-harness was tight and Allum yanked on the rein. The crowd swarmed the carriage and the mourners swarmed the crowd. There were sticks everywhere, rushing and fighting and preventing me from moving forward.

I smelled oil and arcstone moments before a second jar shattered onto the carriage's roof. It erupted and once again, my world burst into flame.

Flames raced down the buckboard and I bellowed as tongues of fire licked my tail. Allum sprang down from his seat but the crowds pressed in on him so he couldn't reach my harness. Steel met steel and swords clanged against the ebony of the carriage, chipping splinters of wood from the frame. One of the Dragon Flight swooped down, blasting fire into the air above the crowd. Another Flight dragon snatched a man from the ground, depositing him safely on the other side of the street, only to have him bolt back into the fray. The sticks scattered at the approach of the dragons but did not disperse and I snarled as a pair of them fell into me, their swords striking metal and wood and dragonbone.

And so, I have mentioned those coals.

The carriage was burning; my owners desperate to

salvage something of their finest cart, and both mob and guards were absorbed in a sea of hand-to-hand combat. I was in the midst of it all and no one was looking to protect me, a fine and useful dragon. The flames stung my wings and I could smell the smoke of dragon flesh, *my* dragon flesh and I remembered Ruby and Summerday and Towndrell and suddenly, those coals roared to life inside of me.

I reared high on my back legs, bellowing as my wings snapped open their full width. I beat down, knocking many sticks off their feet and sending even more scrambling out of my path. I shook my head, the reins swinging wildly and Kellus tried to catch them. He looked so small beneath me and I brought my wings down with another powerful stroke, knocking him to his knees. Another stroke and the wind was my captive. Another and another and suddenly, I was above the street, anchored by the flaming cart. Another and another and it began to rise with me, tipping so that the body of the Prefect slid out and into the mud.

The crowd fell upon it like seasnakes.

"No, Hallowdown!" cried Allum and he gestured wildly up to the Dragon Flight. "He will shatter the carriage! It's the best I have! Stop him!"

A rider astride a large brown drakina swept down to hover at my head. She bellowed at me but I bellowed right back. I was furious at the fact that I was still attached to a flaming carriage and no one seemed to care, not even this noble Dragon Flight. I brought my wings down again and again until the wheels finally left the ground and the cart was airborne. We rose higher and higher until I could see the walls and the gates and the streets and the flames beneath. Above me and all around was the Flight, seven mature dragons blocking my path, their wings buffeting as flames now raced up the poles, catching the fine oils that were used in the polishes and I felt my sides sear with heat.

"Do we kill him?" I heard a rider shout and on the back of a blue drake, another pulled his bow.

Before I knew it, the brown drakina's rider sprang from her back, soaring like a dragon himself through the space in between. Suddenly, he was on my flank, holding on by the harness and bracing himself on the carriage poles. His weight tipped me to one side and I began to sink like a stone.

"Rufus!" cried another rider. "Are you crazy?"

I thrashed my head to dislodge him, for the strain in my neck and wings was too great.

"Fly, night dragon!" he shouted in my ear. "Stay airborne for a moment longer!"

The smoke was sharp and thick and even this high, it was work simply to breathe. Rufus pulled his sword and brought it down once, twice, three times and the harness that held the right pole snapped free. Immediately, all the weight jerked in the opposite direction and the drag caused my wing to bend unnaturally. We plummeted as the carriage swing wildly beneath.

The air stung my eyelids and the heat beat like waves on a rocky shore but with remarkable skill, the rider scrambled under my neck and around my chest, swinging his sword to the braces once again. Suddenly, the carriage was gone, down, down, down, shattering into a thousand splintering pieces across the Prefect's gate.

I soared up to the sky, released but off balance as the rider clung to the harness across my chest. I pitched forward, losing altitude so quickly that I thought we too would shatter across the gate but he swung his leg across my neck, settled into the muscular hump and hollow of my shoulders as if home.

A rider.

I had a rider on my back.

It was heavy and strange but not at all awkward, for his weight seemed to right my balance. It was exhilarating and terrifying at the same time.

He leaned his weight forward along my spines.

"And down, night dragon. You can touch the ground now, without fear."

Down. Down, he wanted me down. I could feel pressure from his legs across my shoulder, seat bones pushing down my spine. It was a natural extension and I angled upwards, throwing my weight into my haunch and beating my wings downward to lessen the impact. When my feet touched the earth, my body lost all strength and I collapsed onto the street. The mud felt good on my charred belly and I barely noticed it when the brown rider left my back. The sticks were still fighting – stick against stick, citizen against centurion, and I realized at that moment that I hated them all except the riders and their Dragon Flight.

I never knew what had happened to the body of the Prefect.

I stayed down for a very long time, until the soldiers and the Flight cleared the streets. Kellus returned to take me to the aviary. I never got mash that night, and the next morning, Junias fitted me with a walking harness and led me to the markets, where I was auctioned off yet again, this time to the Pits. I was glad for the exchange, for in the Pits I could fight and be free of sticks and carts and the dreaded silver band when I died.

LIFE & DEATH IN THE PITS

It was like nothing I could have expected. In fact, it was like a city unto itself, isolated in the mountains between the cities of Bangarden and Salernum. Known simply as 'The Pits,' it was a sprawling complex of caves and underground tunnels leading to and from the bestiaries that housed well over a hundred animals. Sitting atop it all was 'The Crown,' a large circular arena built of limestone, travertine and marble. I could not help but be impressed when I first laid eyes on it on the long road to the underground.

I was perhaps the smallest dragon there, but not the smallest creature by far. As I was led into the tunnels (flanked on either side by sticks riding cerathorns – large armoured four-legged beasts with coats like iron and horns like spears), I saw cages and pens of the wildest variety, containing creatures from sink-lizards to the scaly land monitors of the Remoan deserts. There were creatures like jumpbucks but with razor horns, and creatures like leather-backed phogs with tusks and spines. Many of the creatures had rings pierced through their snouts. I wondered if I would receive such a ring and if so, what manner of tools would be used in the piercing. A two-year old dragon's snout is already strong and hard – piercing such a thing would require strength and no little skill.

And rather than the smell of death as in Bangarden, these tunnels smelled of blood; old caked blood that held together the very stones beneath our feet.

The noise was deafening, even louder than Allum's aviary. These were angry beasts and wild, throwing themselves at the iron mesh in hopes of freedom or a ripping fight and I found it took all of my nerve not to flinch as we walked past. Besides, I could smell trees and grass and fresh air and I prayed that the aviary was as big as Gavius', if not bigger.

It was called the Dome of Dragons.

A huge circular cave that opened to the skies above, containing a veritable jungle beneath an iron mesh roof. Dragons were penned on three levels surrounding the Dome, like the many spokes of a great wheel. All the cages shared one central mesh wall with it and for that, I was grateful. At least to look on trees and sky; to smell the wind and rain. It would be a good way for any dragon to meet his fate then, with a chest filled with jungle air and a memory of sunshine.

I was led up and around to the top level where they kept the youngest dragons and I was relieved to see none younger than I. I suppose it was self-defeating, but the thought of a juvenile dragon sentenced to a life in the Pits fanned those coals once again. I would have been a very angry, bitter dragon indeed if there were any younger than yearlings here.

The sticks turned me out into a pen that was lower but wider than Gavius'. The walls were stone, carved directly out of the mountain rock, and the bedding was straw and dirt. I had a new head-harness, one that allowed me to eat and chew and bite. It had a metal ring under the jaw so that I could be clipped to a cable and led with little resistance. As I have mentioned before, our heads are at the end of our very long necks. For creatures so impressive, we are remarkably easy to control.

The first thing I did was press my face against the mesh wall overlooking the Dome, breathing in the scent of damp soil and old trees. Vines and grasses, flowers and moss, palm trees and cedar and olive pine. For some reason, this soothed me and after the two days of travel, I stretched out by the mesh and studied the roof, wondering if I could, over time, chew my way through the iron as Ruby had done. The thought of chewing anything sounded rather good, and my belly rumbled in the absence of food. Eventually, I dozed and dreamed of seasnakes and lemonwhites and the vast expanse of blue that was the sky.

I couldn't remember the last time I'd dreamed of the night sky. In fact, I couldn't remember the last time I'd seen the stars, nor the winking, waning or wide moons of my father, Draco Stellorum. I knew enough of the world of dragons to know that he wasn't my sire but some things I clung to with a fierce tenacity. I was a night dragon. He was my identity.

Morning brought horrendous screeches of waking dragons, and sticks with whips came to roll open the bars to my pen. Two of them led me out and down a long stone ramp and I passed many pens with many dragons. All watched me with intense, combative stares and I ignored them all, keeping my own eyes from straying too far to the left or to the right. I was led to a small circular arena, not high enough for flying and fashioned out of the familiar metal mesh. Inside, two sticks waited with a hissing blue drake, holding him against the walls with whips and spears. My handlers led me inside, closing the door behind me, the blue and his two handlers. The drake was released and a live goswyrm was tossed at my feet.

Goswryms are awkward creatures with leathery necks and spindly legs. Their wings are frequently tattered (for they like to sleep hanging upside down in caves), but their bodies are disproportionately round and plump and they make a fine meal for any dragon. It tried to run but I stomped down with my clawed foot, stooped to catch its head in my jaws. The blood that sprayed across my tongue was hot and sweet.

Immediately, the blue dragon lunged across the pen, snatching the wrym from my mouth. He began to shred the flesh with his dagger teeth into strips tiny enough for him to swallow and the handlers behind him laughed. I shrank back, puzzled. That goswrym had been clearly meant for me and I snapped my beak at him in protest. He did nothing, merely continued until the meat was small enough to slip past the band down his throat. I looked past him to his handlers, assuming they would rectify the situation but they circled the inside of the ring, one on either side. One man cracked the whip at me, the prodded me with his spear. I swung back to look at the blue, barked once, twice, three times but he ignored me. I sat back to puzzle some more.

The smell of blood was thick in my nostrils and my belly rumbled with lack. Suddenly, I knew what they meant for me to do. They wanted me to fight for my food.

Those coals began to burn once more.

I swung my head toward the handlers once again, growling in a sound that rumbled like distant Hell Down. They raised their weapons but they had not reckoned on my many weeks under the hard-faced man. I lunged and they both staggered back into the mesh wall. I pressed them into it, raising my wings and lowering my head in threat. Shouts now as all the other sticks rushed toward the pen, whips and spears in hand and I brought my face so close to the first man, my mouth open wide, dagger teeth gleaming. He covered his face with his hands as if that simple act would stop my jaws. I did not bite, however. I loosed a long, furious roar that emptied the room of all other sound and echoed until it faded away like ripples on a dead sea.

There was silence now in the arena and I leaned back, let them scramble out of the pen. They slammed and locked the door, leaving me with the half-eaten goswrym and the blue.

I swung my head his way now. He had frozen in place, the wrym hanging from his jaws like waterweed. I snapped my beak and he dropped it into the sand. I lunged forward and snatched it up, shaking it to break its bones before I settled down to shred it with my own dagger teeth.

I knew what they wanted me to do. I knew what game they wanted me to play so I would play it like a master dragon. I had anger, I had cunning, I had been wild and they only had whips and spears. This game, I would win or die trying.

And this time, the blood on my tongue was all the sweeter.

***

In the Pits, no meal came without a price.

A fight, a lesson, a battle, a skirmish. All was intimidation and rage, and while I had the rage in full, the intimidation took a little time in coming. I was young and inexperienced in fighting other dragons. Still, I remembered my talons raking through indigo eyes; remembered the axe plunging into Ruby's head. They were dead because of me and I found that a sickening guilt swept over me whenever I faced a frantic, hungry dragon. But here in the Pits, guilt was a weakness so it quickly hardened into self-loathing which, when fuelled, became fury. It was that fury that gave me the edge in the practice pits. If you succeeded, you were fed. If not, you went hungry. I ate well most nights, whereas others limped to their corners, broken and bleeding and hungry still.

What set me apart from the others, however, was the fact that I did not fear the sticks either. I remembered the thrill of the Lamoan pirates, the rush as I spilled their blood on the decks of the ships. I remembered the crunch of Philius' wrist as my jaws came down on the torch, the smell of burning flesh as I sprayed flames into his eyes. *That,* I reckoned, none of these combatants had ever done. I had a reputation now and it gave me a nerve that the others lacked. I believe the handlers feared me, just a little and that was a very good feeling.

Now, even my dinners had an audience. Sticks would pay for the privilege to watch us fight and kill and eat, and I thought it an odd business to cheer at the defeat of such majestic creatures as dragons. Apparently, they paid more now, as the handlers faced danger and 'certain death' while working with me. I had been fitted with a new collar, one with spikes of steel called a blood-bolt, and in glimpses of silverstone, I can assure you that it looked very menacing around my night-black throat. They also had a new name for me, which once again I must admit was fitting for a dragon of my proud, tragic, terrible nature.

Warblood.

One evening, I was led up a long underground tunnel and the sound of sticks grew louder with each step. There was a large wooden door bolted from the inside that vibrated with the sound of their chanting. *Warblood. Warblood. Warblood.* It rekindled my fledgling vanity and when the door was finally swung open, I burst out onto the arena floor, the sticks wildly trying to control me with ropes and whips. It made, I believe, for a most excellent entrance.

I was in the Crown.

It was the very first time and I blinked as my eyes adjusted to the strange light. The sky above was dark, with my stars and the twin moons shining like beacons. Torches burned along the travertine walls. Columns and arches, stairs and benches and most of all, sticks. Rows and rows of their odd, flat faces seated all around me, many levels up like rocks dotting a mountainside, protected by a web of iron mesh that ran up to the very high ceiling. It was dented in many places and I imagined it was from dragons flying too fast and not making the turns. The entire place smelled of blood and sticks and smoke, and when I reared onto my back legs and spread wide my wings, the entire crowd fell silent.

The only thing I could think of was my colouring. I was a night dragon, the colour of ash and stars and smoke and death. Stealthy and silent, I could steal their flocks in the night. I could murder their children and set fire to their homes. They didn't know that all I wanted was to be free of this silver band and return to the Anquar Cliffs a wildling once more. They didn't know that I would do it or die trying.

I bugled to the night sky, once, twice, three times and the crowds went wild, a roar like the thunder of Hell Down and my heart soared at the sound. My handlers moved forward, using poles to remove the ropes at my head and neck and I lunged at them, causing the crowd to roar more. It was the oddest thing I had ever experienced but I knew that in the Crown, a dragon was expected to perform if he was to live.

I vowed to give them a performance they would not

soon forget.

At the opposite end of the arena, a red drake was ushered in. He was a little larger than me and I immediately recognized him as the ill-tempered drake from the Corolanus Markets. The crowd cheered when he spread wide his wings and roared. I could see the scars from many months of living in the Pits and for the first time in weeks I felt a pang of fear. Life in the Pits was ultimately about killing, a thing that I had never actually done. I was responsible for the death of the indigo dragon, I had aided the execution of Ruby, and while I was guilty of imagining the gruesome deaths of all the sticks I hated, I had never actually taken a life other than a fish. I was all bravado and threat. Now I was being asked to kill and it set my blood racing. Could I do this and if so, how?

The red drake spied me and he let out a bellow that shook the mesh. I bellowed back, knowing that if we'd had arcstone, the entire Crown would be ablaze.

His handlers released him and he stalked forward, hissing and whipping his blood red tail. He was hot, so I needed to be cold. I glanced up at the sky and the mesh ceiling. It too was dented and I swiftly judged the number of wingspans to get there. I spread wide my wings once again, allowing myself to feel the length and width and breadth of the Crown. It was a matter of speed and precision – how soon to reach the sides, how to bank to prevent me from adding another dent in the iron web. He had likely flown in here. I had not. Added to my lack of killing, this would be my downfall.

But what a fall it would be.

Suddenly, there were only two dragons in all the world. My heart was a war drum, my blood the ice of fear but there were also the coals of fury kindling in my belly. I lowered my head, raised my wings and roared.

He leapt through the air toward me, body arched like a bow, teeth and talons leading, wings spread far back. I sprang up to meet him and our jaws clashed as we sought a hold on the other. My talons raked his belly, his raked my chest. I felt fire run like ribbons from the wounds.

In that instant I knew that he was too strong so I launched into the air. As expected, he followed, his wing beats slow and powerful. But mine were swift and efficient for once upon a time I had been a fisher dragon and I knew how to move so that the wind stung my eyes. But there was a ceiling and walls and a floor, not miles and miles of open sky. I would need skill as much as speed.

I began to circle around the widest part of the Crown, faster and faster and faster. He was at my tail, snapping and spitting acid that stung my scales. As we raced, his wing clipped one of the torches and it crashed to the ground, taking bits of limestone with it. At one point I scraped along the iron mesh protecting the sticks. Pain flashed behind my eyes but for their part, the sticks howled with pleasure and I hated them for it.

The red tried to intercept my circles but I was faster and he struck the mesh again and again in my wake. Faster and faster I flew, angling my flight so that it was ceiling to floor now, ceiling to floor in a dangerous ellipse that could kill either one of us with the slightest miscalculation. I counted the wing strokes that it took to go up before the ceiling, and then the sickening lurch of a spiral, counting the strokes before I hit the ground. He matched my speed, his jaws snapping as he sought my tail and I whipped it like the wind to dizzy him. My stomach flipped as I approached the ceiling, banked so sharply that my talons clanged along the mesh. Downward now and I timed it, my heart threatening to burst as the ground rose up so quickly. Barely a wingspan above the floor, I suddenly reversed, lurching upwards and reaching back with my talons, hoping he would be where I expected him to be. He was and I caught his red face and swung him downwards despite his beating wings.

He hit with a crunch and tumbled tail over spine, tail over spine, before finally sliding to a stop in a twitching heap in the sand.

There was silence in the Crown.

I hovered over him, wings beating slowly, blowing bits of sand across the arena floor. His tail whipped back and forth, his legs kicked and thrashed but his head, neck and wings did little more than quiver. In one instant, I had broken his neck and for some reason, I remembered Ruby, flailing in the mud.

Ruby, the indigo dragon and now this warrior red.

It struck me like a poison-tipped spear.

I was a killer of dragons.

The crowd however erupted in cheering, sent coins flying through the air so they fell like hard rain upon us. The handlers entered the arena, two with long brooms to keep me away, others with spear and axe to finish what I had started. I bellowed but they ignored me, moving toward the thrashing red with their instruments of death. I remembered the night in Allum's pen, when Philius had come to call and those hard, simmering little coals began to rage.

Honour, integrity, respect. Things I thought I possessed, qualities I believed would set me in good stead with these sticks, were merely lies to keep me submissive and working. I understood now how they had used pride as both bait and capture. It was clever really. That's why they were masters and I wore a silver band.

When Philius had come to call…

The memory stirred inside me.

I swung my head, scanning the sea of flat faces, finally seeing the torch and limestone burning on the arena floor. I arrowed towards it and scooped the torch in my jaws, tossing it so I could swallow the flames back as far as the silver band. The crowd roared and I soared over the red dragon, spitting acid flame at both handlers and their pathetic weapons as I went. Spear and axe instantly blazed and the handlers scrambled out of the way as I spat again, this time lighting the brooms with the borrowed fire. My mouth burned and my tongue sizzled and the fire from the torch quickly sputtered and died but I was not going to repeat the night in Gavius' fields. No stick would do this because of me.

The blame was mine. Likewise, the blood.

The crowd fell silent as I landed near the drake. His eye rolled up to meet mine and, with wings spread wide, I put a clawed foot on his shoulder. I wished in that moment to have been able to talk the way the sticks talked, to exchange thoughts with such ease and fluidity. Dragons are not blessed with language. We roar, we sing, we bellow, we grumble, but we don't talk. And I wondered if I had finally stumbled on the one true thing that made the sticks more powerful than dragons.

I reached down and sank my teeth into his throat, the one area that has no spines or spikes to protect it, and pressed down. Too hard. Our skins are too hard, so I tore with my clawed foot once, twice, three times until blood sprayed across my scales. I could see the vessels now, red and blue and oozing with life and I bit, severing them as if they were lemonwhites. He shuddered once, then died and I lifted my head, blood dripping from my teeth and jaws.

I spread my wings and bellowed at them now, at the pathetic handlers who thought a broom could stop me. At the pathetic crowds who paid to see us fight and kill each other. At the world of sticks in general and at the injustice of life and power and death and I roared so that the blood sprayed out of my mouth like fire and I hated them with all the fire that was in my belly. I hated myself as well, for my vanity and foolishness and pathetic integrity and in that moment, I vowed to change the laws of dragons and men.

Perhaps it was a good thing that we don't have language, for the crowd went wild – cheering and leaping and throwing coins like the rain. But they didn't know what I was thinking and they couldn't tell what I had just said, for at the next chance I got, and every chance after that, I would kill a stick for every dragon until the scale was even once more.

I let them lead me to my pen but I did not sleep that

night, nor for many other nights after that.

DOME OF DRAGONS

After eight months in the Pits, I was still alive. I suppose that meant I was unbeaten. I never liked to think of the blood I had spilled along the way.

It wasn't because I was stronger. It wasn't because I was more savage. I think it was simply because I was smarter and had a canny recollection of where I had come from and where I was going. I was also angry and I harnessed that anger, made it very small like those coals, using them instead as fuel when I needed them. I killed many dragons because of those coals, when what I really wanted to do was kill the sticks that imprisoned us. In those eight months, I had maimed several men, delimbed one and crippled another but I still hadn't killed. They were careful around me, all the while rewarding my misbehaviour with freedom and food.

When I say freedom, I mean the Dome of Dragons. It was mine for several hours a day then, to fly, to swoop, to sleep and to hunt, for they would occasionally release a wild jumpbuck or daggernewt into the Dome so I could keep my skills sharp. Not often, however. They needed to keep us on the edge of starvation, rewarding us with food if we survived a match and killed. A cruel bargain – death for food. Cruel but effective. We all desired to live.

I don't think they'd ever had a wild dragon in the Pits, only those who had been bred into service to fish or pull carts or whatever else a stick could think of for a dragon to do. I had been born wild. I had fished for my dinner and I remembered back to the time as a fledgling when I had fought off a seasnake and won. Those memories added to the fuel and anger became my core; a hard, sharp white-hot coal of fury and self-loathing and will.

Twice a week I fought to a full Crown, and the theatrics grew more spectacular with each passing battle. There were parades and army drills first to warm up the crowds. Sticks fought each other and I knew that not all were soldiers. I thought of Rue, how he had been bought and sold and wondered if a stick could be sold to fight in the Pits. Regardless, sticks fought sticks then gore bulls and direcats. Then gore bulls fought direcats, and the winners fought dragons and finally dragons fought dragons. Not all would die, but many would and I learned that sticks loved the sight and the smell and the very idea of blood.

Interestingly, dragons never fought sticks. I think the thought of us killing them was something too deep, too visceral, and therefore, too dangerous. Naturally, I thought about it all the time.

My fights were now the finals of the nights. The sticks would lead in a new challenger and the crowd would cheer, wondering if this would be the one to defeat Warblood, the Night Dragon, Jewel of the Crown. The challenger would be released to fly to the roar of the crowd, but then the handlers would douse the torches one by one, leaving a very few to burn in the arena. Then, I would arrive, swooping from the ceiling in almost perfect cover – my scales the stars, my wings smoke in the night sky. Just like with the red drake, I would strike the killing blow almost immediately, leaving my opponent with enough life left for a pathetic parlay once the torches were relit. The crowd never knew my strategy – just the sight of a night dragon filled them with awe, wonder and more than a little fear. It was the easiest job I had ever done and I could have done it forever had it not been for the fact that I hated myself now as much as I hated the sticks.

We never fought in the Dome. The Dome was a place of respite for dragons and sticks alike, and there were many days when I would watch handlers roam the great arena for hours on end. Oh yes, they would clean, they would prune, they would move rocks and rake sand and plant seeds but they would also sleep and spar and laugh and read. I never understood how men who lived in a world of violence and death, could have normal lives beyond that. As I've said, I thought of Rue often, wondered if he could have been a handler like this. Wondered if these men had been bought and sold into such a life or if it was merely a servitum like tending a plow or tilling a field. Something they did in order to have food and shelter and a modicum of purpose.

Like life in Bangarden, I had much time to think.

I had a new collar – not studded like the previous, but buckled leather cased in silver. It was called a clap-lock and I preferred it immensely. I also had a nose ring. It had happened quite suddenly when one day a tray of shredded goswyrm hearts appeared through the food hatch of my pen. Goswyrm hearts are particularly sweet and were a common treat for favoured dragons in the Pits. I never thought to question it and devoured it immediately, licking the tray clean with my sticky tongue. But almost at once, a heaviness came over me and I found my legs buckle beneath. I put it down to the contented effects of the wyrm until the door rolled open and a dozen sticks rushed in.

I was used to being handled by them. I was used to them inspecting my teeth or tending my rare wounds but this was different. A heavy mesh was thrown across my back and the sticks held me down, pinning my wings and keeping me on the floor. My response was sluggish and now I believe they must have treated the hearts with a soporific. I could barely lift my head or lash my tail and before I knew it, a needle was thrust through the septum between my nostrils, which is the only tender bit of a dragon's snout. Fire and light popped behind my eyes and I thrashed sideways, knocking several handlers to the floor. With a roar I rose up like a thundercloud but the sticks had done their job and fled, rolling the door closed behind them.

I shook my head and snapped my jaws, blinking as I

tried to adjust to this unnatural addition. My nose throbbed with the sting of many thornets, more so when I tried to rub it with my wing claw. A ring, I realized. They had fitted me with a ring like a common pit dragon and the coals of my fury blazed anew.

If I had seen it reflected in a slice of silverstone however, I think I would confess to the fact that it was made of very fine hammered steel. Some part of me would have approved, if only just a little.

Another important thing I must confess is the fact that, during my time in the Dome, I had bred a drakina. Several, in fact, given my advantageous colouring and prowess in the Crown. I suppose they were trying to breed for either of those qualities, though I truthfully didn't care. A drake never thinks of eggs or hatchlings, only having more drakinas than any other drake in the territory. They are as important to him as his pride.

A fine drakina had been let into the Dome one day while I was dozing and at first, I thought they meant me to kill her. I had never killed a dragon in the Dome and wasn't sure what to do when an overpowering scent reached my nostrils. It reminded me of Ruby in Gavius' oryza fields and I suddenly understood the indigo dragon and his night visits. The scent was like the taste of lemonwhites – sweet, smooth and overpowering to all other senses. But I also remembered Summerday's tease and Ruby's temper, so I watched her from the branches of a very tall tree and debated what I should do.

She was a year-and-a-halfling, fine-boned and charcoal like dark, dark stone. I don't believe she had ever been in the Dome before as she explored first the rocks and trees and bubbling pond before finding the sand and rolling over in it, enjoying the feel as it polished her scales and spines. My heart ached at the sight of a dragon just being a dragon. We are majestic and charismatic creatures, ill suited to a life of service. I wished the sticks could see that.

I unfurled my wings and soared down from the tree, surprised that I hadn't surprised her. She lifted her head from the sand, blinked slowly and rolled again, lashing her tail from side to side. I sat and watched her for a while, wondering if I should bring her a gift. I had killed a young nox earlier on, one that had been unceremoniously shoved into the Dome and I had broken its neck with ease. (Honestly, I do believe he was happy to see me the instant before he died.) And so, I lifted off and returned with a haunch I was saving for later, reckoning it might serve me better in the belly of the drakina than in my own.

She rose to her feet, shook the sand from her charcoal scales and approached without fear. She put a claw on the haunch and hissed at me, just in case. Language, I marvelled. We didn't speak with words like the sticks, but we communicated. I sat back and watched her as she ate, pondering this lack of language among our people. But before I knew it, she was rubbing her head along my flank, growling and purring in a way that reminded me of Summerday yet again. She was obviously in season and the scents of drakina and nox blood were a heady mix. She snapped at me now and I snapped back, spreading my wings and dipping my head low to the ground. Suddenly, she sprang into the air, rocketing toward the mesh ceiling like a star. I leapt after her and followed, for the first time in a long time flying with someone who wasn't trying to kill me. Soon, we were neck and neck, soaring around the Dome, the envy of all the other dragons who were watching from their pens. She twisted in midair and raked my flank with her claws before wheeling and spiralling downward. I bellowed and followed again until I struck her from above, our wings battering, our tails lashing like whips. We soared upwards now, twisting and spinning in an arc through the domed sky until my jaws clamped down on the back of her neck and suddenly, I knew.

It was like Hallow Fire, I must admit. The flash of light that illuminates everything and threatens to burn all in its rush and quickly we dropped like stones to the sand. Wings and necks entwined we rolled across the floor, crushing shrubs and saplings under our weight and threatening to take down many of the older trees with our tails. Her scales were the wind, her spines the mountains and if we were not banded, our fire would have scorched the earth. Bellow and breath, claw and couple, the mating of dragons is a deadly thing. Even for us, it threatens to consume us, overturn all our majesty and turn us into creatures of instinct and lust.

The mating of dragons also takes a long time and it was dark when the handlers came to separate us. Believe me when I tell you, if I had my fire, they would have all been turned to ash.

I never saw the charcoal drakina again, but several weeks later, I was presented with another one, this time the colour of deep waters. You may also believe me when

I tell you that this time, I was much more savvy, and shared only a very small piece of the haunch. As I've said, I am a clever dragon and was able to breed and still eat twice that day. A few weeks after that a brown and after that, another grey. If it weren't for the Crown, life would have been good for me.

And I could see the sky.

The stars called to me at night, telling tales of the Fat Fish and the Dying Wyrm and most of all, my father, Draco Stellorum. I learned the patterns of his eyes during that time – the Wide Eyes, the Sleepy Eyes, the Winking and the Blinking. Since the Dome was open (with only the iron mesh to keep us in), there was nothing to keep the rains out and when they came, it was magical. As I've said before, water is a dragon's friend and even the fiercest of downpours was a delight. During those times, I would close my eyes and remember when I could fly without harness or mesh to limit me. There were times when I could almost hear the tides and I missed the sound of the sea, the rise and fall of the waves, the smell of the salt on the wind. It was very helpful in keeping those coals of fury alive, otherwise I could have grown complacent. As it was, it only served to sharpen my desire for freedom. I would return to the Cliffs or die in the process.

One afternoon, while dozing in the Dome, I heard a sound and lifted my head to see five shadows cross the mesh roof. My heart thudded in my chest. A Dragon Flight. A Dragon Flight had come to the Pits. It filled my head with all manner of questions. What was a Flight doing here? Was it for fighting and if so, against me?

Surely the riders of a Flight would never watch a match where dragons killed dragons for sport. I couldn't possibly fight a Flight dragon – I wouldn't and I resolved myself to die with honour instead of fight one of them. I'm not sure why I felt that way. I had never met a Flight dragon, not truly. I had saved the great silver drake, but I hadn't met him. However, his rider seemed like a man I could respect and there was much to be said for that.

Unless of course, the honour of the Dragon Flight was all in my mind. Perhaps there was no world in which dragon and rider worked as one, only served and servant. I thought back to Rue and Gavius, to little Tacita and her char sketches in the night. Good sticks, noble sticks, but still I wore a band at my throat.

I glanced at the ceiling mesh. It was almost gnawed through in one corner. Teeth and dragon acid were a potent combination and I silently thanked Ruby for my introduction to the art of the great escape.

Handlers showed up and rolled open my ground-floor door. That was my cue to return to my pen, although I'd often wondered what they would do if I didn't. I never acted on that question and this time, like all other times, I soared down to land on the sand, snapping and growling and they gave me a wide berth as I lumbered in. My thoughts were racing however, and I found myself puzzling over why a Dragon Flight would be in the Pits. There had not been a jumpbuck, nox or daggernewt released in the Dome for me that day. Or the day before, when I paused to think about it.

In my pen, I laid my head down across my claws,

wrestling with my thoughts. I lay for the rest of the day, knowing that tonight I would be called upon to fight and kill and, depending on the challenger, perhaps die. I was nearing three and almost my full size. (Although dragons can grow every year of their life. I have heard of dragons that are bigger than mountains, and dragons that live in the water where sticks make their homes on them like islands.) If I died today, I would never know how big I would have grown had I stayed on the Cliffs of Anquar. So little of my life had been my own choosing.

And so I waited for the rising of the stars and the filling of the Crown and the trumpets and the parades and dousing of the torches and the rush of blood in my veins. And for the first time in my life, I dreaded the coming of the night.

JEWEL OF THE CROWN

It was dark when they came for me.

I needed four handlers now and I moved slowly, reluctantly, down the tunnels toward the Crown. They tried to make me move faster, tugging at my nose ring, tapping my legs with switches, tapping my tail with brooms. My growl echoed in the tunnels and they stopped. I believed by then I had their respect. At least, that's what I told myself.

We didn't use the wooden door anymore – that was for all others and for challengers. The Night Dragon didn't walk in to the Crown. No, I had a special chamber on the sixth level. Originally a cleaner's hallway, it had been reconstructed for me with a long low ceiling, narrow dark walls and a silent drape of linen for a door. But it opened high into the Crown and allowed for an entrance from above, unseen by sticks or dragons, thus preserving the element of surprise for both.

As I waited at the linen drape, I could hear the crowd roaring again, could smell the blood and excitement of other dragons. The torches were still blazing so it was not my time and I tossed my head, rattling the ring and slapping the ropes. I was angry and eager to get on with the night. Victory or defeat. Life or death. There was no other way in the Crown and I was weary of the game.

Music of trumpets marking a new match. My heart leapt to my throat but I steeled it, willed it to grow cold, hard, stone.

"Ruminor smiles on us all tonight," the announcer's voice rang through the Crown, echoing as if there were two. *"For the glory of our new governor, Septus Aelianus, Primar of the Eastern Provinces, we are blessed to bring you the match to end all matches!"*

I understood most stick words by now, enough to realize that the Dragon Flight was here because of an important man.

"Entering the Crown from the north gate," echoed the announcer. *"We bring you Bonesnap – the pride of the city of Belarius!"*

The arena shook with the roar of a dragon and crowd went wild, drowning his war cry with their cheers. *Bonesnap*. I tossed my head again. I would finish him like a sinklizard.

"And from the south gate," the announcer continued, *"His twin brother Bloodtooth!"*

Two?

"Bonesnap and Bloodtooth, Twin sons of Remus and the Eastern Provinces! Together, the sons of Belarius will challenge the undefeated Night Dragon, our very own Warblood, Jewel of the

Crown of Salernum!"

The roar of the crowd shook the walls, rattled the wooden planks as my feet.

I growled, a deep rumbling sound in my chest that I know frightened the handlers. I didn't care. I was angry, doubly so. Two dragons. Two dragons against one, all for the sport of sticks. I ducked my head low and narrowed my eyes, summoning the coals, willing the fury. I would kill them both before they knew I was in the arena. I would kill them as I had never killed before and I felt my blood grow hot in my veins.

"Warblood!" shouted the crowds. "Warblood! Warblood! Warblood!"

Above the crowds, I could hear the cries of the twin dragons down below, trumpeting and bellowing the challenge. From the changes in pitch, I could tell they were swinging their heads, looking between the east and west entrances and back again. They were wondering how large I was, where I would enter, how I would attack. I grunted, imagining the surprise in their faces when I swept down from the sky in the dark. It would last a heartbeat before I broke their necks, but it would be enough.

And one by one, the torches went down in the Crown.

The crowd hushed and I could hear the twins bugling to each other. They were pathetic, lost and helpless and I pulled my chin to my chest, coiling every muscle in my body. The ropes fell away, the drape was swept aside and I slipped into the Crown like a wraith.

I was night. I was darkness. I knew how to ride the air so that my wings made no sound. I was a spirit, a ghost, a shadow. There were stars and the moons, and the Wide Eyes of my father, Draco Stellorum, to guide me. I knew from experience where the mesh walls were, where the pillars and columns were that held up the stands. The Crown in darkness had been my home for months now. In fact, the Crown was more a part of me than the Anquar Cliffs and at that moment, I realized that I was no longer a wild dragon but something else entirely.

Not wild. Not a warrior. Neither and both. I could kill all or none. Dreams of nobility but my life bought and paid for in blood. The sticks hadn't done this. Yes, they had captured me and banded me and forced me to work and now kill or starve, but ultimately, it had little to do with the sticks at all. My vanity had brought me here, to this place. I killed their dragons because I could not kill myself.

Below me, four torches flickered by the four gates and I could see the sons of Belarius, their eyes flashing like beacons on the sea as they swung their heads blindly in the dark. They were green, I realized, and both larger than me but it didn't matter. I had killed bigger. I had killed older. I steeled my will, becoming a creature of death and blood.

I tucked my wings and dropped like a massive stone onto the first twin's head. He crumbled beneath my weight but I did not leave it there. With his face in my talons, I immediately sprang upwards, taking him with me as we disappeared into the blackness. In several powerful strokes, I was at the Prefect's Box where a small candle gave light to the important men. I swung the drake's body into the mesh and with a clang, it dented inward. Inside the Box, the men shrieked and I could see both senators and soldiers shrunk back in fear.

It was a good feeling.

I sank my teeth into the back of the green dragon's neck just beneath the horns. He squealed, writhing and bending the squares of mesh with his powerful talons but the grip I had was savage and sure. With my feet on his back, I pressed him into the iron and shook my head violently, back and forth, back and forth, back and forth until I heard the crack of his neck bones. Squeal became sputter but I did not stop – back and forth, back and forth – until his head came free and I felt the blood spray warm across my eyes.

Bonesnap, I thought with grim pleasure.

And suddenly, a torch crackled to life within the Box.

"Night Dragon," someone whispered.

"Warblood," said another.

I hovered backwards, releasing my grip on the severed head and it thudded quietly into the sand below. The body however continued to flail for several heartbeats, stuck against the mesh by its own talons and spines. Again, like the very first drake I'd killed, the tail lashed and the legs thrashed but the wings merely twitched. The exposed throat pulsed blood into the Box.

"Marvellous!" shouted a man as he rose to his feet. His white robes were splattered with red but he began to clap his ringed hands together. "He is marvellous! I salute him."

The senator from Bangarden.

"Yes, Primar," said another. "Truly marvellous."

"We salute the Night Dragon!"

"Warblood, the magnificent!"

"Stormfall?"

I froze.

Suddenly, a great weight slammed into me from behind, forcing all the air out of my chest as I struck the iron.

It was the second dragon, twin to the first, and I cursed my vanity. In my lust, I had forgotten him and now, in the light of the Prefect's Box, I was visible and therefore vulnerable. I plummeted downwards, spiralling my wings to catch the air until the darkness swallowed me once again. But he had a grip on my neck and fell with me, his back talons raking my flanks and beating my wings with his own. He was larger than me and I knew that if we hit the ground, any advantage I might have had would be lost.

His mouth was wide, dagger teeth tearing furiously and I let him, ignoring the blinding pain as his jaws gnashed and chewed because he finally struck the buckled band. As I've said earlier, I was not savage, I was not stronger, I was merely smarter and once I realized the killing lust was upon him, I leaned into him, pushing the band up between his teeth. He bit wildly, not realizing that it was leather and not skin he was gnawing, metal and not bone. I angled my wings and met the ground with my back feet, springing and taking him with me up, up, up to the far side of the dark arena. Above me my father called. Draco Stellorum, Dragon of the Stars, both Eyes Wide, twin moons full and beaming. I was losing blood, *War*blood, but I was the Night Dragon and I would live or die because of this night.

We flew faster and faster toward the iron mesh. I knew the Crown. I knew the walls like my own scales and, pushing my banded neck into his mouth, I wheeled in midair. Backwards, we struck the mesh hard.

So hard that it dented beneath our combined weight. Behind it, the sticks screamed and bolted from their seats because, at this particular impact, the band around my throat snapped free.

Ping, ting, ting. It bounced off the mesh before hitting the sand.

The silence that fell with it was louder.

A dragon un-banded, loose in the Crown.

I threw back my head and bellowed, bringing up the acid that was always in my belly. The fire came with it, rolling off my tongue and spraying yellow-hot across the face of the green dragon. His eyes burst within his head and ooze ran down his sizzling face. I blew fire through the mesh and the sticks screamed once more. I soared through the Crown, raining fire into the stands and seats and through the arches and exits and doors. The Crown erupted into chaos.

Over the din, I heard the singing of arrows, felt heat rain across my flank as they hit. I saw a torch on the ground, then a second so I circled and swept low, taking out all the torch columns with my wings as I flew. *Bam, bam, bam, bam,* they fell like saplings in a summer storm until there was nothing but moonlight in the Crown, and firelight on the citizens as they thrashed and howled and burned.

Still, I was trapped. There were only two ways out. I

would be free through one or die fighting tonight. I flew high to the ceiling, gripping the iron mesh with my talons, spitting acid on the bars and hearing the familiar sizzle as they weakened and charred. I sprayed fire in a concentrated blast but arrows thudded along my spine and I knew this way would not work for me. I released the mesh and disappeared into the dark shadows, hovering in my night blackness and knowing I had only a few hours until daylight. The only way now was certain death and I hardened my heart for the prospect. Death for dragons was never glorious, no matter how hard we tried.

There were archers in the stands and others on the floor but I could see light flickering behind the large double doors where the processions came through. *The army gate,* I remembered. It was used for the parades and drills and I had no idea where it went but surely not to underground tunnels. When the doors swung open, the army marched out carrying spears and arrows and swords and I took a long, deep breath, steeling my will and deadening my heart. I dipped my head, angled my wing and descended like the night.

The army didn't see me coming until I was upon them, and then I sprayed fire into them, lighting them all like torches but I didn't stop. I flew straight into them, bowling them over as they screamed and fell and crunched beneath me. In a heartbeat, I was through to the other side. It was dark like the tunnels but in the distance, I could see a shimmer of light. Moons, I realized, the Wide Eyes of Draco Stellorum. My father was showing me the way to freedom or to death – which one I didn't know.

Regardless, I half flew, half lumbered through the dark tunnel toward it, my wings unable to fully extend. Arrows thudded into me from all angles but the light was an open arch and I was not stopping.

Swords drawn, centurions rushed from outside, not realizing that I had flame and I burned them with barely a thought. They crumpled to the stone and I felt the crush of them under my feet. Suddenly, I was through the archway into a wide exterior courtyard. Above me, the open sky.

A powerful shock to my shoulder and I staggered, looked down to see a spear protruding from my flesh. A centurion was standing in the archway and I ducked my head and blew, setting him ablaze with one breath. I paused a moment to survey the field – citizens were flooding out of many exits and soldiers were rushing in from many entrances. But there was no mesh; there was no ceiling. There were only the moons and the stars and the great expanse of night sky and my father. I heard the bugle of distant dragons and remembered the Flight.

I tossed my head and sprang into the air, my wings making huge downstrokes once, twice, three times, ignoring the blinding pain from my shoulder and dragging the long spear with me as I climbed. Finally, I was skyborne, soaring over the Crown and then the Dome and the Pits and then the roads and the foothills and the mountains and the clouds.

I looked back to see five dragons flying like an arrow in my wake.

THE CRESCENT MOUNTAINS

From night to morning I flew, determined to stay airborne but feeling light-headed as the events of the battle took their toll.

Stormfall.

The spear in my shoulder was slowing me down, creating drag in the strong air currents above the mountains. Like Rue dragging an oar in the water, I found myself drifting to the side as my good wing beat stronger than my weak. Arrows in my back stung and the blood streaked along my neck from the green dragon's teeth. But I was unbanded and free and could happily die on any one of these great mountains beneath me.

Stormfall.

The Dragon Flight was still following and this puzzled me. They could have easily overtaken me given my injuries but they didn't and I found myself wondering what their aim was.

Someone had called me Stormfall.

I pushed it from my mind and tucked in my wings, plummeting down to skim the crests of the mountains. They looked white, these mountains, like the caps on ocean waves. I had never seen anything like them in my life. While the peaks were white, the valleys were dark and it was the darkness that I was searching for. Night dragons do not hide well in the light.

I angled my good wing, fighting the pain but letting the drag take me down, down, down into craggy valleys. It was magnificent to have the wind in my eyes once again, even if for such a sorry reason. A part of me just wished to close them and let the ground take me. Death would come mercifully quick and I would be soaring through the stars with my father before I knew it. But I was a proud dragon and if there was a way to outwit these sticks, I reckoned I owed it to myself to at least try.

There were trees lining these mountains – bank pines and larches and olive firs growing at steep angles along the slopes. I whipped between them now, knowing this was a dangerous but effective way to become lost in the night. It was very dark, with the clouds passing over the moons, and I risked a glance behind, scanning the skies above for any trace of the Flight. If I couldn't see them, it seemed reasonable that they couldn't see me when suddenly, a streaking branch nicked the tip of the spear and fire exploded behind my eyes. Wildly I spun, crashing into tree after tree until my wingtip struck the slate of the mountain and my belly followed suit, scraping along the stone and moss and bumping off trees and stumps and rocks. I came to rest at a cliff's edge, wedged against a cedar that cracked at my impact but did not fall.

I closed my eyes now. Even if the Flight hadn't seen my undignified landing, they would have heard it and so I was doomed, too weary to hide, too bloody to fight. They would have to kill me for I would not go back to the Pits. The rules had changed and I had changed them. Any dragons I killed would be free dragons, any fight a fair fight and any sticks that got in the way would be a welcome sacrifice.

I didn't hear it when the first dragon landed, nor the second. At some point however, I became dimly aware of voices but I shut them out, determined not to know when the sword fell across my neck. The smell of dragons was strong and I welcomed that smell, let it carry me into the stars. If I am truthful, I do think the last thing I remember was the word Stormfall, and then nothing.

***

It is a strange place, that place between Death and Dying, and it almost seems like sleep. Long, deep, dreamless sleep that is at once empty and disturbing, a twisting world of blurred space and fragmented memory, of insensate calm and unimaginable terror. I was grateful to leave that place, even if it was to hear the voices of sticks once again.

Stormfall. I had been Stormfall once.

I remembered a scrap of the dream – a stick had removed the spear and taken much of my blood with it. Men had climbed over me in my dream, pulling out barbs like nettles and rubbing pine tar into the wounds. In fact, all I could smell was pine tar. When I opened my eyes, I was surprised to see a great silver drake stretched out beside me, fanning his wings in the sun.

He noticed me, cocked his great head to one side and rumbled a greeting. His wings lay open across the rock, the talon-tips crossed beneath him and he looked very regal, more regal than any dragon I'd ever seen. He was easily twice my size and his hide was scarred from many battles. But still, his scales shone like silverstone and I wondered if I knew him.

"Stormfall?" came a voice and I lifted my head to see a stick walking toward me. He was wearing silver armour and a bell of memory began to take chime, calling back a time on the Udan Shore. "Do you remember me, Stormfall? Cassien Cirrus, First Wing of the Eastern Quarter Dragoneers. You saved my life and that of my dragon."

I growled at him, low and deep in my chest. He continued towards me so I bared my teeth, my many rows of daggers that could cut him in half in one snap. The silver dragon growled now. However, he didn't move, didn't change position to threaten or intimidate. The threat was in his tone and I understood it very well, despite our lack of language.

"I thought it was you," said the stick, Cassien Cirrus. "Not too many dragons with your colouring in this region."

He was beside me now, smelling of leather and pine tar and dragons. He reached out and touched my neck where the spear had been, ran his hand along my flank. I remembered the one of the first days in the fishing hut when Rue ran his hand along my face. It had been the first touch of a stick that had not been accompanied by bruises. Like this.

But I was not that dragon any more.

I summoned the fire, blew a curl of smoke out my nostril and the great silver dragon rose to his feet. I snapped at him and he snapped back, our teeth echoing through the quiet valley.

"Enough," growled Cirrus and the dragon lowered his head. "I told you he'd be hard as stone, Ironwing. He wasn't as lucky as you."

The silver drake grumbled and I noticed that he had no band around his throat. Come to think of it, he never had. Of course they were allowed to harness their fire, these Flight Dragons and for the first time in a very long time, my imagination struggled to raise its broken head.

"The others have gone," said Cirrus. "They've returned to the Citadel so it's just us here. You, me and Ironwing."

And he held up a piece of charred meat. It looked like a skoat, a small tree lizard known for sharp teeth and tasty flesh and he peeled a strip for me. I clenched my jaws tight, unwilling to play this game. First Rue, then Junias, then all of the handlers in the Pits. The lure of food, traded for a silver band and work. Or in the Pits – for blood. I was no fool. I would take nothing from this man's hand.

He smiled at me. I could burn him to ash with the fire of my breath.

"You're a clever one, aren't you?" he said. "But look,

Flight Dragons have no band. They can eat what they want, when they want. Ironwing could kill me if he wanted to, couldn't you, Ironwing?"

The silver drake grumbled but did not take his shiny eyes off me for an instant.

"And so, here, I offer you this skoat. It is very tasty and you need the strength."

He stepped forward once again. The skoat looked good, smelled even better.

I pushed myself to my feet. They were shaky but still.

The silver drake growled again.

Stormfall and Rue, Flight Dragons and Riders. Working together for a common purpose. I had been happy once. I had been Stormfall.

I looked around at the sunny mountainside. Trees, rocks, slopes, white cliffs. Above me, clouds and blue. Beneath me, valleys and rivers.

There was no comparison.

I stretched out my wings and leapt into the sky, soaring out and away from this rocky ledge, the stick and his silver dragon with barely a second thought.

And to my relief, they did not follow.

***

Life in the Crescent Mountains was at once different from and similar to my early life at the Anquar Cliffs. Instead of fish, I hunted white ghorns and shaggy noxen and shared with no one. I hunted at night as well, perfecting the arts of soundless flight and killing with a single blow. Instead of a nest on a mountain ledge, I made a lair in a cave I'd found along a cliff face. It smelled of old dragons and I wondered if it was an ancient aerie of some sort. It gave me a sense of belonging, one I hadn't had in some time.

But above all I was free and felt like I did when I was a fledgling. Wild and proud and strong and vain. I had stood up to the dragon rider and his silver drake and had no master now but the wind. It was a good feeling, much needed after so long a slave. I staked my claim on a large tract of land, spitting acid on every rock and tree that I could find. Although dragon acid burned like fire, it cooled to a sticky wad and was the way dragons marked their territory, so I patrolled my borders every night, spitting acid and checking for signs of sticks or dragons.

I was very far from the sea however, and sometimes I could feel the earth force calling me home. I would go one day, I promised, but when I did, I would have to cross the Pit lands and Bangarden, the Corolanus Markets and then Venitus. Even the thought of living with another band filled me with dread.

Dragon Flights were common in this area. Sometimes at dawn or twilight, I would see them travelling in their signature arrowheads across the Crescent Mountains and I watched with interest until they disappeared from view. Of all things in this world, the Dragon Flights confounded me the most – dragon and stick working together without banding. The dragons were harnessed but I wondered if it was more for the sake of the sticks. They were a fragile people, physically – easy to kill, easier to wound. It was a puzzling alliance, a complex one, and sometimes I'd allow myself to think about Rue and our days on the sea, or Tacita and our songs in the aviary. Some nights my dreams replayed these memories. More than once I was back in Bangarden, with a burning carriage on my tail and a brown rider on my back.

There had been a Flight Rider on my back.

Still the thought captivated me. The sensations captivated me – his legs pressing into my shoulders, his hands gripping the spines on my neck. His weight foreign but not wrong and I found my mind turning it over and over, fighting the leap of my spirit every time that arrowhead crossed the sky.

This too I tried to chase from my mind. I was a wild dragon now, only needing to remember the taste of cold mash in order to appreciate the shaggy noxen that were happy to feed me day and night with their warm, bloody bodies.

One morning, as I was flying home with a full belly, I smelled a dragon.

A drakina actually and the scent grew stronger as I neared the aerie. It occurred to me that perhaps my den had history, with dragons returning to nest year after year. It didn't matter now. The den was mine. I had earned it and I would keep it, defending it against any who tried to take it back.

The sun was breaking the dark skies as I landed on the ledge. Her scent was very strong along with the scent of blood and I wondered if she had brought me a gift. I had never bred a drakina in the wild so I didn't know if that's how it was done. It would certainly go a long way to appeasing me, and I must admit that the thought of a willing drakina waiting for my return was a heady thing. It was with great bravado, then, that I lumbered into the small cavern, only to be greeted by a blast of flame.

I shrank back but only for a moment before meeting with a blast of my own and the cavern was illuminated in furious light. Then silence, save the crackling of the stone and the growling of a displaced female. Dim beams sliced the darkness as the sun struggled to rise and I could see her, coiled upon herself, prepared to fight.

She was a beauty, a golden drakina that reminded me of Summerday. A dark sheen on her wings told me she was injured and had sought my den for refuge. The memories of drakinas in the Dome threatened to ambush my reason but still, it was my cave, my nest, my home and she was the intruder.

I pushed my head into the cavern and bellowed at her. She bellowed back, wings held wide, tail lashing. Glorious, like Summerday. Grating like Ruby.

I was larger, could easily kill her had I the desire, but I had hunted all night and my belly was full and I wanted nothing more than to sleep in peace. I pushed my way into the cavern, head ducked low, smoke billowing from my jaws. The tips of my wings scraped the rock, raining bits of shale to the stony floor. She hissed but stepped aside as I hopped up onto my bed of sticks. It was already warmed from her body and I turned several times to settle, curling my long tail around me and laying my head on my claws. I snarled at her.

She hissed again, wings still wide. Looked to the cave's mouth and the rising sun, then back at me. I closed my eyes, not caring. She was no threat to me. I could hear her grumble, could hear her confusion and upset until she grew quiet. After a while, I opened one eye to see she had curled up near the mouth of the cave, her golden back to me, ribs rising and falling with her breath.

She smelled good.

Satisfied, I closed my eyes again and fell into a deep satisfied sleep.

I woke to find her lying against me, her back to mine and I had to admit the warmth was most pleasant. I could smell dried blood and I wondered briefly what had wounded her. It didn't seem fatal, only limiting but that, for a dragon, could be the same.

When I rose to my feet, she awoke, hissing and coiling away from me. I saw how she was holding her wing. Awkward and tender, the leather darkened, the membrane clear. I didn't care. She wasn't my drakina nor was she in season. I'd learned from Ruby and Summerday to keep my distance until she was.

The cave was cold with evening air and when I yawned, my breath frosted as it left my tongue. I stretched and finally pushed past her as I lumbered toward the cavern opening. She hissed but I ignored her, leaping into the darkening sky and forgetting her in a heartbeat.

I was a creature of the night. I was a master of the stars and I soared high, higher toward my father, Draco Stellorum. Some nights it seemed as though I could almost catch him and I wondered what that might be like, to finally become one with the moons. It was so cold the higher I flew, the air so thin, and it made me wonder how he could live the way he did so high above all other dragons. Did he have a lair in the clouds? Did he chase Selisanae, the Golden Dragon of the Sun, into the sea every night?? Did he have a kingdom or territory or lands that he ruled or was he merely an illusion, a smattering of lights that had somehow become real in my imagination?

At night, I was free to think of such things and I would fly for the sheer glory of flying, feeling the cold bite my eyes and the frost burn the ring in my nose until the hunger in my belly brought me back to the earth.

I did think of the drakina once or twice that night. I expected to find her gone by morning so I pushed her out of my mind to focus on the hunt.

That night, I took down two shaghorns – a buck and a doe in one strike and I ate the buck on the edge of the mountain, enjoying the warmth as the blood ran down my throat. As usual, I ate the organs first, then spent the rest of the night tearing and swallowing whole large slices of flesh. I took my time with the bones. I loved long bones as they cracked beneath my teeth and the marrow spilled out over my tongue. There was nothing like it and I marvelled how any dragon could live on mash. Even fish was a sad substitute for nox, unless it was lemonwhite.

Next, I rolled in the snow to clean the blood from my beak and claws. There is nothing like fresh mountain snow for cleaning dragonskin and I realized I was so very content. The only thing I could possibly need might be already in my den. I snorted, shaking the snow from my mane and I gazed down at the dead doe. It would be a good gift, I thought to myself. *If* she was still there. If not, it would be breakfast. Either way would end well for me.

I snatched the doe in my talons and took to the sky.

THE DRAKINA

Once again, I was greeted by a blast of flame.

Drakinas, I thought. They were a puzzle. What could possibly motivate them?

I bellowed at her as I landed on the ledge and she bellowed back, flame licking at the edges of the cavern's opening. It was an orange flame however, not white or yellow hot and I gauged her protest as feeble and unworthy. I ducked my head and pushed inside, dragging the shaghorn carcass across the stone with my teeth. She watched me with wary eyes, wings wide, tail lashing and I could see fresh blood glistening on her wing leather. She had been cleaning it; a natural instinct, I knew. Best to let it scab over and harden. I'd learned that from life in the Pits.

I settled onto the stone and tore into the shaghorn, bolting down great slabs of flesh with relish. I wasn't hungry but I also wasn't overly sympathetic. This was my den and my kill. She was being allowed to stay only by my good will. Best she learn that early on if she was to become my mate.

I looked up at her, licking the blood from my teeth and she hissed at me. Once again, I saw the frost cloud up from her breath and marvelled at the coldness of these mountain winters. So different from the winters in the Under Weathers when the worst that fell was a temperate rain. I remembered the rain well. It had been as much a part of my working life as the dragons. Stonecrop and Stumptail, Ruby and her indigo drake. Dragons moulded and shaped by actions of men. Towndrell was the same, whipped, beaten and left for dead at the side of a road. I thought of Summerday, beautiful and proud and blind now also because of men.

And here, a beautiful wildling, waiting on me for food.

I left her the carcass in an icy puddle of blood.

She was on it before I reached my nest and I must admit there was some satisfaction as I listened to her tear and crunch. I wondered when she had eaten last, when suddenly she spat a mouthful of flames and the carcass sizzled under the heat. The cave filled with the smells of roasting meat before she tore into it again. *Odd,* I thought. Wild dragons did not cook their food. It was not something we did, in and of ourselves. At least, I had never seen in during my early days in the Anquar Cliffs. No, we relished the wild taste and stringy flesh, the blood and the tang of raw. This was a learned behaviour and instantly thought of Cassien Cirrus and his roasted stoat. I narrowed my eyes, studied her all the more closely now as I wondered where she had come from and why.

Perhaps she was like me, returned to the wild from some form of servitude.

There was dried blood on the sticks of my nest so I climbed over them and with my back feet, scratched them off the pile. With one breath I torched them before turning in circles and settling down upon the rest. I laid my head on my claws as the first rays of dawn reached into the cave. My belly was full, my eyes were heavy, and soon I was asleep, flying with my father, Draco Stellorum, in my dreams.

I awoke later that day with the frost settling over my scales but once again, my back was warm. I remained still, watching the rise and fall of her scales as she breathed; the twitch of an eyelid, the curl of a golden claw. She was so much like Summerday and I fell back to sleep, lost in the glorious colour of her.

I awoke later to the feeling of tiny teeth nibbling on my scales.

It took me a long moment to realize she was grooming me, cleaning bits of blood and dried flesh that the snow had not reached and I stayed completely still as her nibbles traced their way along my neck to my cheek, jaw and finally beak. Her hot breath fell across my face and I opened one eye to see her studying the silver ring in my nose. She nipped it with her tiny front teeth and I snarled a warning. She shrank back, startled.

Slowly, I rose to my feet, shaking the frost off my scales and lumbered over to the shaghorn. I pawed at it, searching for anything left that might be raw or wild but it was truly cooked and crumbled beneath my talons. She snaked in, snagging a roasted haunch and dragged it out from under me. I didn't care. I was a wild dragon now, not a slave anymore to leather or wood or steel or cooking.

As she ate, I moved to the cavern's edge, perched at the lip and folded my wings across my back. It was twilight, my favourite time of the day, and I searched for the eyes of my father, Draco Stellorum. There, I saw them. Both blinking as if ready for sleep, pale orbs merely crescents hanging in the skies. The stars glittered as they appeared through the falling darkness and I imagined his wings, covering me the way my mother's did when I was young. Odd. I rarely thought of my mother now. As I swept my gaze over the peaks and valleys of the Crescent Mountains, I felt the earth force tug in my chest, calling me home.

I could follow it, I knew. I could let it lead me back over the Crown and the Dome, over Bangarden and Corolanus and Venitus, out past the Udan Shores to the wild cliffs of Anquar and my people – fishers and free.

I realized that, at some point, the drakina had joined me. She perched on the ledge, wings also folded across her back and I yearned for the language of the sticks. They had words that had the power to change things, while all we could do was trill and bark, warble and bellow. No wonder they considered us beasts. It stirred those coals of anger once again and I lifted my head to the sky and raised my voice in the song of dragons, a song of skies and clouds and waters and stars and solitude and longing. The cold valley beneath me echoed for a moment as the song carried far and away.

Unexpectedly, the drakina also threw back her head and sang, her voice high and musical and rich and moving and I joined, adding my deeper voice and the valley rippled with dragonsong. We sang and sang and sang until the Blinking Eyes moved across the sky and we fell silent to hear the song of the night. Perhaps we didn't need words like the sticks needed words, I wondered. Perhaps our songs were language enough.

My belly rumbled and so when the night had fallen over us, I leapt into the sky to hunt. I caught and killed a large antlered vemison drake and did not eat it. It wasn't because their hides are so very tough. Rather, I relented my opinion on sharing and carried it back to the den whole.

When I arrived at the ledge that morning, she was gone.

***

I have said on many occasions that dragons are not a sentimental people and for the most part, that is true. We don't dwell on the past, we don't dream of the future; we live for the now. For the sunrise and the sunset. For the skies, for the waters, for the hunt and for the next mate. But that morning, finding her gone left me like a stone sinking in the ocean.

But I realized there were other scents in the air.

I dropped the carcass and breathed deeply, tasting the air with my tongue. There was the drakina but there were others – two drakes, no three, and another drakina. There was no blood on the wind so there had been no violence. Her flight, I wondered? And if so, why had she left them? How had she come here? I had marked my territory and the thought of three drakes moving in fanned coals of a very different sort.

I wheeled and leapt into the air, not caring as the carcass plummeted from the ledge to the valley far below. I was intrigued and challenged and more than a little angry. It was past sunrise now and I was as exposed as a night dragon could be. Still, I followed their scent for hours. It was midday when I passed the edge of my territory, later still when I reached a ridge and the smells converged like a wall. I landed, discovered a series of acid wads all along the crest. These were the markers of many, many drakes and as I lifted my head to survey the mountains and deep valley below me, I was astounded.

Dozens of dragons streaking through the air, soaring and wheeling and circling like fledglings. Drakinas in nests lining the cliffs, trumpeting to wayward chicks, cooing to obedient ones. Young drakes in mock battles, preening for the females, jousting with wing and beak. The scents of old eggs mixed with fresh shat floated up along with that of dragon breath and fire. My heart soared at the sight. It was fascinating and glorious and I all but forgot the golden drakina. I had never seen an aerie save as a chick, and now that I was mature, I saw how utterly majestic it was. With one wing tucked over my back and the other gripping the ledge, I leaned forward to get a better view.

Perhaps three dozen dragons, mostly young, some

older, confined to this particular valley. It was wheeling, tumbling chaos, and I swept my eyes over the craggy landscape. It was a large aerie, but not as large as the Anquar Cliffs. White-capped peaks carried on to the horizon and in the distance, sunlight danced across an unnaturally curved surface. I narrowed my eyes, leaned forward even more. It was a dome and next to it, a spire of shimmering, snow-covered gold.

Suddenly, a shadow fell over me and with the thunder of Hell Down, a great drake landed on the ridge, his brown wings held wide in warning. He roared and hot breath sprayed across my face, bringing with it the smells of noxen and skoat and shaghorn. I held my ground and bellowed back, noticing distant dragons circle in for a better view. The brown lowered his head and lashed his tail, the posture of intimidation. I realized that he was almost twice my size, if not more and he would try to kill me in a heartbeat if I dared strike a threat.

But I was a threat. I was Warblood, Jewel of the Crown. Most drakes postured and preened. I killed.

It was daylight and I had no advantage other than the fact that I had killed more than my share of drakes as large as he. An even match, I wagered, and I spread my wings, prepared to accept his challenge.

A second drake rose to the ridge however, blue wings beating a backdraft and he bellowed at the sight of me. Almost immediately, they were joined by a snarling red drakina and a bronze drake. The three hovered in perfect synchronicity and I marvelled at their co-operation. Drakes and drakinas working together to protect their aerie and the thought occurred to me that perhaps not all intelligent dragons were slaves to sticks.

It also occurred to me, then, that perhaps our dragonsongs had summoned them.

A fourth and then a fifth rose up from the ridge, blotting out the sun.

I could win against one, perhaps even against two, but not against all these and not in the daylight. I leapt from the ridge and dipped a wing, wheeling in the air and leaving the aerie for my own lands. While everything in me wanted to, I forced myself not to look back, for it would be humbling to let them win such a simple conquest. However, as I returned to my own lair that evening, I vowed I would investigate further in the coming days. Naturally, at night.

I like to think of myself as a patient dragon but I know that this is not completely true. I do believe I gave it the time between Blinking Eyes and Sleeping, knowing that during the Sleeping Eyes of Draco Stellorum, there would not even be moonlight to give me away. And so one evening during the Sleeping Eyes, I left my lair and flew those many hours, flying by scent and memory alone until my night eyes spied the ridge. I landed silently and gazed down into the valley.

There was nothing.

Not one drake, not one drakina, not one nest of chicks to be seen. I could smell them sure enough, but the scent was days old and I puzzled at the meaning. Slowly, carefully, I sliced through the valley, landing on one of the nests to find the branches cold. I took a deep breath and chirruped into the night. Nothing. I bugled now, the only sound the dull echo as my call bounced across the rocks. The aerie, which had once been filled with life and dragons, was empty.

It was then that I heard the music.

Music like the sighing of stars, notes rising and falling like the ocean waves, plucking my strings like dragonsong from long, long, very long ago.

It was coming from the dome and spire. In the absence of moonlight and with only stars to guide me, I flew for less than an hour before the dome blocked out even those and I soared toward it, lured by the music of the night. There was a low building at its base and I smelled sticks and leather, but the music was not coming from that building. I swept over it, circling instead the great spire capped with snow and pure gold.

Soft and low, coming from within. Pipes…

It stirred something deep within me, calling me the way the night called me. Unlike the pipes, the night and I were one. I was a curious dragon and strong from my life in the wild. Besides, I loved the smell of gold. I breathed it in as I circled the dome, ignoring the prickles of warning racing up and down my spine. This was a place of sticks. I should have flown far, far away. But the music called so I stayed.

In the darkness, I could see holes all along this tower from base to roof. Windows, I thought, or doors open to the night sky. Without mesh, without glass, they were large enough even for very large dragons and the music floated out through them like incense. I spied one such hole near the top and landed, prepared to leap back into the sky in a heartbeat. I peered down.

It was dark but the smell of dragons was strong and after a moment, I could make out nests built into the walls with stucco and wood. Empty nests made of sticks and straw and chaff. I could also smell men. This was an aviary like Gavius' – constructed by sticks to house their dragons. I could smell old leather and old blood and gold and another scent that triggered memories from ages past. My heart ached as the music stopped, echoed away like leaves on the wind.

Below me, a lantern flickered to life.

"Stormfall..."

A boy on the stone floor far, far down. He lifted it so the light fell across his face.

"Stormfall, you've grown..."

Dark face, dark eyes, wild curly hair.

My heart leapt into my throat and I wheeled in the window and sprang into the night, flying as fast as I could to return to my lair and the lands that I had claimed as my own. I settled into my nest by dawn but did not sleep one wit, for my heart did not slow its race, nor did my mind stop its spinning. I could not, I would not believe what it was telling me.

That day at dusk, I left my den to return to the golden spire, finding it still empty of dragons.

There, Rue was waiting for me.

RUE

I watched him from the tower top, sleeping in one of the lower nests with a lantern by his side. He stirred after several moments, rubbed his eyes and stared up at me for a long time. Finally, he stepped to the floor, picked up the lantern and walked out the main floor door. I could hear him outside and I swung on my perch, watching the lantern light swing across the rocks. It stopped on a narrow plateau between cliff and trees and I could see him making a fire on the grass. It was not high enough for snow here and I wondered if the rains would come even to the mountains. If so, warmth and dry wood would not be taken for granted for long.

Then again, the sound of the pipes.

Low and trilling like the music of dragonsong and my heart lurched within me. I leapt from my perch and soared through the night sky, sweeping down over his head like a great black wind. I rose up to the mountains but the pipes were so sad and sweet and they called me with a sharper tug than any rope, so I circled and swept over him again. I heard him laugh and call my name, my old name, my first name before I knew that dragons could have names. I wheeled in the air and dropped to the ground several spans away, wings wide and ready to fly at the first sign of others.

In the light of the fire, I could see him. Lankier, older but still the same.

Rue.

Alive, not dead like Serkus had said. Alive and Rue.

My Rue.

He turned as he sat, lowered the pipe and smiled.

"I can't believe how big you are," he said. "Cirrus was right. You're magnificent."

I shook my head, snapping my mane of spines.

He reached into a pocket, pulled out a gold coin, held it up in the firelight.

"Look," he said. "I still have it, the coin he gave us to enter the Citadel. That was so long ago. We were both so young."

I stared at him. My Rue. I didn't know him.

He looked down, sighed. Slipped it back into his pocket.

"You used to sit on my shoulder, remember? Even when you were too big to do it, you did. Scared all the girls on the docks. You'd scare them plenty now, you're so big. You'd crush me like a beetle."

I snapped my beak at him, like the old days.

"I don't have any lemonwhites for you," he said. "I'm sorry. I—"

His voice caught in his throat and he drew a long,

shuddering breath. His eyes were filling with moonshine and oceans.

"I'm sorry about so many things," he said. "I didn't look for you when Serkus sold you. I was so angry then, so broken and defeated and angry. I left the Shores and never looked back. But I thought about you all the time."

I couldn't smell other dragons or sticks or traps. There was only Rue so I took several steps toward the fire. The stones were warm so I lay down, folding my wings across my back.

"You have a ring," he said and he made a face. I think it was a sad one. It didn't matter. It was my ring. I had earned it, along with my scars.

"Cirrus said you were in the Pits," he said. "That they called you Warblood and that you were undefeated."

I turned my head, nibbled an imagined itch on my shoulder. I always liked the sound of his voice. Up and down like ocean waves. Soothing and musical like a dragon.

"I'm sorry you were in the Pits. I can't imagine you there. You were the best fisher dragon I ever knew."

I was hungry. I hadn't eaten last night or the night before, for that matter, and my belly made a rumbling sound. I yawned to disguise it and once again, Rue laughed.

"I have some dried stoat in the hut," he said, nodding towards the spire and the little house at its base. "It's not much but the riders didn't leave anything and I've had to pretty much fend for myself. I do miss the lemonwhites, though."

I looked at him. Blinked slowly. Marvelled that out of all the sticks I had come to hate in my life, he was not one of them. Even though he had been the one to catch me, the first to put a band on my throat. My Rue.

"I can understand you, you know that?" he said and he poked at the fire with a long stick. "Cirrus told me that Dragon Riders are chosen because they understand dragon thought. He found me in Venitus after a rider told him about a dragon at the Prefect's house. There was a riot in the streets and a dragon almost died. He was the colour of night and stars."

He grinned now, a small sideways grin, stirred the fire so that sparks rose up into the darkness.

"Actually, he said this night dragon lifted a flaming funeral carriage into the air. I said it sounded like something you'd do."

I remembered it vividly. It was an impressive thing, but then again, I was an impressive dragon.

"Cirrus tried to find you but the funeral owner had closed his business and left town. He lost track of you after that but we talked all night. He came to visit a few times afterwards. I was working in a fish shop in Venitus, helping the owners buy and sell Shore fish. We sold to senators who vacationed there with their families. We sold lots of fish."

My belly grumbled at the thought.

"We never bought from Serkus, though," he said. "I don't know what happened to him. Someone told me he was gone. I hope he's dead."

So did I.

"See? Cirrus said you can tell the dragons that will make good Flight dragons. You can almost hear their thoughts, active and sharp. You think all the time, Stormfall. Not all dragons do. Maybe that's why we got along so well. I think all the time too. It's not so good when you're a soul-boy. You're always thinking about what you would do if you weren't."

I didn't know what to do. I didn't know what he wanted. A part of me wanted to go home, kill a nox and eat well, and then sleep for the rest of the night and then all day as well, just because I could. But another part of me wanted to sit and enjoy his company a while longer, listen to that voice that was like the waves. Perhaps it brought back memories of a simpler time and a younger self, when my imagination was as wide as the sea and my feet firmly planted on the shoulders of a boy.

"Cirrus thinks you could be a Flight Dragon," said Rue. He looked up at me. "And he thinks I could be a Rider. He said we should be a team. I'd like that. It'd be better than selling fish to fat senators and their wives. That's what soul-boys dream of when they have the time."

A rider.

I had dreamed lately of the brown rider, his legs across my shoulders, his hand on my spines. Living and working with sticks for a noble purpose, no band of silver at my throat.

But I was Warblood the Undefeated Jewel of the Crown, killer of sticks and dragons.

It was just a dream.

He looked back at the fire, poked it so that ash floated

up to the stars.

"I dream all the time. That night when the pirates attacked the docks, that was the end and the beginning for me. You helped the Flight, Cirrus said. He said you saved his life and the life of his dragon and that he would do his best to find you and bring us together to the Citadel. You can't imagine what that meant for me, up to my arms in fish guts, to hear that a Dragon Rider wanted to help. But maybe you can. You are that kind of dragon."

He had no idea. My imagination had been slaughtered in the Crown. I was nothing but a spectacular killer, all ash and stars and blood.

"I didn't get my soul, see? Even when I left my servitude, I never got it back. I still feel the same as I did before I was free. Ruminor hasn't smiled on me at all."

I wondered if that was my problem too. My father, Draco Stellorum, was aloof, unreachable, implacable. It was hard to believe in stars when your life was filled with blood.

"After the riots in Bangarden, I didn't see Cirrus for months," Rue went on. "And then ten days ago, he showed up again. He said you had been seen here, at South Aerie Four and that if I was still interested in a life as a Dragon Rider, that I'd best get up here as soon as I could. I've been waiting for days."

He looked up.

"But I didn't give up. Not this time. I knew you'd come back. You're faithful and proud and curious. Your mind never stops. I just had to wait. And here you are."

I looked past him into the fire, the yellow dancing

tongues of flame and the twisting reaching fingers of smoke. Men could tame fire, but it was the dragons that ruled it.

He sat for a long while, poking the fire with the stick, watching the embers sizzle and burn. This was the most I'd ever heard him talk. Even in those long nights on the little boat, we mostly fished in silence. He had never been one for words.

After a while, he sighed.

"Never mind," he said. "It's just a silly dream. You're wild and I'm poor and neither of us will be any more than what we are. We're alive and that's the best either of us could hope for."

And he rose to his feet, stood before me as if unafraid. I could kill him with one breath, with one snap of my jaws. He was thin as a reed. Slowly, he reached out his hand, the hand that used to feed me lemonwhites and silverfins and dillies. Trembling, it hovered under my scaly chin and I growled, remembering nets and rings and silver bands.

He turned his palms up, hands empty and open.

So I let him approach, bristling at the brush of his fingers on my jaw. He traced the spikes and spines of my mane, the spiralling steel that was my horns.

"Pebbles," he said as he reached up to my scales with both hands now. "Like smooth, warm pebbles…"

He ran his hands back down my face to my beak, to the ring still lying between my nostrils. Odd how both Rue and the golden drakina had marked it. Truth be told, I didn't think of it much anymore. It was part of my history. Dragons don't care much for history.

And his hands ran down my neck, pausing at the scars from Bloodtooth, at the healed spear wound, the fireburns along my flank. Prizes of my adulthood, I reckoned. Not many dragons lived beyond the age of three. Not in the service of sticks.

He released a deep breath and continued, running his hand up to the hump and hollow where my wings met my neck.

"This is where the rider sits," he whispered. "I can't imagine riding a dragon. I can't imagine flying. It must be terrifying, more terrifying than being in a small boat in a big storm. But then again, you were never afraid of anything."

He was wrong. I was afraid of the silver band.

He stepped back and back again. kicking dirt onto the fire and causing it to crackle and die.

"You should go. Go back to your den or your nest or whatever dragons call their homes. I'll go back to my fish shop in Venitus. It's not so bad."

His eyes were shining like oceans once again. Now, they spilled like rivers.

"You are a fine, fine dragon, Stormfall," he said. "I'm glad I got to know you and I hope you live until you are the size of a mountain."

And then Rue turned and was gone, disappearing into the night like a shadow. I stayed where I was for a long time, wrestling with the war of memory and yearning, freedom and friendship. I must confess that the night was colder without him.

But a Flight Dragon?

There were Flight Dragons at my last match in the Pits to protect the Primar and his company. I hated the Primar and his company. They had orchestrated a battle between dragons for their entertainment. But the Flight had been there only to protect.

There were Flight Dragons in Bangarden, presiding over the funeral of the old Prefect and the skirmish on the streets. I hated Bangarden. The carts and the mud, the mash and the harnesses. The sticks were merely players, using dragons without thought. I was glad Allum had lost his business and I hoped they all burned in the fire started by the funeral carriage. But Junias had been kind and had stood up to Philius to protect Towndrell from the lash. In the riots, the brown rider had saved my life at the risk of his own. Surely, both were acts of nobility, worthy of a dragon heart.

There were Flight Dragons at the Battle for the Udan Shores. The only defense against the Lamoan pirates, they had dispatched those ships with impressive skill. I hated the pirates but the Flight had been against them, burning their ships and dying for the village. Their sacrifice was noble, stirring a deep current of pride in my veins.

And then there was Rue.

I looked up to the sky where the sun was rising over the horizon. No vast ocean horizon but still, the Crescent Mountains were majestic with their snowy peaks and rocky valleys. The sky was huge, with pink and yellow bands streaking across the clouds. I had seen so many different sunrises, each beautiful in it's own way. Like dragons and maybe, just maybe, like sticks.

My territory now was big and impressive and all mine, but it was empty. I had no nests except the one I slept in every night. The golden drakina was gone, leaving an ache that bit like a cold wind. My life was rich but meaningless and I wondered what might change if I were a Flight Dragon.

I would have Rue.

I sat for so long and was so still that a feathernewt fluttered by my face. I snapped and it was down my throat, the first meal in three nights. Small, sweet and oddly satisfying.

Rue and Tacita, Junias and Cirrus. Kindness was like a feathernewt — small and sweet and for me, a rare but satisfying thing.

I rose to my feet, feeling the rush of cold air under my warm belly and in two strokes, I was airborne, circling, rising high above the plateau and the spire and the golden dome. I saw Rue leaving the hut and swept down toward him, silent as the night. But it wasn't night, it was dawn and he turned at my shadow as I snatched him from the path. He yelped and thrashed his stick arms and I flapped higher to get above the trees. It was awkward but slowly, he reached up, grabbing my legs and pulling himself up to my belly. My wingstrokes were sure and strong and soon, he was hanging on to my neck, trying to swing his leg around my shoulder and avoid the many spikes. He slipped, his weight swinging back down beneath me, his legs flailing like a dying bowbuck. He knocked the tops of the trees with his feet and I suddenly understood why Flight Dragons wore harnesses.

I rolled in the sky so that my belly was to the sun and Rue was on top. Slowly, very slowly, I rolled back, righting myself and slowly, very slowly, Rue climbed over me. Finally he was up, sliding his weight into the hump and hollow and wrapping his arms around my neck. It was a difficult balance but my shoulders were strong and heavily muscled from a life of pulling carts and I stayed just above the trees so he wouldn't be afraid. Still, we were very high up and the mountain wind was strong.

Soon, we were over the peaks and ridges that were the Crescent Mountains. He was hugging my neck and while the wind was loud, his laugh was louder.

It was a very pleasant sound.

"Southwest," he shouted over the rush of the wind. "We have to go to the Citadel and that's southwest! Follow the spires! They're the aviaries of the Flight Dragons!"

And he leaned his weight to one side and I felt myself instinctively bank. A little too deeply for once again, Rue hugged himself tightly to my neck. For a fleeting moment, I wondered if dragons could laugh and if so, what it might sound like.

But for now, I was committed. We were going to the Citadel. Cirrus had asked, Rue had a coin and I had a choice. I was a free dragon and needed nothing else. I set my face to the rising sun and flew.

NET OF DRAGONS

I learned much about sticks in those next few days.

I learned that sticks don't like the dark, so I abandoned my nocturnal routine to suit the boy I was carrying on my back. We flew during the day and slept for long stretches at night. I hunted at dusk and dawn and also learned that sticks don't like their shaghorns raw. Rue tried to make a fire once before realizing that I made them much better. Breakfast and dinner went smoother after that.

I also learned that sticks are not sound sleepers. I would find wonderful ledges high up in the mountains but Rue was not as comfortable with the heights so he slept tucked under my wing like a fledgling. In fact, I think he would have been happiest if I had folded myself on top of him like a drakina. It never occurred to me then that he might have been cold. Dragons have thick hides. Sticks, apparently, do not.

We followed the spires southwest and the mountains

grew higher, mightier. The evidence of dragons was greater too and I wondered why they had left the aeries until I woke up one morning covered in snow.

Now, before my time in the Crescent Mountains, I had never seen snow and it had taken much time to realize that it was not its own thing. It made a comfortable nest when I settled down into it but by morning, the heat of my body would have turned it to water and that, on a cold morning, was not pleasant. So I'd always blow a fiery breath across my ledge first, melting the snow and drying the water and avoiding that problem from the start. Rue was happy with this result as well, for I'd learned that wet sticks were not happy sticks. It was not the same with dragons.

So that morning, I shook the snow from my head and gazed around at the ledge and the nearby cliffs. They glistened with pink and purple under the dawning sun and I thought it rather pretty. Dragons are not given to sentimentality but beauty is objective as much as subjective, and we are good at such distinctions.

In those pink and purple skies, I saw a black arrow winging southward and my heart thudded in my chest. We were going to the Citadel, the place where both dragons and riders lived and trained together. Rue thought I could be a Flight Dragon. So did Cirrus. But did I?

Rue stirred and I lifted my wing as he pushed out from underneath. He was wearing the skin of a direcat that had tried to eat us one night. It had been a valiant attempt but still, I was a killer of dragons so the battle had ended before it had begun. For his part, Rue was happy for the new coat and for me, I had been happy to finally taste cat.

He yawned and stretched, running a hand along my scaly neck. It always felt good, his touch, and it brought me back to the days on the Udan Shores when he and I would spend night after night on the big waters. I watched him as he reached down to pick at the remains of a goswyrm I had caught before bedding down. It was frozen and he looked at me, baleful as a pathetic chick. My flames quickly set the flesh steaming once again. He sat down and leaned against my flank, plucking at the sizzling strips and popping them into his mouth. He said nothing, content to chew and gaze out at the pink and purple hues and think.

He was a thinker, he had said. Always thinking. Just like me.

I noticed his hands as he ate. In a few short days they had gone from bloody and raw to callused and strong, all from gripping my neck. His leggings too were tattered from gripping the iron of my hide. Dragon scales are like plates of metal, I've been told; our spines like daggers of steel. I assume sticks exaggerate almost as much as dragons but still, I was happy not to see blood.

The wind carried a scent and I looked to the south, finding yet another black arrow streaking through the sky. Rue lowered the wyrm as he watched, entranced. I knew what he was thinking. I was thinking the same.

"Well?" he said finally. "Shall we follow them, Stormfall? Is this what we want?"

I yawned, making a great effort to appear unimpressed. He knew me too well though and rose to his feet, tossing the last of the wyrm over the side of the mountain. He wiped his hands on the coat and grinned.

"Alright, you lazy nox," he said. "Let's show them what real flying is like."

He laid a hand on one of my horns and swung his leg across my neck, settling into the hollow at my shoulder. It was perfect for sticks, this hump and hollow – few spines, smooth scales, shoulder bones mimicking the bend of a knee. As if dragons were meant to be ridden.

I pushed to my feet and stretched my wings wide, testing the air and the winds and my strength. It was a perfect morning for flying. Rue wrapped his arms around my neck as I leaned forward, enjoying the dizzying pull of the earth on my head, the wind cold against my eyes. I went with it now, springing from the cliff's edge and falling straight down. Rue was silent, no scream, no shout, most likely holding his breath. I knew he hated this, the roaring fall and the sudden, sickening swoop upwards. For me, it was always the best part – that snap of wing leather, that lurch in the belly, the swift rise like the moons over the mountaintops. Flying was freedom. It was joy. It was life.

For a dragon, the best thing in all the world.

And so we flew, my wings beating against the air currents like oars in the water. Rue sat deep in the hollow, holding twin spikes near the base of my neck. His legs followed the angle of my shoulder, feet resting under the curve of my wings. I was young but large and our bodies fit perfectly. Again, as if dragons were made for riding.

We flew just above the Crescent Mountains and I was careful not to swoop or wheel. Without a harness, Rue's seat was precarious – I had once banked too sharply and he had flung forward into one of my neck spines. His chin was still purple from the impact and he was lucky not to have lost an eye. We were also very high up in the mountains and it was winter – the air was so cold at this height that to fly any higher might cause him to freeze. The skin of the direcat kept his body warm but his face and hands were often blue by evening.

I often wondered about how they ruled as easily as they did. Anything could kill a stick, it seemed, even weather. Perhaps they ruled because no one knew this.

So that day, we kept the Dragon Flight in sight as we flew, they (like we) keeping a low trajectory over the mountains. Soon however a second Flight appeared, at first merely a speck on the horizon and growing larger as our paths converged. The first Flight was growing larger as well. It was strange. We were following at a great distance and I had matched speed so we would neither gain on them, nor lose sight. It seemed they had noticed us and adjusted accordingly and the blood grew hot in my veins when I realized I had been seen.

As a night dragon, I was perfectly hidden by the stars. Here, in the morning light, I was a beacon and like one, they were drawn to me. I had abandoned my advantage by flying in the daylight and the thought filled me with sudden and inexplicable terror.

Now, fourteen dragons and fourteen riders filled the sky around us and it was all I could do to remain calm. I could feel Rue hands tighten on my neck, his knees grip my shoulders like a vice. This was no fair welcome to the Dragon Flights, ushering us into the camaraderie of the

Citadel. No, the riders too focused, the dragons too tense. They were working as a team, drawing in a net that would quickly tighten around us, much like a mesh or a pen.

Or a band.

The coals sprang alive in my heart as terror gave way to fury. It was the only way I had survived the Pits.

And I would not be taken again.

Without warning, I tucked my wings and plummeted like a stone, slipping through their net of dragons. Rue yelped but held fast as the earth pulled me down. I let it – down, down, down to the valleys, willing those coals to add speed to my wings. They were at my tail, however – a great green and a brown and I spiralled in the descent, feeling Rue's weight swing against my shoulders. As the mountains grew nearer, a red drake trumpeted from above but I veered away at the last moment, causing the three dragons to almost collide in mid-air.

A grey swept in front of me now and I could see the rider on his back gesturing at us. I dove again, dropping toward a white peak and arcing away at the last moment. A blue soared above me and released a blast of flame across our path. Fighting, I thought, always fighting and my throat grew tight as I reigned in my own fire. Not a Dragon Flight. I couldn't burn a Dragon Flight but as the blood burned in my veins, I felt Stormfall growing thin and Warblood raging now with every beat of my wings

Up now, another sharp sweep and I began to climb, up up up like an arrow. The air was so cold but I narrowed my eyes, thinking of nothing now but escape. I would die before they took me. Warblood would kill. Higher and higher, throat biting with frost, the air so thin that my chest ached. The wind so sharp so that even my teeth ached inside my mouth.

And suddenly, Rue was gone.

It was like the coming of the winter rains in the Under Weathers, shocking and instantaneous and I snapped my wings to halt my climb. I arced in the air, whipping my tail and turning my face to the ground far below. I couldn't see him beyond the circling Flights so I tucked my wings and dove.

It was like diving for Black Monitors, whose young lived deep in the waters. You could see their shapes from high up and a long dive was required to spear them. And so I dove, leaving my heart in the clouds as I sought for and found the dark shape plummeting toward the ground.

Faster, I urged my self, *faster* and I could see him now, gangly arms and legs and cat coat flapping as he tumbled through the sky. All other dragons were gone, all riders gone too. My world became the boy in the sky and my need to catch him. I was a fisher dragon, now fishing for Rue.

And with a snatch of my talons, I caught the coat with one foot. His body flailed and spun out of it but I caught an arm with the other. Awkwardly at first but I swept up and tossed him, catching him at the shoulders in a better hold. We soared around a cliff side, lower now and not as cold. I waited for him to crawl up my legs but he didn't. In fact, he didn't move and as I flew, still desperate to make my escape, my heart lurched in my chest. I spied a ridge and angled toward it, slowing as I approached and beating my wings to hover just above it. I dropped him into the snow and gracefully landed beside him, folding my wings across my back.

The Dragon Flights circled above us now. I ignored them. My world was laying facedown in the snow, arms splayed wide in a sunken pit of white. There was no blood so I reached down to nudge him. He didn't move. I nudged him again, nipped at his cat coat delicately with my front teeth. Still nothing. I reached with a talon and turned him over, his arms sinking back into the snow as he rolled. Still, he did not move to get up.

Death had been intruding into my life since the beginning, since the fledgling in the waters or the unnoticed loss of one sister. Then after that, always, like an insect buzzing around my head in the night. Ruby had died horribly and so had Gavius. I had killed sea snakes and noxen and dragons and sticks. But Rue? Everything inside of me turned to ash at the thought.

The sky grew dark as the great green came down, beating its wings slowly as it lowered toward the ridge. I stepped one foot across my boy and bellowed, head dipped, wings wide. The grey next and then the blue until I was surrounded on this ridge by seven dragons with seven others circling above. I could see the glint of sunlight as the grey rider pulled his bow and all of them followed suit.

I bellowed again, furious and terrified and despairing when I felt a hand on my leg. My heart leapt as Rue pushed himself up and out of the snow. He looked ill, leaned against my chest to keep steady. I hissed at them all.

"That is the night dragon of the Crown," shouted the

grey rider. "He is sentenced to death for the attack on Primar Septus Aelianus."

I hissed again but Rue shook his head, gripping my face with his arms. I let him. I was glad of his touch, if nothing else.

"Stand back and let us carry out our duty," shouted the grey rider. "You will be taken to the Citadel for healing, then you will be free to go."

"No," said Rue. "We are *both* going to the Citadel."

"The night dragon is a killer of citizens," said the rider. "His head will be taken to the Citadel. Stand back."

A bolt thudded at Rue's feet, disappearing into the snow and leaving only a pit.

"No!" Rue leaned his back against me now, began to dig in his pocket. "We were invited!"

And he pulled his hand from his pocket, fingers clutching a tiny object. But they were stiff from the cold and the object dropped into the snow, disappearing like the arrow. He wailed and sank to his knees to look for it.

A second arrow, this time near my lashing tail, and a third into the snow between my feet.

My mouth and tongue and eyes grew hot as I summoned the fire, felt it billow up my throat. I would not die like a nox.

"NO!" shouted Rue and he pushed up from the snow to wrap his arms around my beak. "No, Stormfall! Hear me! No!"

I growled deep in my throat but he had locked me with his dark eyes. I could look nowhere else. My tail lashed from side to side however as the heat boiled my blood but stayed.

"See?" Rue shouted to the grey rider, turning his head while still gripping my face. "He's not what you think. You don't know his story! You don't know him! Look!"

And he thrust his arm straight out, blue fingers clutching a tiny object. It flashed like sunlight against my shadow.

"The coin of the Citadel!" he said. "Given to us by Cassien Cirrus of the Eastern Quarter Dragoneers! To *us!*"

Seven dragons hovered around us. Seven dragons circled above. Fourteen dragons surrounded me, trapping me with their very bodies. My eyes were fixed now on the grey and his rider, smoke curling from my nostrils as I worked to keep the fire inside. Rue had a hold of my mouth. I couldn't kill anyone without killing him and that was something I would never do.

"Cirrus is only one man," said the rider. "He does not speak for the Primar."

"But we were invited," said Rue and slowly, he released me, turning to face the rider, keeping one hand on my horn. "To be trained for the Dragon Flights. Yes, he is wild and I am poor, but we've come trusting your integrity and honour. If you kill him now, even on the orders of the Primar, you'll betray that trust. Is that what wild dragons and poor boys can expect from the Citadel?"

My Rue, a boy of few words. He chose them like swords.

"You cannot deny us," he said. "Not now and not yet."

Fourteen dragons hovering, circling, wings beating a mad wind, lifting the snow and Rue's hair and my smoke.

"We'll let the Citadel decide," said the grey rider. "Come with us and do not fight or our arrows will find their marks."

He yanked the rein and the drake banked sharply, pulling back to join the rest of the Flight. They circled above us, waiting, casting shadows down on the ridge.

I noticed Rue's hand trembling. His whole body was, in fact, but he released a breath, one he must have been holding for a long time. He turned to look at me.

"Don't ever do that again," he said.

It was like an arrow to the heart.

He laid a hand on my neck and swung his leg up into the hollow that used to be home.

Within two beats, we were airborne, the Dragon Flights positioned around us like a net. This time, I did not protest.

It was evening before we made the Citadel.

THE CITADEL

We were made to wait on a large flat plateau that I later learned was called a landing stone. It was growing dark and Rue leaned into me, his body shivering with the cold. I let him, grateful for his company but my mind still wrestled with his words from earlier. I tried to chase them away with the sights, sounds and smells that were the Citadel.

It was not quite city, not quite aerie but a curious mixture of both. Stone towers were built into and out of the mountains, with pricks of lantern-light dotting their spires. Holes were carved into cliff faces – dragon nests, I assumed, and aviaries both wide and tall were staggered throughout the Crescent. Domes rose up from the peaks, their roofs gold and dusted with snow. Arched bridges and aqueducts spanned the valleys and I marvelled at the skill required to construct such things. (Again, perhaps one of the things that separated sticks from dragons. Dragons are not, by and large, builders.) All along the periphery, oil-filled troughs burned, clearly marking the boundary of the Citadel and I could see dragons and riders in silhouette, keeping guard both day and night.

The sky was filled with dragons and my heart soared at the sight. They were moving in all directions – some in Flights, some alone, some ascending to the skies, others descending to the towers but all in patterns, carefully orchestrated and controlled. There was no chaos like in the Anquar Cliffs. These dragons flew with purpose and order. I hated to admit that it was because these dragons had riders.

Beside us, a large brown drake and his armoured rider guarded us and I reined in my temper. I could have easily escaped – leapt into the twilight sky to freedom but Rue's words were still ringing in my ears. While understandable, my fear had turned to fury and I had panicked. In doing so, I had almost killed him. I couldn't blame it all on the Pits. It was my pride once again, threatening to destroy his dream before it had even begun. So, with claws digging into the snowy stone, I stayed. To Rue's credit, he remained standing and did not seek refuge in the warmth beneath my wing.

Sometime during the night, a man approached, his boots crunching ahead of him in the snow.

"Come with me," he said. "They want to meet in Celarus' Landing."

"Both of us?" asked Rue.

"You want to be a dragon rider, don't you?"

Rue nodded.

"How you going to do that without a dragon?"

Without further address, the man turned and walked the way he had come, across one of the narrow stone bridges that led into the mountain.

Rue looked at me.

"Please behave, Stormfall," he said. "For both our sakes."

I growled but it was half-hearted. Together, we followed the man across the bridge to the mountain.

***

Celarus' Landing was a large circular room with a ceiling easily as high as the Crown. Torches lined the walls and high window arches were open to the darkening sky. These arches were obviously made for dragons and the smell of dragonhide was everywhere. But, unlike the Crown, there was no smell of blood. No offal or death, just dragon, leather, smoke and stick and I was grateful for that. For his part, Rue was grateful to be out of the night, although his shivering did not stop. Such frail creatures, I marvelled. One bite and they'd be finished.

There were guards armoured and holding spears, standing by the many doors of this Celarus' Landing. Were they protecting those going in, I wondered, or those going out? It seemed a moot point – Celarus' Landing was the heart of the Citadel. You wouldn't be here if you were an enemy.

Not for the first time, I was glad I didn't understand the politics of sticks.

Other than the guards, we were alone.

Dragons are partial to a rare type of beauty. Colours that please the eye and patterns that engage the mind. As I swept my eyes around the room, I found myself admiring the floor in Celarus' Landing. It was a glass and stone mosaic, a pictorial history of dragons and riders throughout the ages. On the walls were dragon skulls, some almost as large my entire body. I marvelled at the thought of a dragon living to such an age and remembered Rue telling me the legends of Anquarus, a dragon the size of an island, living in the sea.

There was a marble man astride a huge limestone dragon literally carved into the rock and I wondered if this represented Celarus himself. On our way here, Rue had told me the story of Celarus the Swift, lieutenant of Remus and the commander of the first Dragon Flight. His name literally came to represent the one thousand dragons and riders that served the Emperor in peacetime and in war. I remembered the Lamoan pirates, their cannons and swords and I wondered if in Remus, there was ever a time of peace.

I could hear the echo of footsteps and from one of the many doorways, a party of sticks approached. I sat up, ruffling the spines at my neck and lifting my wings from my body. Not in threat – I was not so foolish anymore – but as in a statement of presence, demanding respect. It is the way of dragons. These sticks didn't stop or slow their approach but rather fanned out around me, hands on hips to study me like a specimen to be bought or sold. I growled, feeling like I was back in the Corolanus Markets.

A white-headed wrinkly man in long robes stopped in front of Rue, tapped the ground with a twisted cane.

"Ruminor has smiled on us," said the old man.

"Ruminor has smiled on us all," repeated the others.

Rue said nothing and silence descended into the room.

And so, nothing was said for several long moments. Nothing was done. I relaxed my spines but did slap my tail on the mosaic, just once.

The wrinkly man laughed.

"Magnificent," he said finally. "He's big. How old?"

"Three years or so, Master Dragoneer."

"And you?"

"Sixteen summers, Master Dragoneer."

"Plinius," said the man. "Dragon Master Plinius and I am as old as five of you, boy."

Rue said nothing. The wrinkly man called Dragon Master Plinius grinned.

"So," he began. "Cassien Cirrus, eh?"

"Yes, Dragon Master," said Rue.

"What is your name, boy?"

"Rue, Dragon Master."

"And your family name?"

"None, Dragon Master. I don't know my parentage. I was sold as an infant."

"In Corolanus?"

"Yes, Dragon Master. In Corolanus."

"We don't get many soul-boys here in the Citadel."

Rue swallowed, looked at the ground. I told myself he was admiring the glass and stone.

"And do you have your soul back, Rue Soul-boy?"

"No, Dragon Master."

"Ruminor hasn't smiled on you then, has He?"

"No, Dragon Master. I suppose not."

The wrinkly man grunted.

"What makes you think a soul-boy can be a Flight Rider?"

"Cirrus, sir," said Rue. "He was impressed with my dragon, and then later, me."

"How did you come to meet our Cirrus, then?"

"I worked the waters off the Udan Shore—"

"In Venitus?"

"Yes, Dragon Master," said Rue. "Stormfall here was my fisher dragon. He helped Master Dragoneer Cirrus when the Lamoan pirates attacked."

"I remember reports of that raid," said Plinius. "And how old are fisher dragons, Rue Soul-boy?"

"Young," said Rue. "Up to a year at most. Then they are too big for the skiffs and we have to sell them."

"So how old was your Stormfall when he helped Master Cirrus?"

Rue glanced at me. "Eight months, perhaps, Dragon Master. We could only guess. He was not hatched in an aviary."

There was a murmur from the men.

"Taken from wild, then?" asked the wrinkly man.

"Yes, Master."

"And yet he lets you ride him. Why is that?"

Rue shrugged.

"He trusts me. I trust him. We're friends."

"Wild dragon and soul-boy," said Plinius, tapping his

cane on the mosaic floor. "Both slaves to one master or another, yes?"

Rue said nothing.

"Fascinating. Tell me," Plinius continued. "Did Cirrus mention what he wanted you for?"

"Master?"

"Did he say anything about the war? About Lamos or their dragons?"

Rue frowned at him. "Lamos doesn't have dragons, Master."

"Yes, yes. Yes, of course they don't," said the man. "And why don't they?"

"Well," and Rue swallowed again. "The legends…"

"The legends? Do you mean the history of the Remoan people, Rue Soul-boy?"

"I, I only ever heard it over the fires as a boy…"

"You are still a boy," said Plinius. "What have you learned over the fires of the the myths and legends and history of the Remoan people, of the twins Remus and Lamos and the Golden Dragon of Ruminor?"

Rue said nothing, looked back at the floor.

"Not much, obviously," muttered the old man. "Have you any education at all?"

Rue continued his study of the mosaic.

"No history? No maths? Can you even read, boy?"

"No, Dragon Master," said Rue and he looked up now. "No one teaches soul-boys to read."

"And does that make you angry?"

Rue shook his head.

"That says a lot about your dragon then," said the old

man. "That he would choose a poor boy like you."

"We were both slaves, once," said Rue. "Now, we're free and here."

The old man grunted and now, all eyes fell upon me.

"Interesting colouring," said one man.

"Cirrus said you can't even see him at night," said another.

"He's wearing a ring," came a different voice this time. Lighter than the others and suddenly there was a hand on my flank. I swung my head to growl but it died in my throat. It was a woman and I was surprised. She didn't look like any woman I'd ever seen before. She was as tall as the men and like them, her hair was shorn to the scalp. She looked like a warrior.

"He's been in the Pits," she said, running her palm along my scars. "Cirrus said his name was Warblood."

"He's killed dragons," said another.

"And citizens," said the first. "That's a problem."

The woman tried to lift my lip, perhaps to check my teeth. Dragon lips are tough as stone. I did not let her and I growled again.

She laughed now.

"He's stubborn."

"He's proud," said Rue. "And he's been badly treated at the hands of men."

"A Flight Dragon needs to be handled," said the second. "He needs to respect our leadership and trust our instruction."

"Then we'll handle him," said Rue. "And teach him to trust. He was like that on the docks. He was the best fisher dragon I'd ever trained."

"And how many did you train?"

Rue looked down again.

"Two," he said quietly.

"So you a free boy now?" asked the old man and he tapped Rue on the arm with the cane. "Or are you a runaway?"

"Free," said Rue. "After the raid, my master released me from my servitum. I was almost done anyway."

"A Master releases a soul-boy why? From the kindness of his heart?"

I could see Rue's teeth clench, his jaw work to hold his tongue.

"No…"

"Why then?"

"Because I was angry that he sold Stormfall. Because…"

"Did you hit him?" asked the wrinkled man.

"No."

Now his fingers, flexing and releasing.

"But you wanted to."

"I am as tall as he is and almost as strong," said Rue. "I could have."

"But you didn't."

"He had nothing left. The fishing huts had burned and he'd already sold the dragons. He said it was more trouble to keep me so he sent me away."

"Without your soul?"

"Didn't want it anyway," said Rue, but there was something in his voice. The wrinkled man could hear it too. "Not that way, I mean. Not if I had to work for him for another year."

The old man tapped his stick.

"That's a very bold statement, Rue Soul-boy."

Now Rue lifted his eyes. They gleamed like steel.

"Ruminor gives and Ruminor takes away," he said finally. "If I wait for Him to give me my life, I'll never start living."

"So you *do* have some iron in your spine, Rue Soul-boy." Plinius grinned. It looked like it might split his wrinkled face in half. "That was two years past?"

"Yes, Dragon Master. Two years."

"And what did you do with your freedom, boy?"

"I found a job in Venitus, Dragon Master. In a fish shop."

"So why didn't you take him and fish yourself?"

"Serkus sold him immediately after the raid." He shrugged now. "I didn't try to find him. I had no money and no connections. Besides, the Corolanus Markets are not known for their records."

The old man snorted.

"If you were a Flight Rider," he said. "Nothing would have stopped you from finding your dragon. Your poverty has moulded you."

"I know what freedom tastes like," said Rue. "I will never let it grow cold in my mouth."

The others murmured at that. I growled. These new sticks were proud and audacious. Too much like me.

"Sticks?" laughed the old man. "Sticks? Do you hear him, Master Fisher Freed-Soul-boy-with-No-Surname?"

And the cane struck once more. Rue winced and I growled again. I was weary of growling, felt the heat begin to rise in my throat

"He's going to burn you, Plinius!" laughed one of the men.

"He's going to roast you for breakfast!"

Truth be told, I wanted to roast them all right then.

Rue turned and grabbed my beak and for a brief flashing moment I wanted to roast him too. I lashed my tail instead, causing one of the men to leap lest I take his legs out from under him.

"He won't burn you," shouted Rue. "But don't insult him."

"What if I insult you?" asked the old man. "What if I hit you?"

He struck him a third time.

I swung my head and snarled. The walls of Celarus' Landing echoed with the sound.

"Take care, Plinius," said the woman. "This dragon is angry. I can feel it."

"We can all feel it," said the first man. "He's as subtle as Hell Down."

The old man called Plinius grinned.

"And what if I hit him?"

"Please don't," begged Rue. "Master Serkus hit him so much when he was in training. It was very bad."

The Dragon Master tapped my neck with the stick.

"What are you thinking, night dragon?" asked the old man. "I can hear your anger like Hell Down."

I dipped my head, raised my wings, this time

threatening true. The party of sticks stepped back.

"Stormfall, no!" pleaded Rue but the old man tapped me again, this time on the snout. Rue grabbed my face. "I said No! Respect, Stormfall. He's baiting you."

"Step away, boy," said the man. "Let's see what this night dragon is made of."

He tapped my face again. And again. And again. Rue tried to put his body between the cane and my scales but the old man simply moved around him. The tapping continued.

"I feel it," said the woman. "Watch out, Master Plinius. It's coming."

"Oh I do know."

And he gripped the cane with both hands and brought it down across my head with a crack so that I saw stars. I was a creature of the stars.

I heard Rue's shout echo but it was only an echo, a dream, a vapour.

I was also a creature of ash.

I lunged forward, catching the cane entirely in my mouth, just shy of the man's wrinkled hand. I closed my eyes and willed the fire to rise up over my tongue, creating a furnace of rushing, leaping flame. Celarus' Landing echoed with a roar like Hell Down as smoke rolled from my nostrils. The cane instantly became char in my mouth.

I stepped back and coughed. Ashes floated to the mosaic floor like snow.

The old man had not moved, still held the hilt of the cane in his hands. He stared at me.

And began to laugh.

He laughed so that the cavernous room echoed once again with sound.

"Well done, night dragon!" he said. "Very well done. You have the fire but you also have restraint. *I* would have roasted me in a heartbeat if I were you!"

He stepped forward now.

"Do I have your permission to touch you?"

I swung my head to look at Rue, the men and woman cheered. It was surprising. Rue wasn't my master. I was a free dragon, but still, that was the power of sticks.

I turned back at the old man, narrowed my eyes.

"You understand our words," he said, cupping my spiky chin with both hands. "That's a good sign. Perhaps you will make a Flight Dragon after all. Hmm, a wild Flight Dragon and a rider without a soul. Surely, Ruminor is laughing now."

The man ran his hands along the scales of my face, up over the ridge of my eyes, placed his palms there and held. I was about to growl again but there was a sound in my mind, a whisper, a voice like wind in the sand pines. I knew it. I followed it. It was relaxing, calming, soothing and I leaned into it with both mind and body, inviting it to wash over me like warm, warm waters.

My knees buckled and Celarus' Landing echoed one last time as my entire body folded to the floor.

The old man smiled, stroked my jaws with a touch like summer grass.

"A pity you dragons can't speak," he said gently. "It would be lovely to hold a conversation with you. Any one of you. You are magnificent creatures. Riders are the luckiest people in all the world."

It was true, and I suddenly found myself approving of this strange, wrinkly, white-headed stick.

He turned his face to Rue.

"You will need to choose a surname. Servus, Solus or Liber. Your life, your choice. But you'll need one, for Dragon Riders are not soul-boys with no names. I would choose Solus."

"Yes Dragon Master," said Rue. "Solus."

"Very well, Rue Solus. You and your dragon both will need training," he said. "Make no mistake. Dragoneers are an exclusive guild. You are here now but if you fail in any stage you will not stay. Which, given your unorthodox beginnings, is entirely possible."

Rue nodded as if he were uncertain. I merely blinked slowly, unimpressed.

The old man patted my cheek.

"But I like you," he said. "You don't have fire; you *are* fire."

I let a ribbon of smoke curl from my nostril, making the point, but deep inside my belly, I felt the uneasy glow of embers, the flicker of fire signalling my fate about to change yet again.

THE SKYROOM

Rue learned much about dragons in those next few weeks, and as a matter of course, so did I. He learned how to tell the age of dragons by our teeth and that while our spikes and spines feel like iron, they are really fibre like our claws and scales. Our horns, however, are bone and continue to grow as we do. In very old dragons, their horns can reach the tips of their wings and Celarus' Landing was filled with many magnificent, enormous skulls.

He learned about the acid in our bellies and how it can alternately burn and then heal. He learned about the arcstone that, once swallowed, lives for years in our crops and how the crushed mineral creates a spark when we call the acid across it. And he learned how we need all three working at once to create our fire – acid, arcstone and air. It was the ultimate weapon in a dragon's arsenal.

He confided that he thought it easier to think of our fire as magic. To me, it was just the way of dragons, as natural as breathing or hunting or flight.

I saw Rue rarely in those next days and I knew he was undergoing training on his own. They had shaved his curly head and clad him in leather but still, he crawled into my nest every night, bruised and battered and too weary even to play the pipes. He would slip under my wing and together we would sleep until the blast of a horn woke everyone at dawn. Then he would crawl out from under me, run his hand over his shorn head and stumble off. It was a good thing I was not a worrier, else I may not have enjoyed my first weeks as a Flight Dragon. Which, I must confess, I did.

I shared the novice aviary with three other drakes - a moss green by name of SeaTorrent, a brown called Darkling and a red with a love of food named Majentrix. All were young, perhaps half my size, and afraid of me. Understandably so. Flight Dragons were taken in after their first year but before their second, making me the oldest recruit in the Citadel. I wasn't bothered – my treatment at the hands of the dragoneers was better than I had expected and better than I had ever been given in my short, rather tumultuous life.

It wasn't difficult to stand for their handling – the inspection of teeth, the filing of spikes, the rubbing of sweet-smelling oil into my scales. In fact, I don't recall ever enjoying the touch of sticks as much as I enjoyed this and I wondered if the Emperor's Dragons were treated this way. Meals were noxen, delly bucks and shearers, all freshly butchered and I knew that these dragoneers understood our need for the hunt and kill.

I had been fitted for a head harness that they called a bridle. It was similar to the head harnesses of Bangarden, minus the eye-covers and bits. These bridles were merely a means for the rider to indicate direction and speed, as a dragon with free access to his fire could not in all truth be controlled. Free access to fire also rendered the bit (the name for that insulting slip of metal between our teeth) pointless, for one blast would cause the metal to melt and the bridle would fall apart, useless. This new design was much more comfortable but truth be told, I approved of it less for comfort than for the dignity I was allowed to retain.

And for dragons, dignity is an important consideration.

So after several weeks of conditioning, I was brought to the tannery to be fitted for a saddle. This was a type of body harness that fastened across the chest, with straps along the spine and under the tail to prevent it from sliding forward. It also fit snugly over the hump-and-hollow of a dragon's shoulder, allowing a rider to sit comfortably for long periods of time. Although Rue could ride without one, I had seen what my scales had done to his clothing and skin (not to mention his chin.) A well-fitted saddle would be comfortable for both dragon and rider, although the tail strap took some getting used to.

The tannery was one of the lower complexes in the Citadel valley, and the smell of animal hide was a delight for my nostrils. It had a high dark ceiling with few windows, and dust floated like snowflakes in beams of light cast down to the floor. The walls were filled with rows of saddles, bridles and harnesses and ladders leaned against them leading up to a wooden second level. Some saddles were very large and I marvelled at the thought of the dragons that might fit them.

There were also silverstones reflecting light along the walls and I stole frequent glances at myself. The leather for both saddle and bridle was night-black and I admired how it gleamed against the starry expanse of my skin.

While the tanners tugged and measured, Rue's scent floated in and I let out a call that sounded like the music of stars. The tanners jumped back, startled and they grumbled at me, cursing my name. I didn't care. I called again and again until the wooden doors slid open on Rue's gangly silhouette.

"Stormfall," he answered.

As he approached, I could see he also had been fitted in a uniform of night black. Dark-dyed linen tunic and leggings, leather breastplate, gloves, greaves and kilt of black leather strips. A heavy cloak to keep him warm in these snowy mountains and a satchel draped from shoulder to hip. No armour however, unlike Cassian Cirrus and his iron drake and I wondered if armour was reserved for War Riders.

I was fine with that. Armour would be heavy and I had no wish to be working harder than needed. I was still a free dragon and this experience with the Flights no more than a trial.

He moved in closely to inspect the tack, tugging at the buckles and running his hands along the straps.

"It's good," he said quietly. "The black looks perfect on him."

"He's a vain one, he is," grumbled the Master Tanner. "Always looking at himself in the silverstones."

Rue grinned.

"You'd be vain if you had a pelt like his."

The tanner grunted. "Now, you make sure all the straps are snug but not tight," he said. "Too tight will cause blisters. Too loose will chafe. Both are irritating and you have a bad tempered dragon to begin with."

"Yes, Master Tanner," said Rue.

"Also too loose and the saddle might slip," said the tanner. "It would cause you to lose your seat and falling into those spikes at full speed would not be good either. You're skinny. They would go right through you."

"Yes, Master Tanner," said Rue.

"And here, these are the rings for the draw reins," said the tanner. "But he wouldn't let us put them on. Most dragons don't like them but yours, well he refused."

"Yes, Master Tanner," said Rue.

"Vain and bad tempered. I don't know what Plinius was thinking."

"Yes, Master Tanner," said Rue.

"Now ask him," said the man, and he backed away. "Ask him how it feels."

Rue swallowed and moved close to my head, ran his hands along my face up past my eyes to the hollow beneath the horns. Like the wrinkly man, I heard a sound, a whisper of a voice inside my skull. I didn't like it. I lashed my tail in irritation.

"Oh he will be a difficult one," said the tanner.

"He's proud," said Rue and he leaned against me, his forehead touching mine. My face was now almost as long as his entire body. "I can't assume that just because it works for other dragons, that it will work for him. Besides…"

He reached down to scratch under my chin. I grumbled, but this time there was pleasure in it.

"We have an understanding. This lasts as long as he wants it."

"And when he doesn't want it?"

"I go back to fishing."

Rue laid a hand on the neck strap, slipped one foot up into a stirrup and swung the other over my shoulder, settling in as if home. The leather squeaked as he adjusted his weight.

"How does that feel, Stormfall?"

I grumbled one last time, just for the tanner and lumbered forward, getting used to the feel of the straps along my body. It was snug, as the tanner had said, but made so well that it flexed when I did and held its shape while not annoying mine. The rein fell across my neck and I leaned with it, marvelling at the difference in sensation. Bitted bridles worked by avoidance of pain but this – this was intuitive.

"Yes," said the tanner as he watched my moving. "It fits well. A Dragon Flight is only as strong as the leather that binds them."

"That's not what my instructors say," said Rue from my back.

The tanner snorted.

"Welcome to the Citadel." And for the first time all morning, he smiled. "You are ready. Go, meet up with your Flight."

"Are we ready, Stormfall?" asked Rue from my back. His weight shift and I could tell he was looking at the doors. I didn't need to see him to know that. I could feel it. Intuitive.

I turned as bright light spilled into the dark room. Within three strides, I was leaping out to the sunshine and into the sky.

***

Dragon lessons were not held indoors.

It made sense, naturally. While Rue had some classes inside, dragons do their best work in the open. There were times when we were called into the tannery or the dracorium (a large stone agora for tending injured dragons). There were even times when we would be summoned to Celarus' Landing for presentation or debriefing but for the most part, we dragons worked outside. At stations all along the Crescent Mountains, Flight lessons took place and I could see dragons working in precision within their teams. Sun and clouds were our ceiling, peaks and valleys our walls. They were called skyrooms and were perfect classrooms for both dragon and rider.

As new recruits, we joined the ranks of the first season dragoneers, skipping some classes, making up others as needed. There were upwards of twenty recruits training in the Citadel but we shared a skyroom with only six others, including my aviary-mates Majentrix, Darkling and SeaTorrent. There was another green, a brown and the instructor's large bronze. Seven was the base number for a flight, with some being smaller and others larger, depending on the commission. Master Quintus was our instructor but I wondered if we might see Cassien Cirrus and Ironwing in our lessons. They were the reason we were here and for some reason, I imagined flying with them once again.

"A Dragon Flight does not insist on privacy," said Quintus. He was a tall lean man in bronze armour. Behind him sat his dragon Claysheen, bronze wings folded across his back. "You will be sleeping together night after night after long, weary night, in battle and in peace. You are the Emperor's Skyborn. Abandon any thoughts you may have of leg room or wing room or personal space."

The Emperor's Skyborn. I wondered about the Emperor, what sort of stick would inspire such fealty. I remembered Septus Aelianus, first senator of Bangarden who had spoken so powerfully for Towndrell. He'd become Primar of the Eastern Provinces who had set two dragons upon one. I wasn't sure what to make of that, but I was certain that I hadn't burned enough of his men.

"Stormfall," growled Rue from my back. "Hush."

"Get close now!" shouted Quintus. "Move in. Fall in!"

I looked around at the crew gathered here in the skyroom. We were on a ridge several valleys away from the Citadel, I must admit, it was gratifying to be wingtip to wingtip with dragons who were not trying to kill me.

"I said, fall in!"

The riders of six dragons muttered as they tried to manoeuver their mounts. Wings beat, tails lashed and I hissed as a young blue pressed onto my flank. He hissed back and I snapped.

"Stormfall!" barked Rue. "Restraint. You are a Flight Dragon now."

"He's not a Flight Dragon yet," said Quintus in a voice that carried over the wind. "None of you are. You must learn to control your dragons and they must respond to your commands. If not, there is no place for you – *any* of you – in the Flights."

A rein across the neck, slight pressure of the leg against the shoulder; all ways for a rider to communicate with his mount. But none of us were good at that communication. Majentrix bumped into SeaTorrent, getting stirrups caught in the leathers and others tripped over lashing tails. Riders shook fists at each other and dragons snapped and snarled. I snorted, having little patience for any of it. It was not what I expected from the Skyborn.

"I hear you, night dragon," called Quintus. "And you're quite correct. You are all fledglings when it comes to discipline and training. It takes months for a Dragon Flight to be forged. This is merely to show you the shortcomings of dragons and their riders. But there *is* another way."

I cocked my head. In fact, all of us looked at him, desperate.

"Catch me." He smiled. *"If* you can."

He sprang onto the back of his bronze and

immediately, they took to the skies. I needed but a nudge from Rue to follow, the rest of the fledgling Flight flapping like sea snakes in our wake.

We were fast but Claysheen was faster and I instinctively veered up for altitude. If I was going to catch him, I reckoned, it would be the way I caught all dragons – as a wraith sweeping down from above. But I found myself bound by rein and stirrup as Rue leaned away from my soaring. I could do little but obey and I suddenly realized that the instructor's words had not been literal. I was not *actually* supposed to catch him.

It was an important thing to learn.

At first, we followed like a flock of fledglings, ungainly and disorganized but soon, we fell into a natural pattern, flying behind Claysheen in the shape of an arrow. He broke the wind with his body and we rode it behind him. The wind bit my eyes, stabbed the back of my throat but I have to admit I'd never felt anything like it in my life. Claysheen veered left. We veered left. He angled skyward. We angled skyward. Such speed, such precision, such grace and beauty and shared purpose. In fact, at that moment, there was no other purpose save grace, speed and precision and that, for a dragon, is beauty enough.

Skyborn.

In this arrowhead formation, we flew to the next skyroom. It was a tall peak with a single wooden post rising from the top.

"This post is Lamos!" Quintus shouted as Claysheen banked high above it. "Tomorrow, we torch it to the ground! A second haunch of delly buck for the dragon and rider with the best score."

I banked behind them, confident in the knowledge that tomorrow, Rue and I would retire to the aviary with very full bellies.

As in many things, I was not wrong and this victory was almost sweeter than blood.

***

It was a strange thing then, when we lost SeaTorrent. His rider always pushed him too hard, drove him to fly too fast, banked too sharply. One day, they miscalculated and did not pull up from a dive. He survived with only a shattered wing and shoulder. His rider was not so lucky.

In memorium, we took to calling our flight the Torrent. I thought it was laughable, given our initial ineptitude and the fact that we were named after a clumsy dragon and foolhardy rider but naturally, I had no say. Other than that, the name inspired. For dragons, that is an important consideration.

One week later, the Torrent was summoned to Celarus' Landing. It was one of the last days of winter and snow floated in through the high dragon arches, settling on the mosaic floor for brief moments before melting under our heat. The Landing smelled good – clean and cold and filled with leather. Shadows cut through the shafts of light and I looked up to see the silhouettes of two dragons perched in the arches. One was Claysheen – I knew him immediately but the other was smaller, with a coat that glowed like the late-evening sun. It was tricky to see in the shadows but I could tell that it was a drakina and that she was gold.

"Replacement for Peppe and SeaTorrrent?" whispered Vir Belonnias, Majentrix's rider.

"Probably," said Darkling's rider, Claudio Cloelius. The Flight just called him Cloe. "But we don't need one. We're fine the way we are."

Standing beside their riders, the dragons seemed to agree.

"All Flights are odd numbers," said Vir. "We can't ride with six."

"Why not?" said Urbano Mass, rider of the brown drake, Bruno.

"Because that's not the way it's done, you beet head."

"It's because of the war," said Vir.

"What war?" asked Urbano. "We're not at war."

"Just about," said Vir. "Blame Lamos."

"*We're* not going to war," said Cloe. "We're just recruits."

"It's because of Peppe," grumbled Manillus, rider of Treeheart the green. "They blame us for his death."

"They do not," said Vir.

"Are we in trouble?" asked Urbano.

"*You* will be," said Cloe. "If you open your mouth again."

They all snickered, save Rue. He merely smiled and held his tongue, as always.

Soon, the mosaic floor echoed with footsteps and I swung my head as Quintus and Dragon Master Plinius entered the Landing, accompanied a tall young woman. A scent came with her. *Drakina.* It set my blood racing.

The trio stopped before us. Plinius studied both dragons and riders for a moment before turning to me with his shiny, pebble-like eyes. He tapped his cane on the floor.

"Look, night dragon," he said. "I have a new cane. Do you like it?"

I grunted. A curl of smoke escaped my nostrils.

As for the Torrent, they stared at the girl as though she were a cerathorn. No older than Rue but taller and strongly built with dark hair that fell in one long braid down her back. She was wearing a golden breastplate, cuirass and greaves. Armour when the Torrent only wore leather. But there was something about her. The scent on her metal was speaking.

"We won't stand on ceremony," he said. "Quintus, introduce your rider and get on with it."

"Ruminor has smiled on us," said Quintus.

"Ruminor has smiled on us all," the riders repeated in unison although I doubted any of them meant it.

"In the wake of Paulo Peppe and SeaTorrent, we have been granted a new rider."

The riders looked at the floor, scuffed the mosaic with their boots.

Quintus grinned.

"We have the honour of adding Galla Gaius to our Flight," he said. "She and her drakina, Aryss, have a year of experience with the Vigiles of Vaspar. That's a privilege and an honour for us. Isn't it, Torrent?"

Looked at the floor, scuffed the mosaic with their boots.

"Welcome to the Torrent," said Rue quietly.

She beamed at him.

"Galla Gaius," said Quintus. "This is Rue Solus and Stormfall, his night dragon."

"Good health, Rue Solus," said Galla.

"And to you," said Rue. He'd never been one for words.

I breathed in the scent of her. There was something about her I knew, something from a time past.

As Quintus made introductions, I stretched my neck and breathed on her. She smiled, leaning into my warm breath instead of away, fluent in the way of dragons. I pushed my nose to the leather at her waist, down her legs to her greaves. She laughed.

"What is he doing?"

"I don't know," said Rue. "Stormfall?"

"He's remembering something," said Plinius. "Gads, you recruits have the brains of crickards. Help him to remember, girl. You know dragons. Help him."

She held her hands up to my face.

The other riders gaped as I opened my mouth and took her hands between my jaws, slathering them with my tongue as waves of taste and scent and memory took me back, back beyond the Citadel, beyond the aviaries and the skyrooms to my time in the mountains.

I allowed the colour to form in my mind.

Gold like the breastplate, gold like the sunrise and dragonsong.

Her.

I pulled my jaws away, strings of saliva dripping from

her hands, and sang.

"He knows her," laughed the woman. "Aryss was right. He *is* her Night Dragon!"

Another song echoed down from the dragon arch.

I looked up now as one of the silhouettes launched through the high window, wings bringing her down through the clean and the cold.

I knew her, hard like stone and sharp like sticks, warm like fire and pure, pure gold.

"Oh yes," said Plinius. "He knows."

And he laid a hand on my neck.

I sang again and the answering song took me back to the mountains.

Wearing saddle and armoured bridle, my golden drakina with wing now healed, touched down on the mosaic of Celarus' Landing.

ARYSS

For dragons, the world is a world not so much one of sight or sound but one of scents. Some are rocky, others earthy, some are fleshly and others fire. We can smell when the clouds are about to release the rain or when the earth is under so much pressure it is about to split. I suppose it is similar to the way the sticks can sweep their eyes though a sea of other sticks (who all look the same to dragons) and instantly pick out those they know by face alone. In the same way, dragons can sift through a skyful of smells and instantly pick out those they recognize and those they know.

Aryss was one such scent.

She was beautiful, she was strong, she was skilled and she was clever. She was everything I remembered of her and more because she was a Flight Dragon.

It was early spring – the mountain air had grown warm while preserving the blanket of snow in the high places. With spring came the mating season, and both Aryss and Galla were excluded from the Torrent's aviary, sharing one instead with those drakinas not released for nesting. Dragons caught in the mating fever are creatures of fire and destruction, not purpose and order. It was a pragmatic solution and we were soldiers in the Emperor's Skyborn. Still, she drilled with us and her skills were remarkable. While I spent most of my days with the Torrent, thoughts of Aryss filled my nights. I knew it was the same for Rue.

He would sometimes come back late to the nest with Galla's scent on him and it would set my blood racing. I remembered the girls on the docks, who would smile and wave but never come close. Galla was not like those girls. In-between training sessions, the four of us – black and gold dragons with black and gold riders – would race through the skies beyond the Citadel, wingtip to wingtip to practice our drills. I learned more of cues and response, reining and balance in those times than all the lessons taught by the masters and instructors combined. Perhaps it was my pride but more likely it was the fact that she was forbidden and for this season, however brief, she was mine.

Over the succeeding days, I learned how sticks ran the Dragon Flights and I had to admit, it was a remarkable feat of organization. Flight dragons were usually the products of other Flight dragons, hatched in assigned aviaries until the Spring Tides, when drakes, drakinas and young returned en masse to the Citadel. I realized then, that the aeries I had encountered during my short time as a wild drake were, in fact, these aviaries. This network was called the Draco Curantora, and it was run by a branch of the dragoneers called Curantors. The Curantors chose the drakinas, they chose the drakes, they chose the nesting sites and they trained the fledglings from the central Draco Curantorum near the Citadel. It was an impressive set up, in use for more years than anyone could remember.

Through snatches of memory and Plinius' skill, the Curantors were able to piece together Aryss' story. She had been born of a Flight drake and a wild drakina, hatched with two siblings in the very den I had called my own. But there were (and still are) direcats in those mountains and one had managed to climb down the ledges and into the cavern. The cat had killed both siblings before the drakina returned, and she fought and killed it before succumbing to her own wounds. Barely a fledgling, Aryss stayed in the den until the sound of dragonsong drew her out. It was a Flight, calling out the breeding pairs and the new clutches for their return to the Citadel in the Spring Tide.

"She remembers the sound of their wings was like Hell Down," said Galla. "Somehow, she slipped in and flew with them until they arrived in the Citadel. All the other chicks followed their mothers leaving Aryss lost and alone in the Curantorum. She was raised by my father."

"Umberto Gaius," said Vir. "Quintus served under him, yes? He says he was a great Dragoneer."

"He would have been proud to know I was serving with Master Quintus," said Galla.

"We're all proud to be serving under Quintus," said

Cloe.

They nodded at that.

The sticks were sitting around a small snowy firepit near Aurelias' Peak, running daggers across each other's scalp and wicking the bits off into the snow. Recruits were allowed one of two hairstyles – a long braid or heads entirely shaved. With the exception of Galla, they all chose the shave. There was a certain quiet peace now as they groomed each other like dragons. The rest of us – Majentrix, Darkling, Bruno, Treeheart, Aryss and I – were perched higher up, wings folded across our backs, the sunset warming our scales. I was grooming Aryss, cleaning her spines with my tiny front teeth. Payment for when she had done the same for me.

"Did anyone see the Legions arrive this morning?" asked Vir.

"The First Imperator is here," said Cloe. "Tinitian says they are making the declaration tonight."

"I hope he does," said Vir.

"I hope he doesn't," said Urbano.

"I don't want war," Manillus said. "Not with Lamos."

"I do," said Rue and they all looked at him.

"I want them gone," he continued. "They destroyed the village I lived in. Everything burned. Everyone lost. And there was no reason. They didn't take anything. They would have destroyed the whole city if the Flight hadn't showed up."

Galla leaned forward.

"Did you join the Flight just to avenge yourself on Lamos? That's not a very good reason, Rue."

Rue made a sound. It was like a young drake growling.

"I had friends," he grumbled. "I had dragons. I had a life."

"You have a dragon now," said Galla. "You have a life."

Rue looked down into the fire. I saw his jaw working to control his tongue.

"It's the new Emperor," said Cloe. "He wants war so we go to war."

"He killed his cousin," said Manillus. "That's what the Campari say."

"The Campari don't know anything," said Vir. "They could be tried for treason with such claims."

"Political assassinations happen all the time," said Cloe. "Septus Aelianus had his cousin Maritus poisoned. Everyone knows that."

I paused in my grooming. Septus Aelianus. I knew the name. Aryss nudged me so I continued.

Urbano grunted. "As if being Primar of the Eastern Provinces wasn't enough."

"Not if you want war," said Cloe. "He hates Lamos."

"I hate Lamos too," said Urbano. "But I'm not sure I want war."

"They have dragons now," said Cloe. "Master Willas says dragons were the only thing that gave us superiority but now they have a laying drakina in Nathens."

"A golden drakina," said Vir. "Like the First."

"Where would they get her?" Galla asked. "I didn't think there were dragons on Lamoan soil."

"They stole her," said Vir. "That's what they do."

Cloe spat into the fire. I paused again in my grooming to watch him, curious that their spit did not contain acid. Pointless, I figured. Why have spit that did not burn? And I turned my attentions back to the warm golden scales.

"Cannons *and* dragons," muttered Rue and he ran a hand across his bare head. "Why don't we have cannons?"

"I don't know," said Vir. "Quintus says it's not our concern because it's not our branch of service."

"It *is* our concern," Rue grumbled. "Cannons can blow dragons out of the sky. All dragoneers should be concerned about that."

"You're not a dragoneer," said Galla and she looked at him, grinning. "Not yet."

"I'm an optimist," he said.

"You're an idiot," said Cloe. "Your dragon's too old."

"That's not what Cassien Cirrus said," said Rue.

"We don't serve Cassien Cirrus," said Vir. "We serve Quintus and he says your dragon's too old. He's still wild."

"You lie, Vir," said Galla. "Quintus doesn't talk like that and Cirrus said the Night Dragon could win the war for us."

There was silence around the firepit and she looked away quickly. Ashes rose up to greet the rise of the Sleeping Eyes.

Rue leaned forward.

"What do you mean, Galla?"

"Nothing," she said. "I spoke out of turn."

"When did you speak to Cirrus?"

She glanced up sharply.

"My father trained Ironwing when he was a recruit.

They're here, in the Citadel with the First Imperator."

Rue sat back, brow drawn, frowning. The silence that followed was blanket heavy. Finally, Cloe slapped the fire with his sword.

"We should do a Shadow raid tonight."

The others groaned.

"Not on your life," said Vir. "Not while the Imperator and his troops are here."

"The Imperator is nowhere near the aerie," said Cloe. "And if there's going to be war, we might as well get used to flying in the dark."

"We can get coal from the forge," said Manillus.

"There's no guard at Corantus Five," said Urbano. "They're all in for the proclamation."

A roosting drakina is a fearsome thing. During a Shadow raid, we would attempt to slip through the aeries in the dead of night without waking a single one. It was not an easy task since dragons are sensitive to scent, and the drakinas woke to the smell of us rather than the sight or sound. Quintus suggested that rubbing coal into our skin helped mask our scent as we flew, blending us in to the scents of stone, slate and dragon-scorched rock. It was extremely effective but caused our skin to dry out after repeated use.

"Well?" said Vir. "Are we just going to sit here until the proclamation? Let's go."

"No," said Rue. "Tonight, I'm going to try something else."

Galla glanced at him.

"Celarus' Landing?"

"Stormfall and I can do it."

Cloe snorted.

"You'll get killed."

"Only if they're going too fast and miss," said Manillus. "We saw what happened to Peppe and SeaTorrent."

"They won't miss," said Vir. He leaned back on his elbow and laughed. "No, the worst that will happen is that they might get in trouble with Plinius or his centurions."

"If they get caught," Urbano added.

"The Night Dragon won't get caught," said Rue. He sent a sideways glance to Galla. "You said Cirrus is here, in the Citadel?"

"I saw him," she nodded.

"Good," said Rue. "We'll show him what the Night Dragon can do."

"After the proclamation," she said.

He said nothing so she nudged him with her thigh.

"After the proclamation."

He grinned.

"After."

I growled but Aryss trilled so I resumed the cleaning of her scales until the riders rose to their feet, ending one service in exchange for another.

***

It was early evening when we returned to the Citadel to find all the Dragon Flights on alert. Fires burned along the Crescent and the war flag – a red banner with a golden drakina surrounded by aurel leaves – flapped in the winter wind. We split up, Aryss and Galla arcing for their tower while Rue and I chose to light atop the mountain ridge alongside several of the Campari. The Campari were lone dragoneers who rode without a Flight. For some reason, both Rue and I felt at home with them, perhaps because of our solitary natures. Regardless, as we peered over the edge of the natural amphitheater called Crescent Prime, the sight of over one hundred dragons and even more sticks took our breath away.

"Is that the Imperator?" Rue asked one of the Campari, a hardened man with a dragon the colour of stone.

"That one there," said the man. "The one with the spike-helm."

And he pointed. It was all we could do to make him out, so far below and surrounded as he was by such a crowd, but when he took to the podium, the amphitheater fell silent. Even the wind held its breath.

"Hear, O Remus," he began and his voice echoed through the mountains. *"And hear ye lands of Lamos, let Justice hear! I am a public messenger of Septus Aelianus, Emperor of the Remoan people. Justly and religiously I stand before the most devoted servants of Remus, ye noble Dragoneers!"*

The cheer that went up almost deafened me, being a dragon of unusual sensibilities.

It lasted for a long while, would have lasted longer had not the Imperator raised his gloved hand.

"It's the proclamation," hissed the Camparius. "They always use the same language."

"Let my words bear credit! Hear, O Remus and you too, Lamos – Ruminor also, and all the celestial, terrestrial, and infernal gods!

Give us ear! I call you to witness that this nation Lamos is unjust, and has acted contrary to right. The state of Lamos has offended against the Remoan People with its cannons and its warships and its soldiers. Now, we have witnessed the ultimate act of aggression – a brood of dragons for which Lamos has no precedent nor history nor divine right!"

Booing and hissing rose from the crowd, but the Imperator rose his fist higher.

"This is an act of war!"

The hiss became a roar.

Dragons added their voices, bellowing loud and long into the night.

"It's all myth and legend and shat," said the hardened man. "The High God Ruminor giving Selisanae to his son Remus, not to Lamos."

"That's a bad father," said Rue.

"It's shat." The man grinned. "But that's the High God for you. I only trust in my feet, my stomach and my dragon."

Finally, the roar died away.

"Upon the order of Emperor Septus Aelianus and on behalf of the Remoan People, I have ordered that there shall be war with Lamos. The Senate of Remus has duly voted that war should be made upon the enemy Lamos unless and until they abandon their dragons: I, acting for the Remoan People, declare and make actual war upon the enemy! Which noble Dragoneers stand with me?"

And lastly, one final roar to outdo all others, fairly lifting the snow from the mountaintops. Even Rue was cheering. I didn't share his passion or his hatred for this nation called Lamos, even if they were responsible for the destruction of the Udan Shore. Sticks were sticks. They killed each other as easily as they killed dragons.

I looked for Aryss in the crowded, cheering, bellowing mass but did not find her.

***

There were no Eyes in the sky to guide me as we flew across the peaks and valleys of the Citadel. I was a Night Dragon and as such, didn't need the Eyes of my father, Draco Stellorum, to see the Citadel. For me, it was as clear under the stars as it was in the sun.

Rue pressed low across my neck, fairly hugging the saddle as we swept silently through the night sky. This was why riders' uniforms matched their dragons. They became indistinguishable on our backs, looking almost a part of our wings and spines. At night, it didn't matter but during the day, the sight of a rider carried a weight of a very different sort.

Torches continued to burn along the Crescent Mountains but for the most part, the Citadel was sleeping. The tower of Celarus' Landing was dark, without even a flicker of light to be seen through the many high dragon arches.

I opened my senses to the voices of the night. Stars sang. Wind whispered. Below us, trees brushed and rocks cracked. Snow wept as it dripped away for the spring and I could hear the distant crackle of fire, the voices of men and the heartbeat of dragons. There were no moons to guide me. No lanterns within or torches without. I remembered how I would descend on unsuspecting dragons in the Crown. Blackness in my wings and death at my claws. Warblood, undefeated Jewel of the Crown, Killer of Dragons and Men. How easily he could come back. I shuddered at the thought.

With a shift of Rue's leg, I tucked my wings and dropped like an arrow.

I could feel the dragon arches rather than see them and at this speed, if we hit the walls, we were dead. Rue held his breath and tucked deeply into me as I folded my wings over him. Swiftly and silently, we swept in through one of the arches, my tail following my body perfectly as I followed the curve of the walls. My wings opened enough to keep us aloft, all in utter silence. Skilfully, I circled the Landing, my tail not even brushing the many horned skulls along the walls. Once again, I remembered my nights in the blackness of the Crown, sweeping over the throngs of spectators but avoiding the mesh that protected them.

Rue leaned, indicating we should leave. It was achievement enough to simply have made it in and then out. I ignored his leaning, however, for there was something on the floor.

No one in the room at all; not a centurion, not a guard. It was empty and black as the pitch from Allum's ovens but still I could see with my night-dragon eyes the beautiful mosaic of glass and stone, the history of dragon riders throughout the centuries. In the center of this beautiful floor lay Plinius' cane.

Rue dug his heel into my shoulder but I leaned away, diving silently downwards, wings back, talons reaching.

Down, down and down I went and with barely a scratch of my claws on the stone, the cane was mine. Now, I brought down my wings in a powerful stroke, soaring upwards, seeing clearly the stars through the dragon arches. Within two heartbeats, I was outside and into the night once again.

So sleek, I thought to myself. So deadly. Poor Plinius would beg for his cane back. I would not roast this one. No, I would keep it until he begged.

And so it was with this attitude of self-importance that Rue and I returned to the Torrent aviary, only to find it empty of dragons, save one.

Ironwing, the silver drake, was stretched out in my nest, his wing-talons crossed elegantly in front of him.

And around a firepit circle at the centre, two men were playing dice. One was in silver armour.

They both looked up as we peered down from the ledge.

"Well, come in Rue Solus," said Dragon Master Plinius. "Come in, Night Dragon. And bring my cane with you, if you please."

THE SHADOW FLIGHT

"The Night Dragon and his soul-boy," said Plinius as he approached. "I am impressed, Cirrus. I will gladly refund you your coin."

Rue slid from my back, but kept one hand on my shoulder. I could feel his knees shaking as he bent down to slide the cane from my talons. He did not pass it over but gripped it tightly, twisting it in his trembling hands.

"Forgive me, Dragon Master," he said. "I was…I was…"

His words failed him and for some reason, so did my victory.

"You were proud," said the wrinkly man. "A Flight Rider needs to be proud."

"Of himself and his dragon," added Cassien Cirrus.

The rider rose to his feet, slipped the dice into his silver pocket.

"Do you know what they want of you, Rue Solus?" asked Plinius. "What they want of your night dragon?"

"No, Dragon Master. But I can guess."

"It won't be easy."

"Our lives have never been easy," said Rue. "He's been a fisher dragon and a farm dragon. He's been a pit dragon and a Flight dragon. There is no dragon in the Empire that can do what you're wanting. None except him."

"The Lamoan drakina will be well guarded," said Cirrus. "It won't be as easy as taking the Dragon Master's cane."

"It was just laying there in plain view," said Rue and he held it out.

Plinius took it.

"The cane," he said. "Was not guarded."

"You knew we would come for it. They won't expect us to come for the drakina like that."

"We knew," said Plinius and he leaned forward on his cane. "Because we were told."

Rue glanced up sharply.

"We are a nation at war," said the wrinkly man. "There are espionars everywhere."

"Every man is a soldier," said Cirrus. "As is every woman."

There was only the hiss of the night wind.

"Galla," Rue whispered.

"Galla is a soldier," said Cirrus. *"You* need to think like one. You and your dragon both."

"Flight Riders live to serve," said Plinius. "Likewise their dragons. How do you think we got your dragon here in the first place?"

"Aryss?" said Rue.

The thoughts came together in my mind like storm clouds. Aryss in my mountain den, blood on her wing. Proud, defiant, warm and gold.

"She's a remarkable drakina," said Plinius. "Very clever, very intelligent. Not many could be trusted to return once they've tasted freedom like that."

A sweet, golden lemonwhite for a lonely night dragon.

"Cirrus knew our night dragon would find himself a lair. She tracked him, baited him and brought him in."

Because of her, I found the first of the Draco Curantora, the tower and after that, Rue.

And after Rue, the Citadel.

It had been a clever plan and I had played my part, to the beat.

"I'm sorry, Night Dragon," said Plinius. "But we needed you."

Vanity and pride. Lure them with gold, catch them with ego. Dragons are a predictable people.

"And me?" asked Rue and he turned to the silver rider. "Did you 'need' me too?"

Cirrus sighed, folded his arms across his chest.

Rue was quiet for a long moment.

"We can do this," he said finally. "At least let us try."

"My Flight is leaving for Terra Remus at dawn," said Cirrus. "We've been commissioned by the Imperator to find the Lamoan drakina but she's in Nathens, their capital city. Even if they send one hundred dragons, none will make it through alive because of their cannons. But you can. I know you can. You can end this war before it has even begun. And that's where the problem lies."

He sighed again. The silver drake on my nest grumbled. Almost as one.

"After the massacre in the Crown, the Emperor put a price on Stormfall's head," he went on. "My Flight isn't convinced that we can get into and out of the capital without paying it, maybe in blood. They don't want you, but they don't know you. They don't know what you can do. They think you're wild and unpredictable, that you'll be more of a problem than a solution."

He stepped forward now, laid a hand on my neck and for once, the silver drake did not growl. My heart swelled with pride.

"I've seen Stormfall at work," he said. "In the Crown and on the water. Ironwing and I would be dead if it weren't for him."

Pride, pride, always pride.

I should have learned by now. I should have known.

"We need you, Night Dragon. Our nation needs you. I believe that is why you were born a Night Dragon, to do what no other dragon can do."

He looked at Rue now, knees still shaking. Still a boy.

Cirrus grinned flatly.

"You have my favour to join us, Rue Solus. But first, you must convince my Flight tonight. There's no guarantee that you won't be killed if you come but come anyway. If you succeed, then we fly to Terra Remus where we meet the Emperor's Legion. There's also no guarantee that you won't be killed and Stormfall's head set up on the marble walls as retribution. There's even less of a guarantee that you will be chosen for this commission and finally, if you are chosen, there is almost no chance of either of you coming back."

Rue looked at the ground. I could see the muscles in his jaw twitching. So controlled. So restrained. So unlike me.

"We're leaving at dawn," said Cirrus. "But tonight, we'll be camped at Tarren's Duct. You know where it is?"

Rue nodded.

"There will be three dragons besides Ironwing. Show them what you can do. Impress them with your skill in the night. Hunt, catch them, terrify them, I don't care what you do but don't kill. They think you are Warblood, Jewel of the Crown. Prove to them that you're not. Prove to them that you can do what we cannot."

And with a shake of his silver spines, Ironwing left my nest for Cirrus' side. For such a large dragon, he moved with such grace, such elegance, like smoke. The rider slipped his foot in the stirrup and in a heartbeat, was up. The drake spread wide his wings.

"But this is not Stormfall's fight," he called from Ironwing's back. "This isn't really yours either, Rue. You are both free to decide. Ruminor smiles on whom He chooses and we do what we can with the rest."

The first wing beat almost blew the wrinkly man over. The second had them halfway up the spire, at the third they were out the large dragon arch into the night sky.

Plinius watched him go, before turning to us one last time. His skin looked like parchment.

"It has been a privilege to know you, Rue Solus," he said. "And a pleasure to meet this wonderful Night Dragon. I hope we will meet again in the afterlife. I will drink to your health and you will drink to mine."

He caressed my cheek as one might stroke a child, his eyes shining like tiny pebbles.

"I should not have hit you with my cane," he said softly. "I regret that. My new cane isn't nearly as nice."

He threw a glance at Rue.

"I can't speak for Ruminor. If you succeed, He might just give you your soul back. But then again, He might not…"

He picked up his lantern and shuffled out the door, the cane making quiet tapping sounds on the floor. He was swallowed by the darkness in a heartbeat.

Rue watched him go, did not move for some time.

"I need you to remain Stormfall," he finally whispered in the firelight. "No matter what happens, please stay Stormfall."

He didn't know what he was asking.

He stood until his knees got the better of him and he buckled to the floor beside me.

***

There were no moons to guide me. No Winking Eyes of my father, Draco Stellorum. I didn't need him. Tonight I *was* the night. Tonight I was the darkness.

Impress them with your skill, Cirrus had said.

I was sad when I left the Torrent aviary, a place where I had learned to enjoy the touch of sticks. I was sadder still when I left the Citadel, the last landing stone streaking below me like a fading memory. Sadness and fear, leaving this place of purpose and nobility behind; war before me, my path stained with blood. My heart was racing, too fast, too strong, to the beat of my wings.

Hunt, catch them, terrify them, I don't care what you do but don't kill.

Blackness in my wings and death at my claws.

Please stay Stormfall.

He didn't know what he was asking. None of them did.

They think you are Warblood, Jewel of the Crown.

This wasn't my fight. This wasn't my war.

War meant blood.

Please stay Stormfall.

I ached for Rue as we left his words behind in the aviary.

Stroke by stroke, I left Stormfall behind and stroke by stroke, put on the mantle of Warblood, undefeated Jewel of the Crown of Salernum, Killer of Dragons and Men.

Prove to them that you're not.

I couldn't kill them.

Warblood would try.

Blackness in my wings and death at my claws.

Stormfall would stop him.

"No thinking," Rue hissed over the night wind. "Riders can hear your thoughts like Hell Down."

I tried to quiet my mind. It is hard for a dragon of my intelligence and imagination to be quiet, especially when the blood is hot and the acid scalds the back of your throat.

I was the Night Dragon.

Blackness in my wings and death at my claws.

Bonesnap, I thought to myself and I sifted the air for dragons on the wind. "Hush, Stormfall. Your thoughts."

Show them what you can do.

Back to the fire. I could land quietly. I could grab one or none or all. I could sweep between them and scatter the ash up to the night. There were many, many strategies for proving myself and I wanted to know what he wanted of me, for I could do all of it or none.

Truthfully, I would be just as happy to veer north and let the earth force take me home.

I could see them sitting around a fire beneath a towering aqueduct. Sticks were always sitting around fires and I realized that they coveted fire. It was why they subjugated dragons, the bringers of it.

"Don't kill," he whispered. "Take one, release him into the sky then take another."

I recognized Ironwing immediately. I had saved his life. He had spared mine. We were equals and I found a measure of satisfaction in that. But there was another and it struck me like an arrow in the heart.

Aryss.

Vanity and pride. Lure them with gold, catch them with ego.

Like a spear, I tucked my wings and dove.

Four dragons dozing in the darkness, one raising his gray head to yawn. I caught his face in my talons and beat down my wings, rising us both up, up, up. He was heavy but surprised and swung his back end, his tail lashing and feet raking only air. When he called his fire, I was gone, releasing him and disappearing into the black sky like a wraith. I arced and dove again, but this time they were waiting for me – the men on their feet, the dragons with wings wide. But it was dark and I was the night and I caught a gold drake by the saddle, rose into the air with him even as he beat against me. I wouldn't hurt him, I told myself, though the blood was hot in my veins. I felt the saddle creak as I flung him overhead and whirled, releasing him to dive again.

Aryss next. I caught her by the back of the neck, taking her up, up, up into the starry sky before a blast of fire licked at my tail.

On my back, Rue stayed low, gripping my neck and allowing me my head. Three dragons in the air now and I dodged between them all. Fire lit up the night but I was a ghost silhouetted against the flames, wheeling and snapping and whipping my tail so that I had touched every dragon save Ironwing and left them living.

Perhaps Stormfall had flown with us still.

"Release and down," cried Rue and I obeyed, dropping to the fire with almost no sound. The dragons rushed to land, forming a circle around me with their wings.

Rue sprang from my back as swords and arrows were brought to bear but the great silver drake rose onto his back legs, lighting up the sky with his powerful flames. The riders stepped back as Cassien Cirrus strode into the circle.

"Peace," he barked. "Flight, stand down."

"That was madness!" shouted Galla, her sword flashing in the firelight.

"Insubordination!" shouted the rider of the steel grey. "Cirrus, we should kill them both for that!"

"Did you hear them?" Cirrus he spread wide his arms. "Did any of you hear them at all?"

"It doesn't matter—"

"But it is the only thing that does matter," he said. "None of us heard either sound or thought. They were silent as night."

Rue said nothing, merely looked at the ground.

"Three Flight dragons," Cirrus continued. "Taken like fish from the ocean before any of you even knew what was happening. *That* is what we need for Lamos. *That* is how we take the drakina."

The first colour of dawn glowed over the mountains. The fire crackled and spat ash into the early morning sky. The dragons snarled but as I stood between them, unmoved and undefeated, I desperately tried not to think of what had awakened in me tonight.

"The Emperor won't allow it," said the rider of the grey. "He still remembers the Crown."

"We all remember the Crown," said another.

"This dragon has already faced Lamoan cannons," said Cirrus.

"So have I," said the first.

Cirrus sighed.

"We need him, Rufus. I believe it in my bones."

The riders stood for a long moment before the first slid the short sword into the scabbard at his hip.

"Ruminor have mercy on you, Cirrus," said the one called Rufus. "The Emperor could have us all flayed."

"He could, but he won't."

"You're so sure of this wild dragon," grumbled the rider of the gold drake. "And a soul-boy? How old is he? Twelve?"

"Old enough," muttered Rue.

"Old enough to die," said the rider. He aimed his sword at the silver rider. "This is your measure, Cirrus. We live or we die, because of you. Remember that."

"I won't forget," said Cirrus.

Both riders turned and moved to their dragons. Cirrus waited a moment before nodding swiftly. He kicked snow and dirt over the small fire before approaching to his drake. That left Galla Gaius. She stood like marble, sword gleaming in the dawn's light, long braid swaying in the night breeze.

"I'm sorry," said Rue.

She turned her back and walked toward her drakina, speaking words of comfort and ease. Aryss perched erect, wings wide, tail lashing in the darkness. I could hear her heartbeat racing like a school of silverfins. I had terrified her. No, *Warblood* had terrified her. But I was Warblood *and* Stormfall. Both and perhaps neither.

I hated this. I hated what I had become tonight, what they wanted me to become even still. I didn't know what they would ask of me in the coming days, but I knew that as Stormfall, I wouldn't last.

Warblood, however, would thrive and I wrestled with the fact that I had led so many lives. Stormfall and Snake, Nightshade and Hallowdown, all preparing the way for Warblood the Undefeated, Jewel of the Crown of Salernum. I looked up to the sky. There were no moons but there were stars, scales of my father, Draco Stellorum. Always watching but never doing. Perhaps I hated him most of all.

We flew out at first light of dawn.

***

They were called the Shadow Flight. Not sanctioned, not existing, comprised only of five dragons. There were two silvers – Ironwing and Jagerstone and conversely two golds – Aryss and Chryseum. And now me. I wondered if our colours had anything to do with our selection. Surely there was more to it than that but it was curious. As you know by now, I am a curious dragon.

Both Chryseum and Jagerstone were fine drakes, having reached perhaps eight years but I must admit it was Ironwing who impressed me the most. He was very large, easily ten to fifteen years and compared to my size, I barely came to his shoulder. He watched us with heavy eyes and I could only imagine the life he had seen. It filled me with pride and rage in equal measure – pride that he had lived so long, and rage at the fact that he lived so long because of a stick.

It took us three days to reach Terra Remus and as we flew over the land, it changed from high mountains and deep valleys to limen groves and olive firs. Cities and villages, towns and farms – I saw more of this vain land than I needed, for in every field and on every road, I saw dragons. Cart dragons, carriage dragons, plow dragons and barge. I wondered if they too looked up at us and dreamed of flying.

We also flew over an amphitheater in the middle of a plain. It looked like a small version of the Crown and those coals, long dormant, began to flicker once more. I suppose anger is a kind of fire. One breath and it kindles anew.

It was the morning of the third day when I smelled the ocean. My heart leapt into my throat, my wings beat faster and it was all Rue could do to hold me in formation. I wanted to race ahead of the Shadow Flight, soar high into the billowing sea clouds and plunge headlong into the glorious water. I kept my pace but I believe the entire Flight flew a little faster because of me.

On the third day, the city of Terra Remus grew out of the sea beneath us, with brightly coloured houses hugging its rugged shores. The streets were narrow and steeply sloped, and my heart ached for the dragons forced to pull carts up and down those roads. But it was hard to think of anything but the ocean, the vast expanse of blue stretching as far as I could see. Sea snakes rose and fell on the salt wind, catching heads of fish tossed overboard by the ships that followed the coast. Smelting fires from stone ovens billowed smoke into the sky, fashioning hooks and anchors, spears and rams for the warships. And there were hundreds of war ships, some anchored in the harbour, others docked by the piers, all flying the war flag of Remus.

The war flag of Remus. Golden drakina surrounded by aurel leaves on a blood red banner. I had known two golden drakinas in my lifetime – Summerday and Aryss. While Aryss flew at my left wing, these days she was farther from me than Summerday.

As we closed in on the city center, I was astounded by the sheer number of dragons in the sky and on the ground and on the docks. The city was preparing for war with both ships and Flight Dragons and I had never seen such numbers in all my life. I wasn't sure which made me happier – the sight of the ocean or the sight of so many dragons.

I tore my eyes away from the glorious blue as the silver drake dipped a wing and I inclined to follow. We spiralled downwards to circle a long rectangular building at the crest of the city's highest hill. Red tiled roof supported by marble columns carved in the shapes of rampant dragons. It was called the Curia Terra Remus, I later learned – the Senate House of the Eastern Quarter. Dozens of landing stones surrounded the Curia and on each, a waiting dragon. Cirrus motioned for us to land and we took the last five empty stones.

He leapt from his mount and disappeared up the gardened steps to the building, while a trio of soul-boys moved to work the iron water pump. A trough ran between all the landing stones and very soon, fresh water coursed through like a little river. Flying for three days is thirsty work, and I drank my fill, the little river tending all on the stones. Even Rue knelt to cup it in his hands, splashing some on his face and neck. He missed the ocean too, I knew.

Next came groomers with wooden buckets and scrubbing brushes. They picked at my teeth, sanded my talons, rubbed oil into old wounds and new calluses. It was entirely pleasant, especially with the wind strong on this high ocean hill, and salty and I dozed in the afternoon sun while they worked to polish my scales to gleaming. Dreams of Aryss and shaghorns and life in the Pits made for fitful sleep as Warblood crushed Nightshade under a roof of stones, and Hallowdown collapsed beneath a flaming cart of bones.

I roused to the sound of chains and a familiar tug at my throat.

A band.

I threw my head back, rearing to the sky and wings beating furiously to the second snap of a band around one leg. Rue bolted to his feet as I launched into the air, yanked short by a chain keeping me less than one wingspan above the ground. I roared as an entire Legion surrounded me, throwing a net of linked chain across my wings and dropping me back to the stone in a lashing, writhing mass. Spears and swords rattled before me and I called the fire inside my belly, willing it to leap out of my mouth and burn them all to cinders but the fire stalled – choked to mere smoke as it tried to leave my tongue.

A band.

A silver band.

I raged and roared, tossing my head and lashing my tail and the groomers toppled like tree trunks in its wake.

Kicking and fighting, Rue was dragged off the stone by centurions and higher up, a man in white robes held up a scroll.

"Warblood, Night Dragon of the Salernum Crown, you are marked for crimes against Septus Aelianus, Emperor of all the Provinces of Remus and Imperator of the Known World. Ruminor have mercy on your night-black soul."

NIGHT OF
DRAGONSONG & FIRE

According to Rue, they argued for my life 'til last light of day and the better part of the night. It didn't matter. Stormfall died under the chains and the band, while Warblood was reborn. I didn't grieve the death so much. I think he had been dying all my life. I remembered a time when I didn't have a name, only a starry-black coat and my pride.

So I lost the last bit of Stormfall that night as I thrashed – banded and chained – on the landing stone of Terra Remus. Warblood was whom they wanted. Warblood was whom they would have. The moment this wretched band was gone I would kill them all and burn this city to the ground. My throat was raw from the trying, my talons splintered, my hind leg torn to the bone but I would not give up. I would never give up. I would die on this cursed stone or be free and never return to the world of sticks.

All that night I raged and roared, bellowing and spitting acid at any stick who dared try quiet me. At one point, they sent Rue and then Cirrus but my eyes were filled with blood and I refused to end my struggles. I believe a centurion tried to beat me with a mace but he was hauled off and I was left to thrash in chains and links and bands. The saddle was crushed, the bridle in ribbons and the mesh was now so tangled in my scales that every movement was a fire. Blood dripped from my tongue and sprayed across the stone as accompaniment to my roars.

But I was not alone. Beside me, the Flight Dragons took up my cries, roaring and raging along with me, unappeased by their own riders. Soon, dragons on the hills joined in, then dragons in the valleys. Dragons in the streets, fields and harbours added their voices and before the first Winking Eye appeared above the ocean, every drake and drakina in the city of Terra Remus was crying into the night, drowning out the shouts of men and filling the sky with the anguish of our people. It was a shared plight and if I could have shed tears like Rue, I would have.

It was powerful and poetic and when I had no more strength in my bones, I fell quiet and listened to their cries. Finally after several hours, the night grew silent and still, as if even my father, Draco Stellorum was holding his breath. I could hear the heartbeat of every dragon on the Curia Hill, feel the fire in every scaly breast. It was life and it was death and it was everything in between. I closed my bloody eyes, took a deep ragged breath and sang.

I sang out the song of my people, the music of the stars and the lament of the waters. The song of *our* people, ensnared by our pride and enslaved by the vanity of men. Our majesty and grace, our ferocity and joy, I sang it all through a throat raw and bloody and I know I had never sounded so terrible and so beautiful as I did that night.

A high harmony now to my left. Aryss. I knew it because we had sung together that one night in my mountain cave. Two voices now pierced the darkness, eerie and lilting and brutally sad. A deep rumbling chord next. Ironwing. I could have died on that rock then and there when he added his song to ours. Then Chryseum and Jagerstone. The entire Shadow Flight sang their hearts and one by one across the hillside, every dragon joined in.

No longer raging, no longer roaring; the Dragonsong raced like a mighty wave across the city and the sound threatened to call the moons down from the heavens. Glass shattered in every window, marble cracked in every wall as the sound shook Terra Remus to its very foundations. Every free Flight dragon took to the skies, singing and wailing and beating the air with a roar like Hell Down. I could feel them above me, circling above the Curia Terra Remus in the hundreds, created winds of hurricane force. At some point during the night, my throat failed me and I rested my head on the stone, overcome by the songs of my people.

We were Skyborn. We didn't have words, but we had language. I knew it now. I would ever doubt again.

The sun rose that morning with dragonsong still echoing across the waters. I learned later that many dragons kissed the axe that night. The dragons killed no one, however. Sticks killed. Dragons sang. Ours was the music and the power and the right.

Finally, a procession in gleaming white exited the Curia. They carried poles and banners, scrolls and shields. Rue was with them, as was Cirrus and Galla and they stood before me, waiting for the singing to cease. Ironwing barked and the Flights above the Curia fell silent, save for the thunder of their wings. Still, it was a very long time before the dragonsong died away from the city and the ocean. I was certain no one's hearing ever returned to normal after the Night of Dragonsong.

It took them much longer to remove the mesh of linked chain. I had struggled with such savagery that the metal was embedded in my scales and spines and spikes. I was as raw as I had been after my escape from the Crown but this morning, I felt no pain. Not even when they tore pieces of hide from my flesh to remove the metal, or peeled the ragged leather of both saddle and bridle from my skin. After wearing it for so long, I felt like a newborn hatchling, wet from the shell.

Rue moved forward. He was holding a key. It was to the bands but still I growled at him.

"I hear you, Stormfall," he said quietly. "We all hear you."

Stormfall was gone.

His face was puffy and streaked with glistening lines. Tears. They had happened before, usually with great sadness or greater joy. I didn't care. He was a stick to me now, nothing more. I would kill him as I would any of the others.

"We hear you, Stormfall," he repeated and he edged closer. "The Emperor understands now. He's agreed to lift the sentence on your head. Please let me remove your bands and he will tell you himself."

The morning air cooled my bloodied flesh, the rising sun warmed it. The rising sun was gold. Gold like Aryss and Chryseum. Gold like Summerday the wicked. I missed her now, wished she could have been here for this most remarkable night. I hoped she was dead. Dead like Ruby, dead like Towndrell or Bonesnap or SeaTorrent, no longer victim to the service of men.

Dead like Stormfall of the Udan Shore.

Rue dropped to his knees, covered his face with his hands.

I should have been moved but I was stone. No, after this day, I was ash.

"I hear you, Stormfall," said Cassien Cirrus and he stepped up beside Rue. "But you need to hear me. I'm am going to remove your band."

My heart leapt into my throat. There would be fire there soon enough.

"If you kill me, they will kill Rue. If you fly, they will kill Rue. If you fly and take him with you, they will kill us – all of the Shadow Flight. So I ask you to lay aside your pride, listen to the Emperor and consider his request before you decide. Will you do this for me? Will you do this for Rue? Will you do this for these magnificent dragons who have wept and sung and bled for you tonight?"

His words, echoing like a whisper in my mind. Invasions, always invasions. A dragon was never his own unless he was free or dead.

I growled, a long rumbling sound that shook my chest. Centurions rattled their spears but Cirrus held up his hand, stopping them.

I did not kill him.

After a long moment, he reached down to Rue's side, removed the key and approached slowly. He knelt to examine the band. It also was embedded into the scales of my throat, slippery with blood and ooze. After three good twists, it clicked and band fell away, hitting the stone with a clink.

I slid my eyes over to him.

I could turn him to ash with one breath. With one thought, he would be little more than salt at my feet, cinders floating on the wind. He laid a hand on my neck, ran it across my bloodied shoulder. I did not flinch, but neither would I admit how good it felt. I bared my teeth and snarled. He ignored me, knelt to unlock the chain around my rear leg. The flesh peeled away and it stung bitterly as he worked but soon, it too fell to the stone.

He stepped back and back again, laid a hand on Rue's shoulder, helped pull the boy to his feet. He staggered as he rose, Rue did, and I wondered at that. But I didn't care. I pushed myself to my own feet, the knuckle-claws of my wings bare to the bone and suddenly, there was a hush from the Flight dragons above and beside.

No more saddle. No band or chain or rider.

I threw myself back onto my hind legs, unfurled my tattered wings and blew fire, hot and white into the morning sky. It felt good; the burning breath as it scorched the back of my throat, the searing flame that rolled between my teeth and off my tongue. I sent my fire as tribute to my father, Draco Stellorum, as he closed his eyes for the night.

Above and beside and all around, the last of the night lit up like Hallow Fire. Down the hillside and across the city, through the docks and for as far as anyone could see, plumes sprayed the dawn like a hail of arrows as every unbanded dragon in Terra Remus trumpeted with fiery breath.

Finally, I returned to the stone, shook my mane of spikes and turned my weary eyes upon the riders, one in silver, one in black. They had come to take me to their Emperor, the man who had once been senator of Bangarden then Primar of the Eastern Provinces, now Emperor of all Remus. The man that had me kill two dragons for sport; the man that sentenced me to death for trying to escape his prison of savagery and for treating sticks the way they treated us. The way they treated my people.

My people. The Skyborn.

So in the name of the Skyborn, I would.

I took a lumbering step and the legions of centurions raised their swords, rattled their spears. I took another and then another, finding my one raw leg unsteady but I moved forward. Rue fell in step on one side, Cirrus on the other and together we exchanged the landing stone for the stair leading to the Curia. I left a trail behind me however, a slick of ooze and blood up the travertine steps.

Aryss called as I disappeared beneath the portico.

I did not look back.

***

The Curia Terra Remus was not a fishing hut. It was not a labyrinth of stone tunnels like the Pits, or mesh domes like the Crown, or hewn rock like Celarus' Landing. This was unlike any place I'd seen and it was as beautiful as it was imposing. They could fit many dragons in here.

Marble columns lined the way, easily ten wingspans high and polished to gleaming. The ceiling was plaster, carved with dragons, aurel leaves and scenes from history. The floors were travertine ice and cool to the touch. They echoed with every footfall, hissed as my tail dragged along behind. I felt very small as I made my way through these vast halls, passing one huge alcove after another toward a line of centurions at the far wall.

They stood around a large wooden table that was covered with parchments and papers. I smelled ink and wax and iron and I knew that these were generals in the Emperor's army, poring over maps and agonizing over strategies. They turned to stare at me as I lumbered in, and amongst them, a man in white robes trimmed with gold.

I recognized him.

He turned to face us, said nothing for a long moment. Rue dropped to one knee while Cirrus stood like a statue, eyes fixed on a relief at the far end of the curia.

"Cassien Cirrus, I should have you flogged," said the man, his voice echoing through the marble. "I told you I did not want this dragon here without a band."

"Forgive me, Imperator Augustus," said Cirrus. "But he would not come *with* one."

"He could kill us all with one breath."

"And you could kill him with one centurion."

"I doubt that very much."

"Here, you are equals."

The generals growled now but the thin man raised a brow.

Cirrus took a deep breath, eyes still fixed on the end of the hall.

"You are the Emperor of all Remus," he said. "After last night, the Night of Dragonsong and Fire, perhaps he is the Emperor of all Dragons?"

Emperor of the Skyborn.

It took a moment, but a smile spread across the thin man's face. It was like a knife.

"That is the second act of insubordination, Cirrus. You will not be granted a third."

"Yes, Imperator Augustus," said Cirrus. "Thank you for your patience."

The man stepped forward. Centurions snapped their swords across their chests, generals moved to stand in front but he waved them all away with a bare arm. Fabric swept the floor as he moved toward us, stopping not an arm's length away from my jaws. I noticed the gleam of a golden aurel circlet in his thinning hair.

But I was the Emperor of the Skyborn.

"I've met you twice, Night Dragon," he said. "First, back in Bangarden just before you destroyed my cousin's gate. Then in Salernum just before you destroyed the Crown. I am Septus Aelianus, Emperor of Remus, Divine First of the Sons of Ruminor. I have the power of life and death over all the men and dragons in this province."

He inclined his chin.

"Including you, Warblood of the Crown."

"He is not here as Warblood of the Crown," said Cirrus. "He is here as Stormfall of the Citadel."

The Emperor smiled again.

"Oh, I don't think so," he said. "Look at him. This is the Warblood I remember. The creature who killed Bonesnap of Belarius so swiftly, so savagely, that he tore the head off his body the way I might tear the wings off a moth."

I remembered. It was a good kill.

"I once called you marvellous," he said. "I would no longer describe you as such."

He was wrong. I had never been more magnificent than now.

Clasping hands behind his back, he began to walk a slow circle around me.

"Do you remember how many men died that day in the Crown, Cirrus?"

"Twenty-seven, Imperator Augustus."

"Is that all?" He raised a brow. "I thought it was more. It seemed like more."

"Twenty-seven killed, over one hundred scorched."

The man grunted. He was at my tail now. One lash and I would break both his legs.

"We went to see him, you and I," he said. "I wanted to see if it was the same funeral dragon who impressed all the rich dying in Bangarden, but you? You wanted to see if this Warblood was the same young fishing drake who could disappear into the night sky like the smoke from a fire. It was a bold plan, Cirrus. Bolder even, because you refused to kill him when you were ordered to do so. You could have been executed for that."

He threw a glance over his shoulder.

"Ruminor smiled on you for your boldness that day. He spared your life. As did I."

"Ruminor smiles on us all," said Cirrus.

The Emperor was at my shoulder now. He paused.

"But then he was gone," said the Emperor. "Like the Eyes at Dawn. I wonder how that happened? Ruminor was not smiling then, was he?"

Cirrus clenched his jaw but said nothing. The Emperor glanced down at Rue, still bent like a storm willow. He had not once looked up.

"Is this his rider?"

"Yes, Imperator Augustus," said Cirrus.

"He looks like a soul-boy."

"Yes, Imperator Augustus," said Cirrus. His eyes remained forward. Rue's remained on the ground.

"Imagine that," said the Emperor. "A soul-boy riding a war dragon. What an inexplicable place our world has become."

He dropped a hand onto to Rue's head, patting him

once, twice, three times. It infuriated me. I wanted to snap my jaws around that hand, just like I had Philius', taste the bone crunch under my teeth.

My heart was as black as my hide.

The Emperor moved back to the table, laid a ringed hand on one of the maps.

"According to our espionars," he said. "This is where she is being kept, here, on the fourth hill of Nathens. Are you convinced you can make it there?"

"We can make it, Imperator Augustus," said Cirrus.

"And how long does it take?"

"Five days to cross the Nameless Sea by ship," snapped a general in bronze and leather. "Even a trireme cannot make it faster."

"A dragon can," said Cirrus. "It's three days by dragon."

"You will head out before the fleet," said the Emperor. "If you fail, they will not."

Cirrus nodded swiftly.

"And once there, do you think this soul-boy and his bloody dragon can do what we ask of them?"

"I do, Imperator Augustus," said Cirrus.

"Can you *make* them?"

"They are Skyborn, Imperator Augustus," said Cirrus. "Trained to do the will of the Remoan people."

The Emperor grunted.

"The will of the Remoan people is to eat, drink and let blood in the games."

He turned back as if to study the maps.

"I will rescind the death sentence on Warblood, Jewel

of the Crown of Salernum *if* you are successful in Lamos."

"We will be successful in Lamos," said Cirrus.

"Of course you will," said the man. "After that show, the bloody dragonsong all day and all night, I have no doubt of that. I've never witnessed such a thing in all my life. Perhaps he is the Emperor of Dragons, now. Hmm, Draco Imperator. What an inexplicable world…"

Two of the generals laughed and he glanced over his bare shoulder, smiled.

"We will see if he is Stormfall of the Flights or Warblood of the Crown," he said. "For in the same way he presented me the head of Bonesnap of Belarius, he will present me with the head of the Lamoan drakina."

His smile a knife once more.

"He must become a Killer of Dragons once more to prove to me that he is no longer a Killer of Dragons. What a marvellous, brutal, inexplicable world…"

The generals surrounded him and with that simple gesture, we were dismissed.

***

Killer of Dragons.

Killer of Dragons.

Warblood, Undefeated Jewel of the Crown of Salernum, Killer of Dragons and Men, tasked with the greatest task of all – killing the golden drakina of Nathens.

I perched on the high bank above the harbour, the sun warm on my skin even as the ocean breeze was cool. I breathed it in, allowing the smell of salt to take me back to a happier time. I could see fishing skiffs with young dragons in the prows, some heading out, others returning home. They were oblivious, those young dragons. They couldn't imagine the life that was waiting for them, one of carts and wheels and harnesses and whips. If they were lucky, they would die in a hurricane or in the jaws of a Black Monitor, not under the axe of a stick.

Rue was sitting next to me, arms wrapped round his knees. He had made no move to tend my wounds but I'm not sure I would have let him. It all made sense now; the special training, the night raids. He had known what they wanted of me for a very long time, I suspected. Cirrus too. That was why he spared me that day on the mountain after my escape from the Crown. I gazed at Ironwing, dozing in the afternoon sun, wing talons crossed beneath his chin. He was large, elegant and majestic. But somehow the silver coat seemed a little duller, the armour a little more tarnished than it ever was before.

Next to him, Aryss, fanning her wings in the breeze. As beautiful as Summerday and just as wicked. She was Galla's dragon, working for the Emperor just as her rider was. I studied her, remembering the time I found her in my den. There had been blood on her wing but I never cared enough to investigate. I was still struggling with the thought that it had all been a ruse.

I had hoped to be her drake.

Rue was shaking his head. I could hear whispers of his thoughts but I ignored him, turned my eyes back to the harbour and the boats and the dragons. They were preparing to cross the Nameless Sea with a hundred ships and even more dragons. The ships had red-striped sails but it was the oars that gave them strength and speed. And on the prow of each ship, a dragon tethered to a bronze ram. I remembered how Rue would attach my harness and I would pull the little skiff while he rowed against the tides. This was the same, only bigger.

"You should go," Rue said. He was looking out over the sea as well, likely remembering our time on the water. "Go north. Venitus is north, so your aerie is north too. Go now before they leave. I'll be fine."

Tears. Tiny rivers of water glistening on his cheeks like rivers. Sticks didn't know how much like the elements they were, didn't realize they were made of earth and rain. Dragons were made of wind and fire. Maybe we were meant to be together, uniting the elements in universal balance.

Then again, when so many killed and died, maybe not.

"They won't kill me," he lied. "But if they do, it'll be for the best. Ruminor still hasn't given my soul back so there's no point in living like this. I wonder if there's a place where soul-boys go when they die."

The harbour cliffs were a mosaic of scales. There were more dragons here than in the Corolanus Markets, more than in the Pits, and more even than in the Citadel where they lived and worked by the hundreds. In fact, I never knew there were this many dragons in all the world.

I thought of the golden drakina of Nathens. She likely had no idea she was at the center of a war between nations, between mythical brothers. All she would care about would be her clutch, and I realized that if there was in fact a clutch, then at some point there would have been a drake. Was he still there in Nathens, or was she gravid when she had been stolen?

Had she, in fact, been stolen?

All stories told by sticks. They lied like they breathed, not even knowing how or why.

I had no band at my throat, no chain at my foot. I had no saddle nor bridle nor even rider. At this very moment, I could leap into the sky and be gone, follow the earth force back to the Anquar Cliffs and the aeries of my people. I could do that, return to my home and fight for the Fang and take mates and live until I died a great island of a drake, leaving only young dragons and old stories in my wake.

But then, all these would die.

I remembered the cannons – the flash of the iron and balls of lead that tore dragons apart; that rendered their wings little more than ash and crushed their chests like mountains. These War Dragons knew nothing of Lamoan cannons. They would feed the Monitors and the sea snakes and Draco Oceanus, the great Dragon of the Sea.

All I ever wanted was my freedom.

If I didn't go, Rue would die as well. They would kill him. Even if I took him far, far away, he would never be able to return to the world of sticks. He would be alive but he would be alone. As alone as he'd been all his life.

All he ever wanted was a soul.

Could I give him that?

If Lamos lost her dragon, Remus would reign supreme.
If Lamos had cannons *and* dragons, Remus would be

forced to change.

But all these dragons – the Skyborn that had roared and sung and breathed fire all night for me, those that I had called my people – would be dead.

I stole a glance at him, the boy weeping at my side. In point of fact, he was no longer a boy but a man, as much as I was no longer a young drake. I was a dragon with horns and with a mane of spines and a heart that had been turned to stone.

I watched the water roll down his cheeks.

Water could crack stone. Water could shatter it.

All he ever wanted was his soul.

"My soul," he said quietly. "And you."

I turned my face to his, blew my warm breath across his neck. He reached up a hand to stroke my cheek.

"I'm sorry, Stormfall," he whispered. "I'm sorry for all of this."

And he pressed his face into mine, his tears running across my beak and onto my tongue.

Salt. They were salt. Not like rain, but like the sea.

He was almost a dragon.

We left the shores of Terra Remus at noon.

NAMELESS

It was good to be on the water once more.

The buffeting winds, the leaping whitecaps, the schools of silverfins and bloodbass and lemonwhites. Oh, the lemonwhites. I dove into them, mouth wide, scooping as I used to in my earliest days only this time, blowing the seawater out through my teeth and swallowing as many as I could at one time. It felt good to be eating them, crunching and chewing or swallowing as I willed. I was a dragon without band, free and fighting for my kind.

In fact, it was liberating. Rue had no saddle or bridle but clung to me with both arms, almost a part of my spines now for I was no tame dragon. I was no Flight Dragon, nor Pit dragon, nor fisher dragon. I was not Stormfall or Snake, Nightshade nor Hallowdown. I was not even Warblood. I was, like the vast sea we flew over, Nameless.

The Shadow Flight followed our lead, discarding

saddles and bridles for the necessity of bareback. The colour coordination between dragon and rider was important now, and the riders flattened low along our backs. At a distance, it was difficult to see them at all, which was an effective strategy. We were flying into Lamos, where dragons had never been. If seen, the only way we would not raise an alarm would be as wild drakes, drawn to the nation because of the drakina.

At least, that was the theory.

We flew the first day low to the water and I showed them how to skim the surface for schools of silverfins. Silverfins loved the warmth and were easy to snag with little effort from above. Bloodbass next and I delighted to soar high only to plunge headlong into the depths at the flash of red, bringing up almost a dozen at one time. Rue quickly learned to leap from my back the moment I hit the water and I know the others watched with shock as I caught him on my back once I surfaced. It was a dance – dragon, water and stick, in that order. Rue knew it and danced along. We were more one than we had ever been, both freed slaves serving hard masters. Life was our master. Life and fate and destiny and death. But I wasn't Stormfall any more.

Part of finding my new name, I reasoned. I knew nothing and everything. I was going to kill a dragon to save dragons. Nothing made sense anymore, but then again, I suppose it rarely had.

I also taught the Flight how to rest on the surface of the water. They were mountain dragons accustomed to snow and rock and high altitudes. While these had been like those that had saved the Udan Shore, I distinctly remember Ironwing grooming himself afterward on the sand. Water was a stranger to them.

It came back like I had never left, the tucking of the wings and the forward lean, allowing the waves to hold my weight. Simply by example, I taught them to paddle their feet like the oars of a ship. It felt so good – the water between my toes, splashing on my chest, running down my arched neck. And my tail, steering like a rudder, made weightless by the ocean force pushing up against it. The salt stung the wounds raw from the Emperor's chains but it healed as well. Oh yes, it healed.

There was nothing between sea and sky but a vague difference in colour, a line that cut this world in two. Blue as far as I could see – clouds above, darker dips below. Before and behind, east, west, north and south. Only water and not water and dragons.

And at night, I saw stars.

Stars over the ocean are unlike any stars over the land. They go on forever, longer and farther and deeper because the waters reflect them in the inky blackness. Even with both Eyes of my father, Draco Stellorum, Wide Open above, I was a part of it all, almost invisible in the night. The riders talked for a long time then, discussing plans in soft voices as if not daring to break the spell of an ocean night.

"You sure the maps are good, Cirrus?" asked Chryseum's rider, a short, wiry man named Markus Platt.

"Octarius vouched for them," said Cirrus. "The mercator paid with his life to get the maps to him."

"Why?" said Galla and from my back, I could feel Rue turn to look at her. "I mean, why would a Lamoan mercator want such information in the hands of their enemy?"

"Because he wasn't a Lamoan mercator," said Rufus Dane, Jagerstone's rider. "He was a Remoan espionar."

"The Empire has had espionars in Lamos for years," said Cirrus. "This talk of dragons is not new."

There was a silence as the information settled in.

"So," said Rue. "The maps will take us not only across the Nameless Sea but into Nathens as well?"

"Getting to Nathens will be more than half the battle," said Cirrus. "In two nights, we must pass through the Wall of Moons."

Dane hissed at that, raised his water skin to his lips.

"We won't have stars, Cirrus," he said.

"Ships do it," said Cirrus.

"And ships have rudders," said Platt. "I'm not about to ride backwards and keep a hand to steady Chryseum's tail, that's for gods-damned sure."

The golden drake snorted. So did Cirrus.

"They have the earth force," he said. "That should keep us going in the right direction. The real danger will be altitude. It's hard even for dragons to stay level inside the Wall."

Both Dane and Platt grunted at that.

"Why?" asked Rue. "What is the Wall of Moons?"

"Do you remember back when you were a fisher boy?" said Cirrus. "Of a time when the winds would die and the clouds would come down from the skies and you couldn't see anything or go anywhere because it was all fog?"

"For days at a time," said Rue, nodding his head. "We called it Ruminor's Veil."

"Well, Ruminor's Veil is for dead men," said Dane. "It falls across the middle of the Nameless Sea. You can't see anything, you can't hear anything. It's like flying on a blind dragon."

I thought of Summerday, beautiful and wicked and blind.

"You think you're going up," said Cirrus. "But suddenly, you're going down. I've heard of riders hitting the ocean when they thought they were just under the clouds."

"Sometimes it's two-days thick," said Platt.

"That's all we need," said Dane. "Fly for two days and come out of it right on the shores of Atha Lamos."

"And being blown out of the sky by their gods-damned cannons."

The men laughed quietly, experienced soldiers all.

Rue sighed, stretched out along my back and I knew he was thinking. Still, he fell asleep quickly with the sea rising and falling like the breath of a great dragon. It was beautiful and I was at home, a creature of sea and sky and stars. The Wide Eyes of my father, Draco Stellorum, watched over me as I slept.

Selisanae, the Dragon of the Sun, rose to chase my father from the dawn and that morning, we feasted on entirely new types of fish before launching into the vast blue sky. We flew all day, high enough to taste the clouds but low enough to see shapes of large Black Monitors in the water. I had never been out so far without land in sight and it brought back memories of gluttony, of flashing teeth and storms sweeping me far away from home. When night came once again and with it the Wide Eyes of my father, Draco Stellorum, I was grateful to set down under his sleepy gaze, although I didn't trust that he'd protect me one bit.

We slept in loose formation, close but not touching, heads tucked over our backs. Rue slept between my wings and my neck, warmed by my body and rocked by the sea. I admit I dozed for the most part until I was roused by a sound breaking the waves.

Swiftly, I raised my head, blinking in the blackness.

I could see nothing. The Eyes were wide apart, casting light in different directions and I felt Rue stir as the cold air replaced my head.

"Stormfall?" he asked.

Wrong, wrong, something was wrong. Danger was in the water and I barked to alert the others, pushing up from the surface, wings wide, neck arched, scanning the waves for a sign.

The dragons stirred, Ironwing lifting his majestic head, barely visible in the water's dark sheen.

"What is it?" asked Cirrus. "Ships?"

"I don't know," said Rue and they fell silent, all ears straining to hear something, anything in the darkness. "Stormfall?"

A splash to our left as a rolling hump crested then disappeared into the inky depths.

"Leviathan!" shouted Markus.

"Monitor!" shouted Rue and he grabbed my spines. "Black Monitor. Get out of the water!"

Four sets of wings snapped open as the Shadow Flight leapt to the sky. Suddenly, Chryseum screeched, jerked downwards and the water churned as if boiling beside him. They went for the tail, I remembered and I saw his neck slap from side to side in agony. Golden wings beat the water but a massive shape surged beneath, scales glittering in the moonlight, and his body jerked lower. Red sprayed across the waves.

His rider, Markus Platt, clambered down the heaving spines, sword drawn, hacking savagely at the Monitor's flank. Above him, Ironwing wheeled and dove, plunging into the water like a falling star, talons extended, turning the ocean to steam with his breath. Chryseum screeched again, this time fire billowing from his mouth, illuminating the waves and the spray and the blood. A giant tail slapped the water and disappeared, tugging the thrashing drake deeper and flinging his rider into the waves.

A second Monitor broke the surface now, its many rows of teeth flashing in the moonlight. Platt's scream was cut short and Chryseum's firebreath sizzled as water flooded his mouth. Ironwing leapt back into the night and from high above we watched the golden drake gurgle and lurch before being swallowed by the blood-red waves.

The four of us hovered above, our wings beating like rip currents across the top of the water. It boiled for some time afterwards but neither dragon nor rider surfaced.

"Black Monitors hunt at night," Rue said quietly. "Those were big ones to take a grown dragon."

"We fly all night," Cirrus snapped. "The time for sleep is done."

And he leaned forward, taking Ironwing up into the sky, lit on both sides by the Wide Eyes of my father, Draco Stellorum.

How many dragons had he seen die in his lifetime? Thousands? Tens of thousands? More?

Rue nudged me with his heels and I followed Jagerstone and Aryss into the stars. I felt nothing at the loss of Chryseum and his rider. It was the way of things, the alchemy of life and death and life. Monitors killed to live, to eat, just the same as dragons. Sticks had no power over this and were ultimately at the mercy of death, just like us. No, I admit that I felt nothing at the loss of this golden dragon.

But as my wings took me up, up, up into the shimmering night, I also admit that I was glad it wasn't Aryss who had fed Draco Oceanus that night.

And perhaps that surprised me more than anything.

***

We lost the Eyes during the night as the Wall of Moons settled in.

We flew without speaking, our wings beating a steady rhythm across the water, but the dawn never broke. The sky gradually turned from black to grey to white until we could see nothing but cloud and fog. It was impossible to see the ocean. It was impossible to see the sky. It was impossible even to see the horizon that separated the two.

All was white and grey and rolling, like smoke from a water-soaked fire.

It was a very strange sensation because there were, quite simply, no sensations. Soon, my eyes became blind to anything but white, and I found my ears straining to hear any sound over the sweep of wings. Numb and senseless, even the air was an enemy. It was like flying through an endless vat of tiny needles but I was grateful for the irritation – at least it was something I could feel. I was a Night Dragon, lost in this world of white and grey, this Veil of Ruminor, this Wall of Moons. I desperately wished to settle onto the surface of the water but after the nightmare of black scales, I knew it was still safest in the skies.

So it was all I could do to keep my eyes fixed on Ironwing's great shape flying in front of me. His silver coat reflected the fog, however, and he slipped into and out of my vision as I struggled to keep up. To my left, I could make out the Hell Down shadow of Jagerstone followed by Aryss' sunny glow, but even those were fleeting vapours as cloud passed in between.

I remembered this type of sea from my days as a fisher. The water beneath the fog wall would be as still as a stone, with not even a breeze to move it. It would settle over the docks for days and not a single skiff or barge would go out.

For hours we flew, dizzy and disoriented. Dragons have an innate sense of direction – a tribute to the earth force, Cirrus had said. We can tell if we're level or angled, veering left or veering right, but this? This was like flying without the earth force into a hole and at some point, my mind began to play tricks on me. Ironwing was above me, then below. No, above. Aryss on my left, then on my right, then on my left. I didn't think I was flying differently; certainly Rue made no sudden shifts or leans, but I gradually became aware of the sound of water growing closer. Voices next, not from the Shadow, and I strained to make some sense of our position when suddenly, the sails of a warship appeared before my eyes.

Someone screamed.

Ironwing hit first, cracking the mast like an old tree. I wheeled to avoid the double sails but I struck the top of the second mast with my wing. My talons caught in the rigging and I spun violently around, flinging Rue against my neck at the impact. Jagerstone was on my tail and followed me into the wooden beam, shattering it like cannon fire. I felt Rue's weight disappear and I knew he had been thrown.

All this in less than a heartbeat.

A sound from nightmares as arrows whipped through the sky. Below me, sticks raced about on the deck of the ship, shouting in a strange tongue as timbers and ropes rained down from the sails. Caught in the rigging, I blasted it with dragonfire and was free within moments. Jagerstone, however, was tangled in the canvas, suspended and thrashing above the deck. Arrows shot up at him and I saw his rider pitch backwards, only to be caught in the rigging himself as arrow after arrow thudded into stone-grey leather. Ironwing was free but I could see through the fog a jagged tear in his wing. Wheeling into the chaos,

Aryss blasted archers on the deck while I flew away from it, hoping to spy Rue before the arrows did.

There! His dark head bobbed in the water near the side of the ship. He saw me, raised his hands through the choppy surface. Arrows hissed, bringing fire of their own as they thudded into my neck, chest and side. I sprayed yellow flame across the deck before tucking my wings and diving. I caught Rue's arms and pulled him from the water as arrows whipped past me, peppering my tail with bites. I sprayed the deck with white fire this time, noticing the large eye painted on the curved prow as I flew past.

Lamos.

Rue climbed to my back and I circled down. Jagerstone had broken free of the burning rigging but two barbed spears were lodged in his throat and he flailed through the flames, smashing through oars and deck planks and seamen as he went. Finally, he toppled over the side, the splash sending a wall of water up and onto the deck.

Both Aryss and Ironwing scorched the ship in pass after pass and men leapt from the deck into the water, as if that would protect them from the kiss of dragons. I too swept downwards, setting all bobbing heads alight. Soon, the screaming died away, leaving only the crackling of the flames on canvas and wood and bone. Bits of burning debris floated in the water, and the Wall of Moons swallowed the smoke as if consuming it.

First Ironwing, then Aryss, then I settled on to the top of the quiet water, to wait with Jagerstone as he died. The fog was as thick as ever, but we had no fear of Monitors. We had no idea of time any more, no idea of place or war or drakinas, only a slate grey drake retching flame and blood into the ocean in equal measure. Cassien Cirrus moved his dragon closer, carefully crossed over to the grey drake's back. He himself was bleeding from the head and arm, but he ignored it, pulling one bloody spear out Jagerstone's leathery neck. The drake moaned as Cirrus tried to move the second.

"Rue," said Galla.

"I'm fine," said Rue. He yanked a broken arrow from his side. "Leather."

"You're bleeding."

"So are you."

I watched as the silver rider bent, laying a hand over Jagerstone's eye. He was asking permission and for a moment, my black heart was moved. So I raised my voice in dragonsong, my deep pure notes echoing across the still water. Aryss joined me next, then Ironwing, and we serenaded our companion into the care of Draco Mortis. Cirrus rose to his feet, picked up the first spear and crossed over to stand on the shoulders of his silver. With barely a pause, he plunged it like a harpoon deep into the grey dragon's heart.

Without a sound, Jagerstone's body slipped into the deep.

We sat on the surface for a long moment, numb and pensive, until a crack shattered the silence. Still burning, the Lamoan warship had split in two, both fore and aft decks raised high in the air and the midships submerged. The aft deck disappeared swiftly, following Jagerstone with a hiss of froth and steam and snapping cables. But the foredeck, with its curved prow and great painted eye, took its time. It bobbed and groaned, rising higher into the air before sliding backward, slowly down, down, down into darkness, the Eye of Lamos watching us as it went.

All gone in a heartbeat. In a lifetime of fire and water, ash and blood.

And with that, the wind picked up, moving the Wall of Moons away from us, little wisps of fog spinning in its wake. It revealed a sky bluer than Skybeak over a sea still running with blood. It seemed odd, irreverent even. We had lost Chryseum and Platt, Jagerstone and Dane in less than a day and we hadn't even reached the Lamoan shore. Sacrifices to Ruminor and his Veil.

"One more day," said Cirrus, examining the tear in his dragon's silver wing. "We must push through one more day. Tell me now if you cannot."

"We don't have a choice," said Galla. "We can't float on the sea forever. There's blood in the water and those leviathans will feast on our bones tonight."

"I don't want to fly back through that," said Rue. "Ruminor's Veil is for dead men."

There was something in his breathing and I turned my head to look at him. His eye was swollen, his lip split in two and his leather was glistening darker than dark. I knew it wasn't from seawater. My heart of stone that had been broken by Rue's salt tears was turning to ash.

With bleeding limbs and charred hearts, we took to the skies.

We were over Atha Lamos by dusk.

LAMOS

Atha Lamos was a port city, a ship-building city, a cannon-making city, so we made a point to fly very high above it. Below us, the lights of the city's torches made a complex pattern like the spokes of a carriage wheel. I remember Rue had once said that Lamos was shaped like a hand and Remus like a boot. Lamos, he had said, always reached to grasp the boot of his brother Remus who, being a boot, strove to crush the hand of his brother Lamos. I wondered how a legend of brothers could cause these peoples to go to war. Then again, the war was over dragons. Of all the possible causes, I suppose only dragons would be an acceptable one.

Atha Lamos was also an island, the largest in a chain of islands that flanked the northwestern coast of the nation. It was built around a harbour that, from the air, resembled a perfect circle. It was as if one of the Wide Eyes of my father, Draco Stellorum, had kissed the water, leaving an imprint in the ocean floor. Perhaps there had been three moons at one time, three mothers to the twins. Perhaps one had thrown herself into the sea after the battle between brothers, a sacrifice for peace in hopes for her children.

I suppose my imagination was returning and I wondered why. There was no hope left in me, no life and my heart was as inky as my coat. But I had pride still. Perhaps there was enough of that for all of me.

We flew silently over this ship-building city, grateful for the blanket of stars that cloaked us. I was invisible, Ironwing near so but Aryss was the sun streaking across the sky and I knew we needed to land soon. Fortunately, this set of islands was an archipelago, as craggy as the Citadel and we settled on a peak overlooking the rugged coastline. A small herd of mountain shaghorns had watched our approach with curiosity, never having seen a dragon before, and we each snagged one as we flew past. After three days of fish, I was happy to be eating meat and I let the blood run down my chin with grim pleasure.

The leftovers we roasted for our sticks. It seemed the only blood they enjoyed was in their sport and so we sat that night with full bellies but raw bodies, numb to everything but the senses of the night. The rush of the mountain wind, the roar of the tides below. The Eyes were wide, the night was warm and while we couldn't risk a fire, Ironwing held one in his open mouth. It was like a great kiln and the flames billowed and danced over his tongue with each breath.

Cirrus rolled out the map.

I had never seen a map before and it was intriguing to

me. It was drawn on oiled animal skin, so it would keep the ink if wet, and there were sketches of land, water, mountains and beasts. The Nameless Sea separated Remus from Lamos and it looked indeed as if a hand were reaching up to grasp a boot. I could see the circular harbour that was Atha Lamos and all the little islands like blobs of ink. The mapmaker had been careful to draw leviathans and the Wall of Moons in the water, dragons on Remus, cannons on Lamos and a great many ships on both sides of the sea. There were also a great many symbols and I remembered that sticks had a complex language that included the transmutation of words into ink on parchment, paper and skin.

I growled softly. Part of the reason they ruled as they did, I supposed. Dragons could only transmute fire.

"Here is Nathens," said Cirrus, pointing with a grimy finger. "Two days to fly, and we'll stay to the mountains. Less chance of being seen."

"We could fly at night," said Rue. He looked very bad. His eye had swollen shut and his breathing was loud and wet.

"We might," said Cirrus. "But it's hard to hide on land in the daytime. Easier to be in the sky."

"People don't look up," said Galla. "Not usually."

"They must expect dragons," said Rue. "Now that they have a laying drakina. Her scent will call drakes from everywhere."

"They have a dragon master," said Cirrus. "And according to the espionar, he's Remoan."

Galla hissed but Rue nodded.

"It makes sense," said Rue. "Who in Lamos can tend and rear dragons? They have no experience."

"We will kill the drakina," said Galla. "Then we will kill her master."

"Maybe we free the drakina and kill the master," said Rue.

They both looked at him.

"Why not?" he asked and rose to his feet, laid a hand on my neck. "The orders are to keep Lamos from getting dragons."

"The orders are to kill her," said Cirrus.

"But dragons killing dragons is not the way to end a war," Rue insisted. "It just prolongs it."

I looked at him now.

Much had changed in these past weeks at the Citadel, in the Torrent then the Shadow Flight, at the Curia and in the Nameless Sea. Hope and betrayal, life and sudden death. I had changed but perhaps more importantly, so had Rue.

"Lamos doesn't deserve dragons," he said and he stroked my jaw, cupped my spiny chin. "But neither does Remus. We treat our dragons very, very badly."

I grunted and smoke curled from one nostril.

"We're soldiers, Rue," said Cirrus. "And we have orders."

Rue didn't turn to look at him.

"You've disobeyed orders before."

"We're all that stands in the face of open war," Cirrus said. He folded the map, tied it with a leather strip. "How many of our people would you see die when the life of one dragon will stop it."

"Two dragons so far," said Galla. "Chryseum and Jagerstone. This drakina will make three."

"And two men," said Rue.

"Three," said Galla. "The espionar paid with his life. You said so yourself, Cirrus."

"I'm sorry Rue, but we kill the drakina and then we go home."

Rue sighed, stroked my face.

"It never ends with one," he said. "It only begins." My heart swelled at his words. Here was the Rue who had been my kindred spirit, my stick, my fellow freed slave and I was happy to have him back. I arched my neck, pushed my long face into his body. He gasped and staggered back.

Both Cirrus and Galla bolted to their feet.

"I'm fine," said Rue. "It's nothing."

"Show us," commanded Cirrus.

Reluctantly, Rue peeled back the layers of leather that protected him, revealing a puncture wound in the middle of his chest. The bruise was the size of his fist, but the wound was puckered, round and oozing.

It was from me.

***

I remembered the instant it happened. We had been flying blind and I had struck the warship's mast, spinning violently as the rigging caught my wing. The impact had slammed Rue forward into the spikes of my neck and punctured the leather at his chest. Cirrus was certain that there were several ribs broken, but what worried him most was the sound of Rue's breathing. If a lung had been pierced by either spike or shattered bone, then Rue could not ride, and if Rue could not ride, then the mission, whether deliverance or deathstroke, was lost.

While it was still deepest night, Cirrus took Ironwing to find the brine clams that lived on rocky shores and shallow reefs. They had a poisonous jelly inside their shells that could be used to slow the spread of infection and hold back the sensations of pain. He hoped the Wide Eyes would light his path but left us the map in case they didn't.

Aryss was agitated for much of the night, grumbling and lashing her golden tail behind her. It was annoying, especially since she was next to me and would frequently lean over and nip my shoulder or neck. I didn't understand, nor did I care to. A heaviness had settled onto my chest and I knew it was because of Rue.

Galla had built a small altar of stones and had not moved from it, rocking back and forth on her knees as she prayed. Rue watched her, propped up on his elbows, resting yet not at rest. At the first light of dawn, the tall woman pulled her sword and lifted it to her neck, slicing her long dark braid clean off. She laid it across the altar.

"Why did you do that?" asked Rue. His voice was strong but I could hear a catch in it.

"I asked Ruminor to accept my sacrifice," she said.

"You sacrificed your hair?" said Rue.

"The braid is a token," she said. She rose to her feet, touched her forehead with the flat of the blade and slid it into her belt. "If he spares you, he may have me."

"That's a stupid bargain," said Rue. "I'm not dying."

She moved toward us, knelt before him. Beside me, Aryss began to nibble my mane.

"It's the only one I can give," she said. "I have only two things of worth – my dragon and my hair. I will never sacrifice my dragon."

Aryss' nibbles quickly turned to bites and I growled, lashed my tail this time.

"Your life is worthy," said Rue. "And you are a skilled dragoneer."

She took his hand in hers, spread her fingers in between his. Golden and dark, like stripes along a dragon's back.

"I'm sorry, Rue."

"It's my own fault," he said. "I'm not a rider. Not really."

"No, I mean…" She leaned down, kissed his forehead. "For Aryss. For me. All I ever had was the Flight, until you."

"Did you ever love me?"

"From the moment we first met," she said. "It wasn't strategic."

"I know." And he blinked slowly.

Aryss trilled in my ear, nipped again. I grumbled but she leaned into me, rubbing her cheek along my neck. Her purrs quickened my blood like a pulse. She was acting as though she was in season and I wondered if it had anything to do with her rider.

"You're the only one who ever made me feel beautiful," said Galla and she straddled him, pulled at the fabric of her leggings.

"You're the only one who looked at me as anything other than a soul-boy," Rue said, helping her.

"Has your soul come back yet?"

"Maybe it never will," he said.

"I don't want to lose you."

"I'm not dead yet."

"Really?" She grinned sadly. "Prove it."

And he reached up with his hand, pulling her face down to meet his.

Their behavior was curious. I had never seen sticks mating. Had never really let my mind consider the thought but now with Aryss writhing against me, it was all I could do to ignore them. It was almost beat for beat, blood for blood, the passion of dragon and rider. I remembered the old man Plinius and how he reached into my mind like a wave upon the shore and made my legs buckle in response. Sometimes when we were flying, I just knew where Rue wanted me to go, how he wanted me to fly, without a single cue from rein or leg. I hated that sensation, resisted with every scale on my night-black body. Just another of the ways sticks controlled us dragons, with the power of their thoughts. I wanted to observe more but when Aryss arched her back to welcome me, all my observations quickly turned to ash and stars.

Sometimes I think too much.

Regardless, while the sticks mated quietly, the dragons did not. I believe we may have altered the rock formations of this particular island, perhaps caused a small landslide that killed a few more shaghorns. There was a distant boom that sounded like cannonfire but we were occupied with the entanglement of tails and limbs. It was the first time I had mated with a drakina that was not banded and I'm convinced that because of our fire, there is one patch on the peak where still nothing will grow.

As I've said before, the mating of dragons takes much time and it was noon before we flew back up to the peak. We had snagged two other shaghorns and shared them with our riders. Mating for sticks seemed to be as consuming as it was for dragons and they ate their fill on the meat we roasted. Or perhaps, Rue did not eat as much. I stretched out in the warm coastal sun and slept until the air grew cool and the Eyes rose over the waters.

By nightfall, neither Cirrus nor Ironwing returned and the sticks talked in terse, low whispers. Finally, Rue rose to his fee and approached on unsteady legs.

"Stormfall," he said and he held out the map.

I breathed it in – the scent of ink and leather and Ironwing. I knew the silver dragon's scent well by now but I opened my mouth, closed my jaws over the map, tasting it, inhaling it again and again, imprinting it in my very scales.

"But be careful," he added. "Because you must return before morning. No matter what, if you don't find them by first light, you must come back. We must go on, otherwise it's all in vain."

It was all in vain, I thought. Remus, Lamos, Ruminor, sticks, me. We were all vain. I don't know who was worse.

With a powerful stroke of my wings, was up in the dark sky above the peak. It was comforting to know that Aryss watched me go.

***

I followed the route we had taken back along the island chain – over the waters and craggy peaks and distant villages. It all looked the same, I thought. The same as Remus from the sky and I cursed the sticks' need for nations and boundaries. They were possessive. They lived to possess. Lands, noxen, barns, even other sticks. Dragons possessed nothing but territory and even then, could share as long as there was enough food and drakinas to go around. And with our great wings, we could easily find new territory for aeries and nesting and hunting. The sticks had carts and carriages and ships – surely they could move as easily as dragons.

I wondered if pride were somehow involved.

And so it was with such philosophizing that I followed the scent of the silver dragon until the distant flickering spokes of Atha Lamos came into view. However, I also smelled fresh water and my tongue suddenly reminded me of its existence by sticking to the roof of my mouth.

It was late, it was dark and I was thirsty so I followed the scent down, sweeping over the clay rooftops as I never had done in Bangarden or Venitus or Terra Remus. This was remarkably similar to those cities however, even to the smells and sounds of a city at night. Soon, I found myself circling above a public fountain in a town square, surrounded by mud-brick homes and lit only by the Wide Moons.

Silently, I landed on the cobbled street, listened to the

waters as they splashed and bubbled in the fountain's pool. Ocean water was drinkable for dragons but fresh, *ah,* the smell of this was sheer bliss. It was both fountain and well, and I lumbered forward, dropping my jaws into it, drinking deeply and enjoying the cool, refreshing streams as they ran down my throat.

A new scent met my nostrils and slowly, I lifted my head. A woman stood mere paces from me, wrapped in tattered linen and holding an amphora in both arms. She had not seen me in the darkness and was clearly terrified at finding a dragon in the city square.

She was not a Laomoan monster. She was not at all like what I had been led to believe by Rue and the others. In fact, she reminded me of Avea, Allum's wife from Bangarden. I reached out my beak. Her eyes widened, the clay pot trembled in her arms, but she did not scream or run or faint. I breathed in the scent of her clothing, her hair, her skin, reasoned that she was a mother of children from the milk on her robes. Breathed out on her face to gift her the scent of dragons.

The amphora slipped from her arms, shattering on the stone of the road.

I snorted and gathered myself to launch into the night sky, careful not to flick her with my tail as I went.

I followed the smell of the silver dragon into the city and I felt my heart sink. This was not good. Surely there were brine clams along the shores closer to the Mating Peak and I vaguely remembered the boom of cannonfire almost hidden by the chaos of mating dragons. I soared now over the vast dockyards and the scent of iron filled my nostrils. There was also the salt and the fish and the wood oil and the smoke. Other than the iron, it was the smell of my youth.

One pier was brightly lit, a beacon of activity in an otherwise quiet night so I angled toward it, hearing the sounds of a crowd echoing across the water. From the deck of a large ship, a treadwheel crane lifted a large net over the dock. Sticks waved torches beneath it, and between the netting a great mass gleamed like silverfins.

My heart stopped its beating as I winged my way towards the net. It was what I had feared, what I had know, deep in my deepest heart of darkness, for I was a creature of the night and the ash and the stars.

Blackness in my wings and death at my claws.

The silver in the net wasn't fish.

I swept down over the crowd, raining fire across their murderous heads. They bolted, screaming in all directions and I torched them as they ran, burning the people, the dock and its wooden treadwheel. Up I circled into the night sky, watching the flames races across the oily pier before I bore down once again, this time scorching the ship and all its crew in this pass.

I was the night. I was the nightmare.

I was Nameless, primal dragon of the night and the ash and the stars. I roared in fury as I sprayed both docks and ships with white fire, the purest and hottest of all the fires we can breathe. Cables snapped and canvas raged under the heat. As I flew, I sprayed my white fire along the netted body of Ironwing, the most majestic of dragons, so that he would suffer no more from sticks. I heard the boom of a cannon and in a heartbeat I whirled, the iron ball streaking past my belly. I followed it to its source, sending a blast of white fire into the black mouth of the Lamoan warship before wheeling back into the sky. It burst into flames with one, two, three explosions behind me and I rode the blast of heat and light up high above the dockyards into the coolness of the night.

Other cannons fired now from other ships but I was far out of reach and their iron destruction whipped beneath me to rain down on other far parts of the city. Below me, fires raged along the docks and ships blazed as they rocked on the waters but it was nothing. Nothing compared to what they had done, to how carelessly and thoughtlessly they had slaughtered the most majestic of dragons. As if he were a sea snake. As if he were a wyrm.

And in that moment, I hated them all, more than I hated the Remoans. I vowed to Ironwing that I would kill this traitor drakina and her master and all the sticks that dared defend them. I would smash her eggs and devour her fledglings and fly with Aryss to the Fang of Wyvern where I would sing the dragonsong every night and burn every ship that ever dared pass.

The sun was stretching her fingers of pink into the dawn sky when I returned to the Mating Peak. I was not a stick. I had no words. I had no language but I lowered my head as Rue and Galla rushed toward me and they knew what I knew. And I sang for him, for noble Ironwing, elegant and proud, majestic and regal leader of the Shadow Flight of Remus. Aryss sang too and together we let Lamos know that if they dared court dragons, dragons would come.

And we would deliver the fire.

THE FOUR HILLS

Those next days, we made our way to the Four Hills of Nathens. We flew all day, all night, all day and all night again, following the mountains as they followed the map. We stayed just below the clouds and while it was very cold at such an altitude, it served to keep our riders awake even at night. One of the moons was waning and it was more difficult for Aryss to see in the dark. She flew just beneath and slightly behind me, our wings beating the same rhythm, catching the same winds. While we saw many towns with many flickering torches, they were for the most part distant and that eased my mind. I had announced the presence of dragons loud and clear to the people of Lamos and in doing so, lost the element of surprise. For a night dragon, it was a bad strategy.

Nathens was the capital city of Lamos and I remember Cirrus speaking of how it had originally been built between the Four Hills as a tribute to Fulcanor, the god of forges and fire. Back then, the mountains had breathed fire, frequently spewing flame and molten rock out the top. Lamos, brother of Remus, refused to move his settlement and ultimately sacrificed his daughter, Nathena, to appease his god. Apparently, it was an acceptable sacrifice, for the mountains ceased their eruptions and the liquid flame quietly turned to arcstone. The Four had been quiet for decades, if not longer.

I thought about Galla's sacrifice – her token and her bargain – and wondered if my father, Draco Stellorum, was waiting for a similar gift from me. How many dragons would die to appease him? Would I die to secure peace for my people? Should I?

I have said before, dragons are not a sentimental people. Perhaps, it was just me.

As we approached Nathens, it was easy to see the Four Hills from the glow of the city surrounding them. In fact, it reminded me very much of Terra Remus for there was a large body of water in the distance. I tried to remember the map, if it was a part of the Nameless Sea or new water entirely. What was distracting, however, was the smell of arcstone rising on the wind. It made sense. If the Hills had once coughed fire, then the sticks could easily mine arcstone from the earth for their cannons.

My heart tightened at the memory – the warships and the crowds and the high net of silver.

I never knew what happened to Cirrus. This was one time when I cursed the imagination of dragons.

Lights from the city stretched on and on and we were quickly losing the cover of night. One of the Hills was very near and looked to be unpeopled and wild. There were four very tall columns on the peak and as we winged closer, I could see that they were statues, one facing each direction and as tall as a dragon from beak to tip of tail. I could feel Rue tense on my back as I swept through the darkness toward them. It was blacker than black under the Winking Eyes of my father, Draco Stellorum – one miscalculation would mean a broken wing or shattered skull or worse. He held his breath as we bore down.

Like the dragon arches of the Celarus' Landing, I sliced between the columns just as easily as we had that night. Immediately, my wings snapped to stop my forward motion and I was pleased that Rue did not jerk forward at the force. I dropped silently to the warm, dry stone and the drakina circled once more before landing beside me, her golden claws touching the ground moments after mine.

No one had heard us. Certainly no one had seen. Our position from this first Hill gave us a perfect vantage point – I could see the city of Nathens spread out like a wheel, lanterns and torches flickering like stars. Just like stars, I thought, as we settled down for our first sleep in two days. I spread my inky wings over dragon and riders as my father, Draco Stellorum, slipped away under the skirts of the dawn.

I wondered where he went, that great starry dragon I called my father. To his lair under the sea? Perhaps he was devoured by the Selisanae, Golden Drakina of the Sun, only to return again each night, reborn or regurgitated. And not for the first time, I thought of my mother.

I closed my eyes, hoping that thoughts of the aerie, the

sea snakes and the Fang of Wyvern would carry me off to sleep but a fleeting scent drifted through the night, and after that, I could not sleep because of my racing heart.

It was the scent of a dragon.

***

A wall of dark cloud was moving in from the east and I could smell a storm on the wind.

It was difficult to wake Rue that evening. His breathing had grown worse and now, as the sun dipped behind us and the sky grew red, Galla knelt beside him, rubbing his shoulders and calling his name. It was not the first time I'd thought he might die. The first time was after the Lamoan pirate attack, when Serkus had beaten him and I'd not seen him for years. The second time was after his fall from the net of dragons, when I'd caught him in midair. They were so fragile, these sticks. A sip of black water could kill them as easily as a whiptail. As I watched Galla try to rouse him, I realized that I didn't want that to happen. He was my stick. I needed him.

More.

I needed him more than I needed the sky. More than I needed the sea or the stars or my pride. He couldn't die.

She ground her knuckles into his chest and he opened his eyes with a gasp.

I had seen many dragons die in my short lifetime. Sticks were different. I remembered Gavius and his children; the way they had hugged me and kissed my face after the plow on the hillside. Their loud screams and louder silence as the little house collapsed under the indigo dragon. The smell of death from Bangarden and the wailing of the people as they poured from the walls. The shrieks of the soldiers as they burned in the Crown. So fragile and yet they ruled the world.

The net of silver moved me to fury but what of noble Cassien Cirrus, First Wing of the Eastern Quarter Dragoneers and leader of the Shadow Flight? Surely he was dead as well. Why didn't I mourn for him? Why were some sticks enemies and others, idols? Did the hard, cruel stone of life shape them as it shaped dragons? Were they as helpless as we?

Galla helped Rue sit up, passed him a skin of fresh water. He gulped it greedily as she put a hand to his forehead. I could feel heat coming from him. He was earth and sea, now he was becoming fire. If ever a stick turned into a dragon, it would be Rue.

I looked over at Aryss. Between the large statues on the peak of the hill, she was watching the city, her gaze intent and fixed. She was magnificent, I realized, the setting sun causing her scales to gleam like molten fire. I thought of Summerday, glorious, wicked and blind. I thought of the drakina and her seven chicks in the Anquar Cliffs. This was the gold that dragons loved, not jewels or trinkets or crowns or treasures. The gold of a fiery soul, pure as anything in the sea or the sky or the stars.

This drakina I was to kill was gold.

I moved beside Aryss to cast my eyes out over the sparkling city. An angry wind was picking up, bringing scents of arcstone, dragon and Hell Down. I could almost see her, this rogue drakina I was meant to kill, and I lashed my tail, tossed my head so that my mane of spikes slapped against my neck. Rogue dragon, indigo dragon, death dragon. No dragon could ever be understood by sticks. They laid words on us to reduce us to the size of their language. This drakina was either slave or free; trapped against her will, or simply doing what dragons did, sitting a nest and hoping for life. I could free her as easily as kill her although I had vowed to Ironwing her death. The thoughts warred within me but I was used to that.

"We'll do a sweep first," said Galla. She laid out the map, was struggling to hold it down with palm and knee as the wind threatened to lift it from the rock. "Take a look at that fourth Hill where the drakina is being held."

"How is she being held?" asked Rue. He was hugging his knees and to me, looked very young. "In an open pen or roofed building?"

"It doesn't say," she said.

"You'd think that if the espionar actually saw her, he'd have drawn it on the map."

"Maybe—"

"Is she laying or has she laid?"

"I don't know."

"Because if she's laid, then we have eggs to consider. Or even hatchlings."

"I'm not Cirrus. I don't know."

"He should have told us. That's important information."

"He didn't."

"And now he's gone, leaving us with a map that

answers no question but where."

"It's enough."

"And if she's not there?"

Galla said nothing, looked down at the map.

"If we can free her," he said finally. "We free her."

"If," said Galla. "And if not, Aryss and I will be decoy. The guards will think their dragon escaped and give you a better chance."

"To free her."

"Yes. Fine. Whatever you want."

I would kill her. I had made a vow.

Rue staggered to his feet when a fit of coughing caused him to double up. Blood splattered on the rock at his feet. He straightened, drew in a deep, shuddering breath. He wiped his mouth with his sleeve.

My chest tightened within me at the sight. He was dying. This boy that had saved my life, shaped me the way waves soften a stone, was dying.

"Stormfall and I should go alone," he said. "That was always the plan. That's why Cirrus wanted the night dragon."

"You're not well."

"Well enough for this."

"Can you even ride?"

"I can ride," he said and he laid a hand on my neck. It felt good, almost like the first days. Life had turned me to stone since then. Life had turned me to ash.

He couldn't die.

"I'm coming with you," she said, folding the map and slipping it back into her golden leather.

"In case we fail?"

"To make sure you don't."

They stared at each other for a long moment, before he reached a hand toward her. She took it, allowing him to pull her to her feet. She reached into a leather pouch, produced three fingers of slime and wiped it across her face. It shimmered like gold in the twilight.

Rue grunted, pulled out a pouch of his own. Soon, his face was as black as my wings and I understood their strategy. If possible, we were meant to be seen as wild dragons, not a Remoan raiding party. Lamos might think twice if wild dragons brought a rain of fire and destruction on their lands.

I had already given them a taste of that at Atha Lamos.

I could smell the gathering clouds, the coming storm, the fury of Hallow Fire and the terror of Hell Down. It was like a billowing wall moving from the east and as the sun fled over the mountains, I looked up at the statues that had been our guardians during the day. I hadn't truly seen them earlier but now, on the verge of leaving, it was important to me to study them. To truly see them, mark them in my mind like a memory stone.

They were statues of men, facing the four directions of the world. The one with face to the south was of a man with arms raised to the sky, holding the sun in his hands. The one with face to the west was the same man, holding a sword in one hand and a severed head in the other. The one with face to the north was the man stomping a dragon under his feet and the man with face to the east was holding a dead child in his arms. Such beauty in tragedy and I wondered if this were a common thread in all of life. Sacrifice and fury, death and revenge. Perhaps this was not a thread, but simply life. Perhaps there was nothing beyond these mortal things.

I snorted as Rue climbed onto my back. I was a Flight Dragon and this was a time of war. I would kill this drakina like a nox and move on.

With the wind biting at my eyes, I leapt into the sky. The eastern statue watched as I went, dead child of stone in his arms.

***

The wind was loud but my pulse was louder. Flashes of Hallow Fire split the sky and my wings strained against the clouds. I couldn't get there fast enough. Deathstroke or Deliverance. I didn't care which. Stormfall wasn't flying tonight, nor was Warblood. I was Nameless like the sea and I knew it wasn't only the drakina's fate that would be determined tonight.

The Second Hill of Nathens was crowned by an extensive complex of buildings. Curia, ramps, walls and agorae. It was clearly habited, with lanterns flickering between marble columns and torches whipping in the stormy wind. They had no emperor, I had heard. Not like Remus. Lamos was ruled by a council of rich and powerful citizens, and I wondered which of them had given the order to secure a dragon. A bold move, clearly inviting war. We gave it a wide berth and continued east.

On the Third Hill of Nathens, a solitary temple rose

out of the mountain, with columns and pillars, arches and gates. Smoke from incense that struck my nose like a wall. Another statue towered over the complex, this one helmed and holding a golden spear. I debated snatching it with my feet as we flew but I restrained myself and we pressed on toward the fourth.

Below us, the city sprawled in the darkness, shutters closed over windows to keep out the wind and blowing sand. I could smell her now, dragon scent mixed with shearer blood and arcstone. I wondered if it were deliberate, masking her scent the way the Torrent coated their dragons with coal for the night raids. There would be no need to mask her, I reckoned. There were no other dragons in Lamos to hide from.

The Fourth Hill now. It was the largest and also the hottest and I angled my wing to ride the rising air around it. The scent of arcstone was very strong and I could smell deep molten fire even in the coolness of the night. How the sacrifice of one small child had kept this mountain from blowing was entirely beyond my understanding. Stick gods were even more confounding than their sticks.

There were no moons, only Hell Down and Hallow Fire. As I swept around the peak, I could see that this complex was in three sections. A long ramp zig-zagged its way up the hillside to enter through a façade very near the top. It looked like a temple built into the face of the mountain, complete with columns, pillars and arches but I could tell that the bulk of the habitation was within the mountain itself. In some ways, it reminded me of the buildings in the Citadel – half rock, half construct and I wondered if it were hot inside because of the arcstone. I could certainly believe these mountains had breathed flame.

Maybe long ago these mountains had birthed dragons.

I swept across the middle section now. Marble arches and a large stone circle opened to the night sky. I could see two torches faltering in the wind and in their light, a small gathering of men guarding an entrance that led back into the mountain like a great open mouth. One man was butchering a shearer, while the others stood and watched. I think they were soldiers but none of them were looking for enemies. None of them were expecting dragons. They were barely awake. Still, I was grateful for the angry clouds and buffeting winds and I began to think how I would kill them.

On the far side of the stone circle, a half ring of steps like a great outdoor amphitheater. It was very similar to the Citadel's Crescent Prime and I wondered if those rich rulers ever watched their dragon fight. If so, I would gladly stop at the Second Hill and kill them on my way home.

Dragonscent wafted on the whipping winds and I could smell gold. She was gold. Gold – rich and beautiful gold and something tugged at corner of my memory. Gold and arcstone, arcstone and gold. But as I've said before, dragons can sift through a skyful of smells and instantly pick out those they recognize and those they know.

This one, I knew. Somehow, I knew.

Rue bent, squeezing with one leg and I obeyed eagerly, wheeling in mid-air, tucking my wings and diving like a spear. I took the man with the butchered shearer first, crushing his head in my talons as I plucked him off the stone. No one heard over the roar of the winds. No one noticed, wrapped as they were against the buffeting of the clouds. Silently, I dropped the man over the side of the Fourth Hill and wheeled again, setting my sights on the next.

I was an arrow – no, a cannon ball, dropping towards the group of men at reckless speed. I could feel Rue's knees tense as he tucked himself deep into my back. Like Celarus' Landing, like the First Hill of Nathens, I streaked seamlessly through the stone arches, talons extended, just as a flash of Hallow Fire cracked the clouds.

Two men looked up and I must admit I revelled in their expressions before I landed, crushing them under my weight. I snapped the third in my jaws and flung him over the open side with a toss of my head. Immediately I launched back into the air, taking the last man up with me, my talons piercing his throat as easily as a shaghorn.

Such fragile creatures. Dragons were far superior.

Soundlessly I released him into the night sky, the eventual thud of his body masked by the wind and Hell Down. I was Nameless of Many Names, the Night Dragon, Killer of Men and Terror of Flocks. I circled, returning to the arches and the wide circular ring of stone. My talons touched down and I dropped, head low, wings wide, waiting for more to rush from the cavern mouth. They didn't and I could hear the faint beat of wings as Aryss landed atop the arch above me.

"Rue!" Galla hissed down over the wind. "What in Hadys are you doing?"

"Stay there!" he hissed back. "Guard the door!"

"This is not the plan—"

"Go," said Rue.

There were two torches struggling to hold onto their flame in the whipping winds beside me. I swung my head and closed my teeth over the first, feeling it bite the roof of my mouth before it sizzled and died. Another step and I chomped the second and the landing stone plunged into utter darkness. This was what I needed. I was the Night Dragon. The black was my father, the clouds my cloak. So many years ago, I had fallen from the storm on the shores of Remus. Now, I was falling from the storm on the peaks of Lamos. It was fitting and poetic and altogether perfect for what I would find inside.

A doorway-without-a-door hewn directly into the mountain and I snaked carefully toward it, swinging my head with each step. I could feel Rue press down against my neck, could feel the racing of his heart against my skin. My eyes adjusted to the blackness as I moved into the cavern, seeing the chiselled walls, the bricks and beams added for reinforcement. The ceiling was very high and it carried along the same angles as the arches and the smell of drakina was very strong.

Soon, this cavern became a great keep, a dragonhold of brick and arches and iron and mountain rock. I could smell blood and shat and I slowed as the rustle of chains echoed off the stone. There was no light but I needed none. Several wingspans ahead, I could see a pale nest of straw and sticks, the glint of her tail moving as she turned. More chains now and she lifted her great head, breathing me in with a rumble and snort. On my back, Rue was frozen, more a part of me than ever before, terrified and spellbound in equal measure. Together we watched as the drakina spread her glorious wings across the nest and stretched her head toward me, spines flattening along her neck.

She trilled.

My heart thudded in its cage at the sound. She was music. She was beautiful and proud and magnificent and wicked and everything I remembered and more.

Rue let out a long, ragged, wondrous breath.

"Summerday?"

FACELESS

Summerday. It was Summerday.

My heart soared at the very memories of her. Of a wicked young fledgling perched on a bar, nibbling the weeds from my mane. Of a proud, glorious drakina pulling a pilentus under whip in Bangarden. But here, now, and very much alive, Summerday breathed in my scent. And trilled.

Rue slid off my back, paused only to steady his legs at my side.

"Summerday?" he repeated.

She hissed, shrunk back onto her nest, turned her head away from him. The rustle and clink of chains made me furious and I wonder how long she had been imprisoned this way.

She hissed again as Rue reached forward to ease a stick from the nest. He slid back and held it up to me and with a sharp puff of breath, I lit it. The new torch blazed to reveal a majestic dragonhold with a high arched ceiling and braced stone walls. Many dark doorways led into the mountain itself and I could smell men and iron and arcstone. Along the walls were carcasses of shearers and shaghorns, tallybucks and goswryms. In one corner, tall urns stored water.

I studied her now, my glorious Summerday. A great wide leather collar bound her throat, keeping her tethered by a long chain to the wall. Beneath it, I could see the requisite silver band, her scales almost grown around it and I wondered how she was even able to eat. There were perhaps four eggs cradled beneath her legs, all speckled like large pebbles. One leg was chained as well and while she could move about the nest area, I noticed claw marks on the stone floor.

Life turned dragons to stone. Stars to ash, gold to coal.

She hissed again and coiled back on the nest, teeth bared, tail lashing. She was as blind as ever but I wondered if that had made her senses sharper, keener.

And then Rue reached into his satchel and did something I hadn't expected. He pulled out the pipes and began to play.

I watched Summerday carefully. Watched her head lower, watched her eyes close. She was back in happier times on the shores of Udan of Venitus, when she fished like the rest of us and was queen of the docks. She grumbled deep in her chest and finally, turned to face to him, reaching out her beak and breathing him in.

Summerday.

He lowered the pipes, laid a hand on her muzzle, ran it

under to scratch her chin. She purred and my heart leapt at the sound.

His hands deftly moved to the collar and the large buckle there, dropping it to the floor with a thunk. She shook her mane of golden spines, snapped her beak in satisfaction. He lowered the torch to study the chain at her leg when suddenly, her head lilted in the direction of the cave. She trilled.

"Gods be damned," came a voice from a dark doorway. "The soul-boy and his black snake."

My head snapped up as the no-faced man stepped into the light.

***

His voice was the echo of nightmares.

I boiled the acid in my belly. I willed the arcstone into my crop. Master Fisher Brazza Serkus. There would be dragonfire tonight or I would die trying.

Master Fisher Brazza Serkus. I hated Master Fisher Brazza Serkus. Every scale on my night-black hide hated Master Fisher Brazza Serkus.

He lit a torch on the side of the wall and the dragonhold was bathed in warm, radiant gold.

Two guards accompanied him, with helms, breastplates, greaves and shields. With a hiss, I dropped my head low and raised my wings, lashing my tail behind me. I revelled in their faces. I filled them with terror.

They hesitated only a moment before fanning, pointing spears toward me as if that might stop me. Most likely, they had never seen a drake before, certainly never a war dragon and I did not need my vanity to know I was surely an impressive sight. In three strides, they could be dinner. In one breath, they would be char. "I would never ever, in all of my years, have thought of this," Serkus said, stepping into the room. "That your snake would have survived for so long. I did tell the old man he was a slippery one. I did say."

His face was no longer raw, but puckered and tight. One eye was pure white, while one ear gone altogether. He had no hair on one side of his head.

Tonight, I vowed I would finish the job the pirates had started.

"It was him on the docks the other night, wasn't it? The 'wild dragon' that torched Atha Lamos. He's already a legend in Nathens. But you, soul-boy? A dragon rider? That's comedy. Or is it tragedy? Lamos does love its theatre."

"You?"

I didn't need to look at Rue. He had frozen in place, eyes fixed on his one-time master.

"What?" said Serkus. "You so surprised?"

"Why did you do this?" Rue gasped. "You sold your dragons! You sold your ships! You lost everything to the pirates!"

"I lost everything because of you!"

"Me? What are you saying?"

Summerday trilled and Serkus moved over to her, took her face into his arms. It was as big as he was.

"That's my beauty," he said. "You caught that big,

black snake again, didn't you? You a fine girl, you are."

He didn't look up at us, continued to stroke her elegant face.

"They were coming for my dragons, you shathole. I made a deal with them – ten thousand denari for three young dragons. But you and that damned Flight ruined everything."

"That's not true. Their cannons—"

"Greedy," he snapped. "Thought they'd just take what they wanted, cut me out of the deal and pocket the coin. Lamoans are greedy that way. I've learned that by now."

He snorted and gazed down at the drakina.

"It doesn't matter," he said. "I got here, didn't I? She's already had a clutch so if you've come here because of some cursed Flight orders, then you've wasted your time. And likely your life."

Four eggs, likely just laid.

Acid. Flame. Teeth to the throat. Talons to the belly. It came back like a tide.

"Who's going to train them?"

Serkus shrugged. "Not all Remoans love Remus."

"Let her go, Serkus," said Rue. "She's served you too well to end up like this."

"She adores me," he said and he lifted her chin, gazed into her unseeing eyes. "Always has. Some dragons are loyal to their masters."

All the ways I could kill him. "If she adores you," seethed Rue. "Why do you chain her?"

"In case she changes her mind. She is just a dragon, after all." And I was so very good at it now.

"Her mistress, that Bangardian horanah, died of the plague. I found her again in Corolanus. No one wanted her. She was blind, already pregnant and ready for the Kiss of the Axe. Picked her up for five denari, took a skiff, crossed the gods-damned sea myself. I became their dragon master and saviour all at once. I live like the bloody emperor."

He looked up at me.

"But she needs to be bred again, see. I knew she'd attract a drake or two, but Ruminor piss-in-a-pot, the Snake? That's not what I ever imagined."

Sticks have no imagination. Dragons, however, are unequalled. I had imagined all the ways I would kill him ever since that first day on the docks.

"Why are you here, boy?" he asked. "It's not for Remus, certainly not for dragons. Not for nationalism or pride or duty or any shat like that. So what is it? Ruminor still got your soul?"

It was a bitter, long moment as I realized that a part of him was right. The Citadel and the Shadow Flight, the lessons and the dogged quest. Rue was noble and brave and valiant and kind, but he was also much like a dragon. He wanted what he wanted. In the back of his mind, this had been a last attempt to win back his soul.

"Let her go, Serkus," Rue repeated. "We don't want to kill her. We don't even want to kill you. I don't care about Lamos anymore. I don't even care about Remus. Keep the eggs. Just let Summerday go."

The no-faced man smiled. I didn't know that was possible, given his lack of face.

"Not today," he said.

A scream from outside, shouts of men and the roar of a dragon. I coiled back on my haunches and snarled, feeling flames scald the back of my throat. Summerday snarled too, swung her head in my direction and bared her many dagger teeth. But she was banded and chained. I could kill her in a heartbeat.

"Rue!" Galla's voice echoed through the dragonhold. "Archers! Fly!"

Brilliant light flashed from the front of the hold and I knew that outside, Aryss was battling Lamoan guards. Inside the hold, the two soldiers hoisted their spears for a throw but I sprayed a blast of my own and they screamed as their armour melted under the heat. Serkus whirled for the doorway but Rue bolted after him, fighting to get a hold and tackling the older man to the ground. Summerday lunged but so did I, snapping my teeth across her neck and dragging her off the nest and away from the men. She bellowed and braced with her feet, scattering the nest and raking the stone with her claws. One of the eggs rolled out after her, instantly cracking as it dropped from stick to stone. Grey claws and yellow slime seeped onto the floor.

Even though she was blind, somehow she knew.

Suddenly, she dropped her shoulder and rolled, using the tension of the leg chain to pull me into her. Suddenly we were a snapping, writhing mess, slicing flanks with our claws and biting flesh with bloody teeth. Pain popped behind my eyes but I had been a Pit dragon. I knew when to use the pain to my advantage, to harness it as if from a vat of coals. She roared at me, her jaws wide, tongue curling so I pushed my face into her open mouth and called my fire.

Summerday was a fisher dragon, then a carriage dragon and finally a breeding dragon. She had worn a band all her life, likely never tasted arcstone, never blown flame or even spat acid. She could never have been prepared for the power as I breathed sizzling, raging dragonfire down her throat.

She yanked backwards, shaking her head and blinking her unseeing eyes. She didn't know to release it and kept her jaws tightly shut as she backed away, smoke billowing from both nostril and teeth. I could see flame red burning her from within but more than that, I watched her throat expand as the flame met acid.

"No!" shouted the no-faced man. Rue had him in a choke hold against the wall. "Not my Summer, no!"

She shook her head again and again, her throat now swollen like a fat sea snake when suddenly, the silver band snapped and dragonfire burst from her mouth in a great torrent, white hot and scorching everything in its path. The straw and sticks of the nest caught easily, engulfing the remaining eggs in flames and the cavern filled with the sickly stench of burning yolk.

Guards appeared at the doorway but I rained fire across the rock. They disappeared.

The drakina retched and retched again as she tried to suck cool air into her lungs. Finally, she sank to the stone, blinking and bewildered and spent. I lumbered over to her, placed a foot on her neck, talons constricting to the point of blood. I bellowed at her to stay down.

"Don't kill her," the no-faced man moaned. "Please don't kill her! She's a good girl."

"You're killing her," hissed Rue. "Give me your key so I can free her."

More guards from another door and I roared, spraying fire at them as well. Beneath my foot, Summerday shuddered, retched again before pushing up to her feet. I let her. She shook her head, snapped her jaws and a wisp of flame rolled off her tongue.

"You'll take her back to Remus," said Serkus. "She'll die there. What do you do with a blind drakina?"

"Stormfall will take her far, far away," said Rue. "Back to the land where free dragons fish for themselves under the stars. Give me your key."

Voices shouting in a strange language and out of the dark entrance of the hold, I could see a set of guards marching in formation towards us. I swung around, dropped my head and raised my wings in threat. They lifted bows, arrows already nocked.

"Tsirkos!" one of the soldiers shouted. *"Tha échoume skotósei aftó to dráko?"*

"You think they're going to let you keep a dragon now?" hissed Rue. "After this? She's as dead as we are unless you let me free her."

Serkus turned his face, barked an answer in the tongue of Lamos. He tugged a pendant around his neck, passed it to Rue. It was the key. He slipped over to Summerday's side, laid a hand on her thigh and ran it down to the chain that had puckered and torn her flesh. She snapped at his touch but with a twist and a click, the chain fell off onto the floor. Rue stepped back as, for the first time in her life, the golden drakina was free.

"Tsirkos!"

Snarling, I swung my head back to the unit. I could melt their golden plates with one breath. Could tear their heads from their bodies; puncture their throats with my dagger teeth. All the ways I could kill them.

But there was a sound behind me, a gasp and gurgle and I turned. Rue's eyes were wide, brow furrowed as Serkus stepped back, the tip of a small blade glistening in the firelight.

"Off to Hadys with you, boy," he hissed. "Without a soul, that's where you go."

My roar deafened the wind, louder than Hell Down as I watched Rue stagger and drop to his knees.

"Skótose ton!" shouted Serkus. "Kill them all!"

Arrows whipped across the narrow space, every one of them thudding into my flesh and I roared again, sweeping a rain of flame across the unit. The first row flailed to the stone but the second, another volley of arrows were loosed my way, striking face, neck and chest. My vision blurred as a bolt pierced just below my eye and I tossed my head, calling the fire again but more metal barbs had punctured my throat and the flames sputtered with little effect. This, I realized, was where I would meet my father, Draco Stellorum as the second row of soldiers raised their spears.

Suddenly, a blast of brilliant light from behind turned them into silhouettes and heat struck like a wave. Lumbering in through the mouth of the hold, Aryss sprayed the unit from behind until every last man was writhing on the stone floor, skin flayed, armour melting. I could see her through the smoke and flames, riddled with arrows but golden rider still on her back.

"Rue!" Galla cried.

Serkus whirled and bolted for the nearest doorway but a blast of flames cut him off. I swung my head, blinking from the brilliant light and the arrow under my eye. To my shock, I saw Summerday, head low, wings high, tail whipping like a banner, smoke curling from her mouth.

"Now, my lovely," said the no-faced man and he raised his hands to her. "I'll be back, I promise. See, look what they did to your nest. To your eggs."

She snaked forward, following the sound of his voice and cutting off his escape from the hold.

"You're my queen, my empress, Selisanae of the Sun."

Her trills became hisses and her head swung from side to side as she stalked him, herding him away from the door and toward me. I growled and dropped my head, summoned the fire and held it like a furnace in my jaws.

"Don't you dare," Serkus snapped. "You are forbidden to kill me! My dragon won't allow it. She will kill you if you hurt me! Summerday! Show him!"

She was beautiful and proud and magnificent and wicked and everything I remembered and more, for she was a drakina and for the first time in her life, she was free.

"I raised you, Summerday! I trained you! I —"

She spewed her fire in a sudden burst, setting her master alight like a flailing torch. He screamed and staggered towards me, arms waving over his head. With great pleasure, I added my flame to hers, white hot this time. In a heartbeat, the blackened body of Master Fisher Brazza Serkus teetered and fell, shattering into kindling across the stone floor.

Of all the ways to kill him, this was the best for it was well and truly dragon. "We go now!" shouted Galla. "Rue! Get up now!"

He was sitting on his heels, face blackened, arms loose at his side. He looked up slowly, shook his head.

"No," he said. "I'm Rue Solus. Soul-less, the soul-boy. It doesn't matter."

As he spoke, blood pooled up on his tongue.

"You saved the drakina!" She leapt from her dragon, rushed to his side. "That's what we came to do. Ruminor will smile on you, I know he will."

"I can't walk," he panted.

"But you can ride."

She slipped her arm under his, lifted him to his feet.

There was noise at the mouth of the hold. Another unit preparing arrows and spears. I remembered this from the night in the Crown but I couldn't do it with Rue on my back.

Two drakinas, two riders. They could do it if I made a way.

"Stormfall, wait!" cried Galla.

I turned away from them, spread my wings and took first one step, then another, launching myself into the dragonhold and blowing fire as I went. The soldiers shouted as arrows peppered my forehead, bounced off my horns, pierced my wingleather. Just like the night in the

Crown, a spear thudded into my shoulder and sent pain stabbing up with each stroke of my wing. I was Warblood, Undefeated of the Crown but I was also Stormfall of the Citadel. I was Snake and Nightshade and Hallowdown and Nameless and free. I was everything I had ever been, every name, every place, every circumstance.

I steeled my head, stayed low to the ground, and they either scattered before me like chaff or were trampled beneath me like straw.

And suddenly, I was out into the night, soaring over the dark circle of stones. Above me, the skies flashed and roared. The wind filled my chest, stung my eyes, soothed my rage. I noticed motion on my right. It was Aryss, Galla leaning low across her neck. And on my left, Summerday, flying free for the first time in her life. On her back, my Rue.

My heart rose with my wings. We had done it. We had saved the drakina of Lamos and I had saved my wicked Summerday. Surely, my father, Draco Stellorum, would be proud of me now.

I should have known better. I should have known.

A flash of Hallow Down and a last volley of arrows whipped past my head. I heard a cry as Galla pitched forward, then back, sliding from her mount to disappear into the black sky below. Aryss arced a wing and followed.

My heart sank with her but I turned my face to the Nameless Sea and flew.

SKYBORN

The storm did not abate all night and I took us beyond the First Hill of Nathens. I didn't trust that Summerday could navigate between the statues without damaging herself or lose Rue in the violent winds. I also resisted torching the Second Hill of Nathens, along with those politicians so eager to enslave dragons in the service of their nation but my appetite for burning stick had been quite sated. I pressed eastward, following the mountains until I spied a flat plateau far below. There were no signs of habitation so I took us down as the first light of dawn stretched her fingers across the sky, pushing the flashing clouds ahead of them. Still, dawn was far away and the winds were very angry.

Summerday could fly surprisingly well without sight and she touched down immediately behind me, almost in my tracks. Rue was slumped over her neck and when he didn't move to dismount, I must admit to a tightening in my chest. I feared he had been impaled on her spikes and spines. I crooned at him. He didn't move. I nudged his hand with my beak. It didn't rise to meet me. To her credit, Summerday lowered to the stone and this action alone caused Rue to slide from her shoulder, leaving a dark slick along her golden scales.

Even when his body thudded to the ground, he didn't move.

I sat back to watch him.

There was little warmth in his body and the wind was cold. An easy explanation, so I stretched out beside him, ignoring the discomfort as the many, many arrows dug deeper into my hide. A dragon's skin is thick, thicker than a Lamoan arrow is long, and it would take many barbs to do real damage. The one below my eye was problematic and my inner eyelid twitched and spasmed. The barbs in my throat would need to be removed as well, else I'd never throw fire as I needed.

Odd.

Thinking about myself made it easier not to think of Rue.

The paint had streaked off his dark cheeks but stayed under his eyes, across his forehead and in the cracks of his lips. His mouth was partly open so I lowered my beak, breathing the smell of blood on his tongue. The wound on his chest had ceased weeping and I laid my chin on his punctured breastplate, unaccustomed to the new and terrible weight pressing in on my own heart.

Ever since that morning in Celarus' Landing, when Plinius had touched my mind with a voice like whispering trees, I had fought Rue's thoughts inside my head. He had only ever been a fisher boy. He was no threat, he could never harm me, yet I had fought to stay separate from him, to stay safe. To stay my own and to keep my mind free from the invasion of the sticks. They had bought and sold my body but I had always been the sole master of my mind. I had been too proud to let him in and now, as he lay here growing cold under my head, I regretted that my pride that had denied him such a little thing.

We're alive, he had said. That's the best either of us could hope for.

And now he was dying. Would it have been so bad?

I nudged my face beneath his unmoving hand so that it rested on the ridge of my eye socket. I closed my lids and remembered.

I remembered life on the docks with Summerday and Skybeak, flying so fast that my eyes burned. Catching so many blood bass that my throat would stretch like a fat senator overtop the silver band. I remembered the skiff on the water, nights under the stars, song of the pipes across the waters. Cannons and fire and Serkus and then Corolanus. The day my life ended was the day it had truly begun.

I remembered Gavius and his little ones. They had been kind to me. Tacita had drawn my portraits. Their screams had grown quiet under the flaming roof.

I remembered Towndrell, the whip of his master, the carcass on the side of the road. The most valiant, most faithful, most honourable dragon I had ever known.

I remembered Ironwing, stretched out in a net, caught

like so many silverfins going to market. Elegant, strong and noble. I'm glad I never saw him die. I'm glad I burned him in a proud dragon pyre.

But most of all, I remembered Rue. Rue with the wild curly hair and big teeth, slicing lemonwhites and teaching me to fly like the wind. I remember the pipes, how music seemed more his language than words and I wondered if that was why I understood him, for dragons are creatures of music and song. Even now, when I think of Rue, I hear his songs and I sing them.

I was older now and I had lived. Rue had been right. It was the best I could have hoped for.

Summerday stretched out on Rue's other side and my heart ached for her too. I never knew her before the Udan Shore. I never knew how she had been brought into service of such a man as Serkus, or how she had survived as a blind dragon in a vain city. Even this night, she had lost her young in the battle and yet, here she was, grieving for a boy she barely knew. She had carried him here, she who had never had a rider on her back. I was honoured to be grieving in her company.

The storm was fleeing now at the onset of the sun. Selisanae of the Sun, chasing the storm with her beauty and warmth. Life wasn't beautiful or warm, I thought, but then again, I had known two remarkable golden drakinas in my lifetime, so perhaps in some small way, it was.

It was a very long time, then, before I felt something against my eye ridge. Something weak and feeble, but moving.

Rue's hand.

Stormfall, he said.

I open my eyes, noticed his, round and glassy like pebbles. My heart thudded in its cage.

Stormfall, he said again, but he wasn't speaking. His lips had not moved, the blood caked and blowing off in the wind. *I have it.*

His voice in my head.

I crooned, allowed my tongue to trill like Summerday. Truthfully, I could have sung.

My soul, he said. *Ruminor gave it back...*

I breathed in his scent, that of blood and leather and oceans. Oceans. Seas. Big water. Rue.

It was like sunlight through treetops, memories not mine flashing behind my eyes. Faces I didn't know, old women I'd never met, children and bowls of soup and then standing on the blocks at the Corolanus markets. A younger Serkus and the fishing huts and the threading of nets and the removing of shells and the wonder of dragons. The lure of dragons, the delight of dragons, the training of dragons.

And then me.

And you, Stormfall, he said. *Brave dragon. Clever dragon. Loved dragon...*

Loved dragon.

Loved dragon?

Love?

Look. Selisanae, he said. *She's coming to take me to Ruminor...*

I looked and I saw.

Sunlight, reaching her long fingers across the horizon,

pink and yellow and orange and red. Selisanae, consort of my father, Draco Stellorum, sharing the sky and trading night for day without ceasing. She was coming for us on the beams of the dawn, flashing in and out of sight like a vision, hidden in the brightness the way I was hidden in the stars.

It was a golden dragon.

Summerday raised her head, trilled. The sunlight answered back as a molten shadow appeared from out of the light.

My soul... said Rue. *Is free...*

Aryss the magnificent lowered from the sky, the body of her rider in her claws.

And it's singing...

His hand stopped.

Wings beating a strong low rhythm, she laid Galla Gaius on the stone beside Rue, arrows riddled across the gold-clad back. And so we sat for most of the morning – Aryss, Summerday and I, not willing to leave but not wanting to stay. The drakinas took turns pruning the arrows from my scales. I'm not sure I felt them anymore. Soon, there was a small pile and I set them alight with a puff of my breath. I looked over at my boy and the woman who had been his lover. Whatever Ruminor did with souls, wherever he took them, I hoped that Rue's was somewhere he could sit on the sand and play the pipes all day.

Loved dragon.

He was my boy. I had loved him.

I set them alight as well. He and his woman and his

pipes. Music and honour and love and fire..

Aryss the magnificent sang a dragonsong of mourning, and Summerday the wicked joined in. I chose to watch the fire rather than sing, as it crackled and roared, sending ash up into the clouds. In fact, I'm not sure I had a voice. We stayed until nightfall, Aryss, Summerday and I, until the fire was little more than embers and bone, and the sky was filled with ash and stars. Ruminor had not accepted Galla's sacrifice. Her hair lay on an altar two nights west, while two bodies fed my father, Draco Stellorum, with their ash. He was as greedy as Ruminor was cold. Ember and bone, ash and stars. That was the music of life.

As the sun disappeared under the cloak of darkness, I felt the earth force tug inside me once again. I had no rider, I had no purpose but I had two drakinas who had never been free. Finally, after so many years of delay, detainment and detour, I was going home.

So I, Draco Stellorum, launched into the night, Selisanae on either side.

***

We flew for two days, sleeping on mountain peaks during the days, hunting shaghorns in the valleys at night. Summerday was an amazing hunter. Living in the dark made her other senses sharp and she could 'see' by heat, scent and sound better than most dragons could with their eyes. Aryss was ever vigilant, rarely sleeping, always watching and I wondered if she grieved the loss of her rider as I grieved the loss of mine. I could well imagine.

We had all lost our sticks, I realized one evening as we left the Mating Peak for the Nameless Sea. While Summerday was grieving the loss of a very bad man, he had been *her* very bad man. He had treated her as an animal, but she had been *his*, saved from cruelty in Bangarden and from life in the soulless markets of Corolanus. Above all things, dragons are loyal. Perhaps that is what makes us to amenable to life with sticks. Our characters are larger than their shortfalls.

Water is a great conductor of sound, so when I heard the thunder and boom coming from the west, I knew it was not the storm. The Remoan fleet had made Atha Lamos and cannons were firing long and loud across the waters. Soon, we could smell smoke and iron and burning flesh, and I debated changing our route to avoid the island altogether, as the battle was undoubtedly going on around it. I chose not to, however. There were dragons in the fray, noble dragons who'd been given no choice. Dragons, who had alternately raged and then sang with me on the Night of Dragonsong and Fire.

Because of that night, I would give them a choice.

It was evening as the lights of Atha Lamos came into view and we flew through acrid smoke to perch on the highest crag above the city. The sun was sinking over the moon-shaped harbour, painting everything in hues of red and orange. There were ships as far as I could see, all the way to the western horizon – Lamoan ships and Remoan ships. I could tell them apart by the eyes and the dragons. Flashes of cannonfire alternated with dragonfire and the thunder of both threatened to tear apart the very sky. The air was filled with arcstone and fire and iron and oil and blood.

My heart leapt in its cage at the sight of hundreds of dragons wheeling and soaring in the skies. It was chaos but it was war, as ship rammed ship and cannons barked death with every iron ball. Ship dragons tangled in rigging, thrashing and flailing and sinking along with their vessels. Flight Dragons swept through the skies, torching docks and homes and ships as they went. Riderless dragons, ragged holes blown through their wings, crashing into those same docks and homes and water, trailing plumes of smoke as they went.

Just like under the indigo dragon, houses echoed with the screams of children.

I remembered the number of ships and dragons assembled for battle in the skies above Terra Remus. Now, there were half. These were the same drakes, the same drakinas, who had struggled with me under the nets of Terra Remus. They had raged with me, then sung with me, then lit the night sky with their fire. The same dragons, warriors all.

Dragons fighting. Dragons dying, all for the vanity of men.

I couldn't leave them but I couldn't stop them so from my vantage point, I closed my eyes and lifted my voice in song. Mournful and rich and melodic and sad, my song rang out over the moon-shaped harbour, carrying across docks and water alike. My drakinas joined in, adding their voices, sliding up scales and down octaves as our music carried on into the night. We didn't have words. We didn't have writing or maps or language, but we had music and in that music, we spoke victory and loss, sadness and rage. We sang fire and water, earth and sky. We wrote the history of the Battle of Lamos and told the story of Selisanae of the Sun and wove the tragedy of the lives and deaths of dragons in every land. It was marvellous.

When I opened my eyes, dragons filled the skies before me, first a few, then dozens, then more, rising high above the cannons, hovering in place and listening to our song.

Riders, kicking but powerless as Flight Dragons left their aerial attacks in a valiant act of corporate disobedience. Most swept low, allowing riders to leap off into the waters; others, whose riders continued to kick and haul on the rein, rolled mid-flight, disposing of them in altogether unceremonious fashion.

Shipsmen rushed to release ship drakes from harness lest their ships be capsized as the dragons took to the air, joining the growing thunder in the sky. Some ships came with them, creaking then cracking at the end of their tethers, splashing into the churning waters far, far below.

Dragons without riders swooped high above the city, darkening the twilight like a tattered cloak. Soon, ship fought against only ship, man fought against man alone, as every single dragon above Atha Lamos abandoned the battle to join the thunderous flight. They took up the dragonsong of our people and once again, just like in Terra Remus, it threatened to shatter every window and deafen every stick. The cannons targeted them, firing in an attempt to take them down but they succeeded only in raining destruction on the city of Lamos in the form of iron hail. The sky was black with the thunder of their wings and even the cannons were deafened as every eye in Atha Lamos looked to the stars.

As the last of the red disappeared beneath the horizon, my father, Draco Stellorum, stretched his wings across the land. Draco Stellorum and his Eyes, the moons of Remus. And Lamos. And now, me.

I rose up on the highest mountain above the city, stretched wide my starry wings. I was the Draco Stellorum, Dragon of Stars. I was also Draco Cinis and Draco Fumari and Draco Mortuis. I was a dragon of smoke and ash and death and all things dark and deadly. But like my father, I had the Eyes, my moons, my own Selisanae of the Sun. Aryss and Summerday, drakinas of fire and strength and pure, fierce, gleaming gold.

You know how dragons love their gold.

With that, I launched into the night and called my people to follow.

They did.

DRAGON OF ASH & STARS

When there are a hundred dragons in the sky, it is Hell Down and Hallow Fire. It is the winds of a hurricane and the roar of the storm. We blot out the sun, we blacken the clouds, we churn the sea like foam. It is a magnificent, terrifying sight.

In honour of the Torrent, I called them the Thunder.

I followed the earth force northwest. We did not stop to sleep, not once, not even when we passed through the Wall of Moons. As a blind dragon, Summerday's equilibrium was excellent, and she kept the Thunder high and level. I had not forgotten losing Jagerstone to the ship and Chryseum to the ocean. I was flying with a hundred war dragons. I didn't want to lose a single one.

Days later then, we were finally free of the Wall of Moons and approaching the southern shores of Remus. The earth force was calling me north but I couldn't help but track west, just a little. There were two reasons for this. Firstly, we reached Terra Remus on the fourth day after leaving Atha Lamos and as we flew over the city, we called to every dragon down below. Whether Flight or working, whether banded or free, we called and they responded. We created chaos in Terra Remus that day and added to our number perhaps twenty Flight Dragons who abandoned their riders and as many cart dragons who lifted their plinti and carriages to the skies. We torched those carriages and watched them seed the clouds with ash and dust.

The second reason we flew over Terra Remus was entirely juvenile and vain. But then, you do remember that while I had lived a difficult life, I was still at that point, quite young.

I was then, and am still, vain.

I took my one hundred dragons on a flight across the roofs of the Curia Terra Remus, where I shat as I flew over the clay tiles. Trust me to say that we did not need language in that moment, for the hundred following did exactly the same thing. Part of me wishes I had circled back for a look but I prided myself in knowing that our point had been well and truly made. I also knew that I'd never have a reprieve from the Emperor if I ever fell afoul of the centurions again, so it was a good thing I never did.

Day after day, we flew along the coastline, calling to any working or fisher dragon we saw, snagging cliff bucks from the shores and fat fish from the sea. I knew that when we finally stopped at the Cliffs of Anquar, we would need to free those still in harness, saddle or band. Truth be told, I hadn't given it much thought but the more dragons that left the earth for the skies, the more it became apparent that while they were free of service, they would die very quickly if not freed from the trappings of service. I remembered Bloodtooth cracking my band during our battle in the Crown and I wondered if I could teach such a skill to another, all without the benefit of language. That would be an interesting development for I was not sure I could sing that particular skill.

Regardless, the earth force beat steadily stronger with each stroke of my wings and I pressed the Thunder long and hard without a rest. None of the dragons disappointed. They had no idea where I was leading them, but followed – no, *joined* me in the anticipation. Day became night, water became sky and the smell of salt and fish and freedom was life in my chest.

My father, Draco Stellorum, watched as we flew under the Wide Eyes of the Moons and I remembered how Rue had spoken of the First Dragons. Selisanae, Nerisanae, Stellorus and Anquarus and I had listened with keen interest. Memories of the Cliffs and the nest and my mother and sisters led me with a ferocity that I had thought reserved for the Pits and I let myself wonder what I might do if I found the Fang of Wyvern occupied by another drake. I would leave him, I reckoned. After so long fighting in the service of sticks, I knew that I would never stoop to fight over territory. The world was big. My world was bigger.

And all this time, both Aryss and Summerday flew with me, one at my left, the other at my right. My moons, my Eyes. Golden and fierce and mine.

One night, with the Cliffs so close, I took the Thunder down onto the dark sea. The impact of such a number of great creatures displaced much water and caused such a wave that I knew any Monitors in the area would leave us in peace. Silverfins however, were another story and we ate an entire ocean of them, barely sating our hunger from such a trip. We slept on the waters that night, a hundred of us rising up and down on a warm, welcoming sea. With Summerday's head across my neck, I was almost content. But with home so close, there was a fire in my blood that would not, could not, be doused until I set my eyes on the Cliffs of Anquar.

And so I waited for the first light of dawn, held my breath as the sun's rays painted those daggers first purple, then red, then glorious gold and my heart leapt into my throat at the near-forgotten sight. I had only seen them from a distance once in my life, on that dreaded day when I traded the aerie for adventure. They truly looked like the spikes on the back of a great dragon. So many islands rising sharply out of the sea, waters crashing at their base, vegetation sparsely scattered along ridge and crest. Beyond the cliffs, a stretch of land extended beyond the horizon, made golden by the sun. I had never seen it before and I wondered if it was inhabited like Remus or wild like the dragons. Anquarus could easily have made his home here.

As Selisanae of the Sun made her way out of the ocean, the sea snakes found us, swooping and worrying and raising their cries to the heavens. The memories took me back to my mornings as a fledgling – sea snakes and sunshine and gleaming over it all, the Fang of Wyvern. I would have laughed had I been able.

In the distant dawn, I could see silhouettes circling the

cliffs and my heart leapt into my throat at the sight. Wild dragons.

The sea snakes fled as I rose on top of the water, beating my wings and barking to the Thunder. They had slept soundly, but within minutes the sky was dark and the waters churned beneath them. Those distant silhouettes whirled and grew larger as the Wild dragons took notice and rose to meet us. I prayed there would be no violence – there were enough cliffs for all. But then again, I would never have expected so many to abandon their sticks and follow me home, either. I knew so little about my people. We are unpredictable as we are proud.

The Fang was between the Thunder and the Wild, so I rode the air up, up, up to its pinnacle with Summerday and Aryss on either side. It was, for the most part straight, striated rock, but moss grew in the ledges and on the peak. I circled first then landed, waiting for the largest drakes and drakinas to meet us. Soon, the sky grew black under wing as both Wild and Thunder circled each other, bellowing in agitation and threat. The air was sharp as a spear.

Two drakes, a blue and a brown, wheeled above me before dropping to the mossy peak, wings wide, head low. Behind me, Aryss barked and Summerday hissed and I snapped at them both. I had been a working dragon for too long. I had a different plan.

I raised my wings but bent them inward, arched my neck and averted my eyes, gazing at the mossy stone at their feet. A deep, respectful bow, an early gesture of respect. The sticks had enjoyed such things and these dragons, having lived their entire lives in freedom, deserved it.

The drakes fell silent, unsure of their next move, when first Aryss then Summerday bowed as well. In fact, with over a hundred dragons in the air, there was little sound save the beating of wings and the crash of waves against the Fang. A shadow crossed the sun as a drakina landed between the drakes, larger than either of them and bringing with her a scent from my youth.

I dared look up.

Almost as large as Ironwing, my mother towered over me, as dark as the Cliffs of Anquar. She lowered her great head, scarred as if from some terrible battle, but I realized that it was just life and that she was old and magnificent and strong. I studied her grey scales, the spines and spikes that had never been filed, the throat that had never been banded. She breathed in my scent, made a rumbling sound deep in her chest and my heart threatened to burst from within. She leaned forward, opening her mouth wide and ever wider, strings of saliva swinging between rows of dagger sharp teeth. I resisted the urge to shrink back and those familiar jaws clamped over my head.

Fish oil and arcstone. The fragrance of my youth.

As long as she didn't regurgitate bloodbass all over my head, I would be fine. Suddenly, she released me and threw back her head, warbling a song into the morning light. I followed suit, singing the dragon song with a joy I had never known and soon, the sky exploded as both Thunder and Wild joined the chorus. It was glorious and we alternated singing with blasts of fire, and the sky flashed light then dark with the smoke of our breath. Dragons wheeled and danced in the sky, dove into the waters, tugged at what little remained of harness and rigging. Young dragons flitted around the outer rim, bold yet equally terrified and full of the vigour of youth.

I had been the same when I was young.

Suddenly, a bellow rippled in from the outer dragons and a boom that shook me to my core. A second and then a third as iron balls whipped through the air past me into my mother. She barked and leapt from the Fang, a gaping hole in her chest. Blood sprayed from her heart as slowly she spiralled down, down and down into the water below.

Cannonfire.

I sprang into the sky, furious and wheeling to see a huge fleet of ships moving northward. Lamoan ships. I could tell from the cannons and the great glaring eyes. But Remoan ships as well, with their golden drakina sails, outfitted with Lamoan cannons. It made no sense, but as I coursed toward them, my wings beating faster than my rage, I realized that I had caused it. Me, the Night Dragon of the Crown. I had ravaged the Lamoan docks and freed their golden drakina. I had called the dragons of Remus and they had come. I had shat on the house of the Emperor and united two warring peoples under the banner of fear.

This was me. All me. Nameless, riderless, limitless, free. Dragons were a threat to both brothers, and they had followed us here to destroy us all.

I barked to the Thunder, I bellowed to the Wild. They followed me and we dove toward them like a hailstorm.

Boom and flash of cannonfire. Breath and crash of dragonfire. Almost two hundred dragons bore down on the fleet and soon, the sky was filled with black.

Smoke and fire, the smell of iron and arcstone. This was why they mined the arcstone, to out-breathe dragons and I felt it burn in my throat as I carried the fire to them, eager to torch every one of their pathetic skiffs. The balls whipped like leaden arrows and next to me, a brown drake was struck. I tucked my wings and dove, spraying flame all across the lead vessel. I didn't care that it had a golden drakina sail, that it was Remoan not Lamoan. It was stick and it would burn.

Up into the dragon-dark sky, wheeling and plummeting again, the fire pouring like rain from our mouths. The cannons boomed like many mouths, coughing flame and lead and iron. Dragons were like schools of silverfins. Too many to miss, and one after another, they splashed into the sea. They did not go quietly, however, and their thrashings crippled as many ships as our flame.

I'd lost sight of Summerday and Aryss. I hoped they'd stay well out of the fray but I knew otherwise. Aryss was a Flight Dragon, her skills unrivaled but Summerday? How could a blind drakina who had only known captivity survive such a battle? A ball tore past my head and thoughts of drakinas went with it.

The ships had reached the Fang of Wyvern. The cliff face was pitted as both dragons and iron balls slammed into it, and I must admit I despaired of ever claiming it as my nesting site. The fact saddened me, then angered me and I bore down once more, raining fire across the eye of a

Lamoan warship. Aflame, it carried on to crash into the Fang, shattering and scattering wood and men across the surf.

It was then that I saw the eye.

Larger than anything painted on the ships, a great yellow eye opened beneath the waters.

And it roared.

It was not the roar of cannonfire. It was not the roar of Hell Down. It was the roar of an earthstorm, of the very Cliffs and the rocks and slowly, just like an earthstorm, the Fang of Wyvern began to move.

Thunder and Wild fell away as the sea began to churn and boil, and the cliff rose up beneath me. All along the archipelago, cliffs that had been homes to dragons for hundreds of years shuddered and sank, while the Fang rose higher and higher. The warships pitched on the churning seas, sucking inward as a massive shape pushed out of the ocean, spray and foam roiling like a cauldron. It was the largest dragon I had ever seen and with a flash like Hallow Fire, I realized it was Anquarus of the Sea. The Cliffs were his spines, the Fang one of his horns and his tail carried on as far as the horizon. As he rose, winds surged and sucked all around him and dragons were sent spinning through the air, some crashing into the water, others into the iron scales of his body. When he spread wide his wings, they lifted water and weeds and fish and silt with them, only to rain back down to the waves like a waterfall. With a roar that was like the heart of Hell Down, he turned his great yellow eyes to the ships.

They shattered under his claws, were sucked into his

jaws, crushed between his iron teeth. He flung his great body onto the fleet, sending giant waves crashing on both sides, capsizing the others. He thrashed and gnashed and when he finally blew his ocean-blue flame across the remaining ships, they instantly turned to ash and blew away on the hurricane wind of his breath.

After many hours, all that was left was the sound of sea snakes and hissing water.

He was the size of many mountains, had to be hundreds of years old. He gazed up at us, past us, to the gleaming gold of Selisanae above and with a roar that split the earth in two, he brought his great wings down, forcing both dragons and water out from under them. A second and then a third and I wondered if such a weight could be carried but his wings were as wide as the sea and soon, he thundered into the sky, blackening the clouds and obliterating the sun with his bulk.

It was noon before he was out of sight and the roar of his passing finally died away into wind and silence.

It was longer before any dragon was able to breathe, longer still before any of us could move.

A pitiful warble echoed across the water. I looked to see Summerday resting on the surface, wings wide, eyes unseeing. I flew over to settle next to her, nudged her throat with my beak. She exhaled deeply, then again, and I realized that there was no way I could tell her what we'd seen. There was no song, there was no comfort, but there was life and there was freedom, and I nipped her spines to calm her. She hissed at me, but she settled once Aryss lit on the water beside her.

Eventually, the Wild swept back over their former home but there was nothing, merely white sand and blue waters made brown with silt. We lost many dragons that day and I must admit that their bodies fed the sea creatures for weeks afterward. Those remaining settled back onto the waves but Anquarus had destroyed the greatest natural aerie I'd ever known. In truth, Anquarus had *been* the greatest natural aerie I'd ever known.

All of us, both Thunder and Wild were united in one common plight. We had no home.

I could see the golden strip on the horizon. It was land of some sort. Perhaps there were dragons. Perhaps there were men. Either way, it was a place we needed to go, for neither Thunder nor Wild would last long floating on the waves like debris.

With a bellow, I spread wide my wings to capture the winds. Aryss and Summerday did likewise and together we rose into the sky with all of the Thunder at our backs. We soared toward the Wild. They were circling over the emptiness where the Cliffs been, and hissed and barked as we streaked past. I ignored them, focusing now on the strip of land in the distance.

Gold before me. Gold on either side. The sky above was gold as well, under the gaze of Selisanae of the Sun and you know how dragons love their gold. I was free, a night dragon of ash and stars, fire and smoke and pride.

But most of all, fire.

***

Now, I am old.

I am the oldest of all the dragons. I do not breed anymore. I do not hunt nor do I fly, for even moving disturbs the trees and the rocks and the young dragons all around me. I'm rarely hungry, rarely thirsty and I have roots growing under my belly and moss beneath my wings. Perhaps it's trying to make me a part of the earth, much like Anquarus was a part of the sea. It doesn't matter. I won't be here for much longer.

We called the land Nerisanos, after Nerisanae the First Drakina of the Earth. It was a good name, an ancient name befitting this ancient place. There were no sticks, no cities, no civilization of any sort. There were mountains as high as the Cliffs of Anquar. There was fresh water and forests and plains and beaches. There was fish and shaghorns and coarse shearers and goswryms. There were few sea snakes and I must admit, I didn't miss them at all.

Our dragons stretched out across this land and soon, there was no distinction between Thunder and Wild. All were Wild because all were free. We bred and nested and built our homes up on the tallest peaks and in the deepest valleys. I bred both Aryss and Summerday and our young were alternately sunny gold or starry black or striped both, and soon, a night dragon was not a rare sight. We sang each night, telling the stories of our lives around fire pits like the sticks used to do. I rarely thought of Rue, but when I did, my song was all the sweeter.

I don't sing anymore either.

I lie across the flat, mesa-topped peak of a mountain for there is no nest or ledge, lair or den big enough to hold me. I sleep during the day, enjoying the warmth of the sun all along my sides. My horns are so long that they touch my back, twisting like roots in the ground. Young dragons fly over me, play in my spines, nest in my scales. My skin is like stone, my eyes like silverstone, my claws like flint. I'm not as large as Anquarus but it doesn't matter. As I said, I won't be here for long.

I'm going to my father, Draco Stellorum. I know now that he is one of the Veternum and his name not Draco Stellorum but Stellorus of the Stars. He is real and I will find him.

I'm not sure when, but one night I will rise. I will shake the moss and the trees and the rocks from my body and when I spread my wings, no one will know that the sky has disappeared, for the stars will be my stars, my scales will be the night. I will crack the mountain when I leap into the air, each beat of my wings will create a hurricane. I will brace my eyes against the cold as I rise higher and higher and I know I will see not just all of Nerisanos, but Remus and Lamos as well. I will see what it is that a map is based on, and I wonder if it will be long and flat or curved and round. I suspect curved, but I am a dragon given to great imaginings.

I imagine flying with my father, Draco Stellorum, through the stars; soaring through the night sky as if it were water and chasing Selisanae of the Sun. I long to sing once again with the moons, the Eyes, my dear golden drakinas Aryss and Summerday who met my father far earlier than I. When I think of them, my entire chest aches and the mesa-topped mountain trembles with the grief.

I am a vain dragon, a proud dragon, and now an old dragon. I have lived with vice and with vigour and while I could go on, I am eager to see where the stars will take me and how high I will fly before the cold turns me to ice.

And sometimes I wonder if I might meet Ruminor, the harsh father of sticks and cruel breaker of bargains. I would scorch him with my breath until he is ash and I will blow him on the wings of the wind so he could never steal souls from young boys again. I will set the heavens on fire with the flames of my breath and perhaps the stars will burn for me as I light them. Selisanae would burn, I know this to be true. I wonder if my father, Draco Stellorum, would join me or if he would watch, as he always watches, while I battle a god and win. Perhaps that will appease him. And then again, perhaps not.

As you can tell, I have much time for thinking.

And perhaps when I burn the heavens, I will burn my father too, perhaps I will take his place. Draco Stellorum Cinisi. Dragon of Ash and Stars. Then, the young drakes will gaze up at me and wonder what I think and make songs about the moons, my Eyes Aryss and Summerday. I will not be too proud to hear them.

And so until the day that I rise, I stay. My breathing shakes the treetops, my heartbeat moves the tides. I have lived a good life but even now as I gaze up at the stars, I grow restless.

Listen for the wind. Turn your ear to the roar of distant Hell Down.

I move.

Finis

If you enjoyed this novel, I would be honoured if you would leave a review somewhere. Unlike Stormfall, I am not too proud.

Other Books by H. Leighton Dickson

To Journey in the Year of the Tiger
To Walk in the Way of Lions
Songs in the Year of the Cat
Swallowtail & Sword
Cold Stone & Ivy

ABOUT THE AUTHOR

H. Leighton Dickson grew up in the wilds of the Canadian Shield, where her neighbours were wolves, moose, deer and lynx. She studied Zoology at the University of Guelph and worked in the Edinburgh Zoological Gardens in Scotland, where she was chased by lions, wrestled deaf tigers and fed antibiotics to Polar Bears by baby bottle! She has been writing since she was thirteen and pencilled her way through university with the help of DC Comics. She has three dogs, three cats, three kids, one horse and one husband. She has managed to keep all of them alive so far.

A Hybrid author, Heather has several Indie novels on Amazon along with the Gothic thriller series, COLD STONE & IVY published by Tyche Books. She also writes for Bayview Magazine and is a photoshop wizard when it comes to book covers.

Come join the conversation at
http://www.hleightondickson.com
or on Facebook at
http://www.facebook.com/HLeightonDickson

DRAGON OF ASH & STARS

Printed in Great Britain
by Amazon